NOT *THAT* GUY

FELICE STEVENS

Published by Good Man Press

Edited by Keren Reed
Copyediting and Proofreading by Flat Earth Editing
Additional Proofreading by Lyrical Lines
Cover Art by Reese Dante
Photography by: Emma James Photography
Model: Devon
Digital ISBN: 979-8-88949-096-8
Paperback ISBN: 979-8-88949-097-5

DEDICATION

To my family

ACKNOWLEDGMENTS

Thanks to my wonderful editor, Keren Reed. To Hope and Jess from Flat Earth Editing, you are the best. To Dianne, from Lyrical Lines, I couldn't do it without you. And to Reese. Thank you for everything and more.

And always, every day to the readers who choose to pick up my books, you are the reason and make it all worthwhile.

PROLOGUE

One year earlier

WESTON

Sometimes I wondered why I let myself get talked into doing stupid things. Then I remembered that it made my senior partners happy.

Take panel discussions—always boring as hell. Five of us sitting under hot lights, droning on about estate planning as it affected marital property in a divorce, meant I was ready to partake in the evening festivities.

The one good thing was the assurance from the coordinator of the event that as a panelist, my bar drinks would be comped, and I sure as hell had taken advantage of that generosity in the form of two straight vodkas. A light tease of perfume invaded my space, and I looked at the beautiful redhead standing by my side.

"Can I get you a drink?"

Deep-set blue eyes swept up and down, and damned if they didn't dismiss me. "No, thanks." She hailed the bartender, ordered a Chardonnay, and walked away.

Stung, I held out my glass. "Make it a double."

"Well, well. Lost your touch? Who would've ever thought the great Weston Lively would get snubbed?"

What the— I spun to my left and came face-to-face with the arrogant smirk of Brenner Fleming. Eyes narrowed, I casually sipped my drink before answering.

"Planning to shoot your shot with her? Why don't you go for it, Fleming? You always did come in second to me, no matter how hard you tried. I'm sure nothing's changed."

It had been like that since law school. Fleming and I had been one-two in class rank for all three years. I was the editor-in-chief of *Law Review*, and he'd taken that same position on our school's *Family Law Review*—the first of its kind in the country and pretty damn prestigious as well. Not that I'd ever say that to his face. Our rivalry for best in class was well known and had extended to our fraternity, where each year we'd battled for president, with me winning two of the three years. At graduation I'd given the valedictorian speech, and I'd seen from the podium how he'd seethed. Less than a percentage point had separated us.

But I'd come out on top.

I'd never been that competitive, but something about Brenner got my juices flowing. His unconcealed disdain for me—unwarranted, in my eyes—had always been a catalyst to make sure I never failed. I'd studied hard and partied harder once exams had finished, but Brenner would never join us. He was a lone wolf whose scorn for me showed in his scowl every time we said two words to each other. He thought I was a spoiled, rich brat, and he never failed to sneer at my antics when the weekend rolled around. And I thought he was boring and judgmental as fuck. We didn't click and made no attempt to hide our mutual dislike, which only grew each year.

His hard jaw working, he finished the rest of his drink and beckoned for another. "Maybe in law school that might've been true, but now I always win."

A familiar face peeked over Fleming's shoulder. "Don't tell me you two are still going at it? You're both rich, successful, and gorgeous. Why are you acting like idiots? Maybe you're gonna whip 'em out and measure 'em to see who's got the biggest dick? I mean, I wouldn't mind…" A grin split the man's handsome face. "How the hell are you, Weston?"

"Bailey Marks. I'm good. How's it going?"

He stepped past a scowling Fleming to give me a hug. Always a bundle of fun, openly gay, and never lacking a date, Bailey was in our class and a member of our fraternity. He'd often act as the buffer whenever Fleming and I would get in each other's faces.

"It's going well. Being a solo practitioner means I gotta keep my fingers in every piece of the pie." His eyes twinkled. "Or cake, if you know what I mean."

"Jesus, Bailey." Brenner's brows shot up. "You haven't changed a bit."

"Neither have you, Brenner," I told him. "Still the same tight-ass you were almost fifteen years ago." The liquor had loosened my tongue, and I wasn't giving a damn. "You need to get laid."

His scowl deepened. "That's always been your answer for everything. Some of us are particular about their bed partners."

Maybe that was it. Pure and simple jealousy. I'd had no shortage of women, and far as I knew, Brenner rarely dated. We were at opposite ends of the universe except in the classroom, the two of us fierce competitors, though I doubted he was running from the same devil.

"As I recall, you didn't exactly have them breaking through the doors for your charms. My guess is, that's probably still the case. What's the problem? You're a decent-looking guy."

A flush rose over his face, and I smirked. No matter how many years had passed, it was still fun to get a rise out of him. Truth was, I was straight, but I was sure the women found Brenner hot as hell. Six foot two, big blue eyes, a full head of thick, wavy dark hair, and a body he obviously took care of. I'd seen plenty of women and quite a few men tonight give him the eye. Not that I'd ever tell him.

Brenner's stormy eyes dismissed me, disdain oozing from every pore. "The day I explain myself to you is the day I lie down and stop breathing."

Probably to break the tension, Bailey broke into our face-off. "Well, if either of you wants to take a walk on the wild side, I'm here for it." Bailey winked and waggled his brows.

Leave it to Bailey to say something outrageous. Laughter burst from my mouth. "What? I've never been with a man."

"First time for everything, and I'm offering to pop your cherry. To teach you. Both of you." A pink tongue swiped at his full lips. "Back in the day, I used to have dreams of you and Brenner."

"You're cute, Bailey, but not my type." I patted his cheek. "Maybe Brenner'll take you up on it."

A snort greeted my ears. "Fuck off, Weston. Bailey, you know I love you, but not like that."

By this time, I was four vodkas in and feeling no pain. The music started, and people moved to the dance floor. Bailey grabbed my hand and Brenner's.

"Well, if we're not going to get horizontal, at least come dance with me. Give me a little bit of fantasy to take home."

"I'm in, but you know Brenner. He's a dud. He'll never do it. Plus, he can't dance." My words brought a flush to his face and had the desired effect. Brenner gulped his drink.

"Fuck you. Let's do it."

Wide-eyed, Bailey grinned. "Oh man, come on. I'm ready to be the pastrami in a Lively-Fleming sandwich."

The bar wasn't restricted to the panelists and bar-association guests, and the floor was crowded. I hadn't danced in forever and was itching to let my inhibitions go. While my partners were always women, I didn't give a damn if I was seen dancing with a man, and to my surprise, Brenner seemed to feel the same. Bailey got his way, and Brenner and I danced with him in the middle. He ground his butt into me first, before he turned to give Brenner the same treatment. At some point, we attracted other male and female partners. A large group formed, and we all ended up dancing with each other. Bailey thrust a shot in my face, and I swallowed it and then another. Out of the corner of my eye, I watched him repeat the same with Brenner.

The music thumped, and the lights flashed. Hands grabbed my ass. Lips grazed my cheek. God, I was turned-on. It didn't even matter who was touching me at this point. I was so damn horny, I couldn't see straight. I needed someone. Anyone. A round ass pushed into my hips, and I slipped my arms around their waist. My dick was rock hard, and I knew they could feel me. They didn't pull away, and we ground and bumped each other. Then light flashed over dark, wavy hair.

It was a guy.

It was Brenner.

I didn't fucking care.

Adrenaline rushed through me, and I kept a steady rock of my pelvis into his ass. His head fell back to my shoulder, and I closed my eyes and pressed my face into his neck.

"Oh yeah," he panted, and I knew he hadn't the slightest clue it was me holding him.

Fuck, he smelled good. It must've been the drinks that led me to lick his neck. The taste of his sweat and heat burst on my tongue, and I nipped at the tender skin, feeling him shiver in my arms. Goddamn, it was hot. I did it again, and my dick jerked.

"Let's go upstairs," I breathed in his ear.

"Oh God," he groaned, continuing to grind his ass into my aching dick. Heat poured off the two of us. My hands reached lower and brushed against his groin. He was as hard as I was.

"Fuck, Brenner, you want it."

Hissing, he jumped away and faced me. The colored lights revealed eyes blown wide and an open mouth. "West?" he gasped, paling.

I stood still as the bodies rocked and danced. My control was slipping. It didn't matter that it was a man. Or Brenner.

I needed to feel.

"Upstairs," I croaked.

Without a word, Brenner took off across the dance floor, and for a moment I stood rooted to the spot, watching him thread his way through the dancing throngs. My feet had a mind of their own, and I traversed the space and caught up with him as he fled into the elevator. I slipped in after him. He kept his head down and didn't look at me. Not when I followed him after he exited the elevator, nor at the door to his room.

Blood rushed through my veins, and I was on fire. Reckless. What the hell had taken possession of me, I had no clue, but I'd never wanted...never *needed* anyone like I needed Brenner Fleming.

Huge and hazy, Brenner's eyes pinned mine. He waited by the door, his chest heaving. He licked his lips, and my dick throbbed. A matching bulge in his pants let me know I wasn't the only one ready to explode.

"West?"

His whispered question roared in my ears. I took a step forward, and he swayed toward me. I crowded him up against the door. "Oh, yeah." I couldn't stop myself from touching him. "I need to know."

"What...ohhhh." He sighed, then froze as I buried my face in his neck again, lips pressed to the rapidly jumping pulse.

"Inside," I rasped. My head spun, and my heart pounded. I was on a roller coaster hurtling for an unknown destination. No way off.

Brenner's hands shook as he touched the card to the reader, and we entered the dark room. My mouth crashed into Brenner's, and after his initial gasp of shock, his throaty groan sent an electric current straight to my dick. Was it strange kissing a man? I didn't give myself a chance to think as Brenner's hot, wet tongue touched my lips and his hungry, needy sounds vibrated through me.

"West," he gasped against my cheek. "I've never–"

"Me neither. But I have to..." My fingers went for his belt, and he hissed as I unzipped his pants and released his thick cock. Heat rose from his skin, and I couldn't take my eyes off my fingers wrapped around him. "Oh, fuck."

Why I hadn't expected Brenner to reciprocate I had no idea, but his large hands yanked at my zipper and pulled out my throbbing dick. A moan of pleasure spilled from my lips, startling me, but I couldn't stifle it.

We stood like two statues until we began moving in unison, each of us stroking the other from root to dripping tip. That same overwhelming, soul-stealing sensation swept through me, and soon we were humping each other, our hips snapping. My mouth latched on to Brenner's neck while he tangled his fingers into my hair to hold me steady as he pumped the length of my aching shaft with a hard and steady hand.

"Fuck...fuck...oh, my God." A blast of hot come spurted from his dick, and he shivered and keened. The wildness in his face set off my orgasm, and faster than I could blink, it ripped me apart from head to toe. Our breaths mingled, and feeling my legs start to give out, I leaned heavily on him. The gallop of his heart pounded alongside the stuttering rhythm of my own.

"Get off me," he rumbled, giving my shoulder a half-hearted push.

The high had begun to recede, and in the dim light spilling through the windows and the half-open curtains, I gazed at my sticky hand. A hand that had been holding Brenner Fleming's dick only a minute ago.

"We were drunk," I stated. "This doesn't mean shit."

Head bowed, Brenner couldn't meet my eyes. "No kidding. I never said it did. You're still an ass."

"Congratulations, Fleming." I washed my hands in the bathroom, then tucked my shirt in my pants and zipped up. "For once, you came first."

I shut the door behind me.

CHAPTER ONE

The following year

BRENNER

"Please, Brenner? I've got a massive hangover from my brother's bachelor party. There's no way I can make it to my nine a.m. meeting."

Starting the week by having to fill in for someone who'd called in sick was never high on my list of things I liked to do. But Seth was a senior partner's son, and it didn't matter if he was a giant pain in the ass or a slacker. Which, to his credit, he wasn't most of the time. Still...

"Shouldn't you have thought of that before you soaked your brain in tequila?" I sipped my coffee, looking over the morning headlines, each one more depressing than the next.

"Yeah, but how could I say no? Plus, there were strip-pers with the biggest—"

"Spare me." I rolled my eyes. "I know all about bachelor parties."

"You do?"

"Yes, of course," I responded with irritation. "I'm not a monk, you know."

"Could've fooled me. I've been here five years, and I don't think you've ever mentioned a date or even a hookup. You've gotta be ready to bust a nut."

A lecture on my sex life was not something I either wanted or appreciated. "I don't speak about my personal life. That's why it's called personal. Also, please try and remember—I'm not one of your bros. I don't need all the dirty details. And you don't exactly have a good track record with women."

"At least I have one. You and I are different. I'm twenty-eight. You're thirty-nine."

There were a great many differences between me and Seth other than our age, but I wasn't going to bother to list them. It would take way too long.

"Thanks for the reminder. Anyway, I'll do it, but you owe me a very large iced coffee. And make sure your ass is in bright and early tomorrow morning."

"I will. Promise. It'll be an easy one for you."

"I've said it before. No matter how it looks on the outside, divorce is never easy. At one point, these two people thought they loved each other and would spend the rest of their lives together. We're part of the cleanup crew—the aftermath of the crash and burn. I always tread lightly."

"I know. I'm sorry."

I grimaced. "And Jesus Christ. Didn't you remember one of my first rules? No meetings earlier than ten a.m."

"Uh, yeah. Oh, I forgot. The opposing attorney can't—shit, I gotta go." Hacking and gurgling noises on his end made my stomach turn. "I'm gonna be sick." The call ended, and I was left with the image of Seth tossing his cookies. My sausage-and-egg breakfast sandwich suddenly didn't seem as appetizing as it had only moments ago, and I dumped it into the trash.

I checked my watch. I had just enough time to open the file he'd emailed me and try to familiarize myself with the case. Two young people whose parents hated their choice in spouses. That never boded well. I checked the firm and saw the name of the attorney handling the case had been crossed out, with a note from Seth: *New opposing counsel.*

"Who the fuck is it?" That must've been what he'd been about to tell me when he'd lost the contents of his stomach. I scanned the file, but there was only a phone number with no name. Obviously, Seth's brain had been on the bachelor party rather than his case. My intercom buzzed.

"Yes, Tanya?"

"Seth's nine a.m. is here, but he's not in yet."

"I'll be taking it this morning. Please put them in the conference room."

"Okay."

Roman and White was a boutique firm I'd joined after I graduated law school. They handled all aspects of family law, and I'd been thrilled to receive an offer to work for them. I'd turned down the rat race of the huge, white-shoe law firms, wanting a less hectic, less competitive environment. Roman and White were well known in the family-law field, and they boasted some high-profile clients. Making partner was the culmination of all my hard work and the dream of being a lawyer—one I'd had since I was a kid. In the intervening years, I'd paid no mind to the petty infighting of the senior partners, and though the shine had somewhat worn off, I remained grateful every day. I was living a life I'd only dreamed of as a child and took nothing for granted. Headhunters kept trying to recruit me, and while I wasn't averse to leaving, I did have a sense of loyalty to the firm.

I picked up my legal pad and pen and stopped by Seth's office to get the printed file. While everything was online, I preferred to have paper in front of me.

"*Old-fashioned,*" Seth always joked.

I opened the conference room door and saw our client, Rodney Fuller, seated with his father, whom I knew from the intake meeting. The soon-to-be ex, Jill Swanson-Fuller, sat opposite them with an older version of herself, ostensibly her mother. A tall man stood with his back to me, studying the legal treatises in the bookcase. Rude of a colleague not to even bother to acknowledge that I'd entered the room. That put him one rung up on my shithead ladder.

"Hello. I'm Brenner Fleming. Seth Roman couldn't make it this morning, so rather than postpone the meeting, I'm filling in."

The man snapped to attention, and finally turned, greeting me with a wicked grin and predatory green-gold eyes reminiscent of a big cat on the hunt. "Weston Lively."

I swore my heart sank to my feet. It couldn't be. *Fuck. Not that guy.*

I remained mute, damning my traitorous body. Sweat popped up and ran down my spine, my nerve endings firing. It was all I could do to keep from trembling. Uncomfortable silence grew between us until I blinked and got my shit together.

"Hello. Nice to meet you."

A slash of brow rose high as if to say, *So we're going to play that game, are we?*

"Same. I'm also new to the case. The Swansons called me in last-minute."

My nod was curt. "Shall we start?" I sat by Rodney. "This seems like it should be—"

"It's not. If you were going to say simple," Weston interrupted. "My client has uncovered assets Mr. Fuller was attempting to hide."

"That's a lie," Rodney burst out. "You just want to take everything from me and leave me penniless so you can be with your boyfriend."

"There is no boyfriend. I never cheated on you. But I know about that Swiss bank account. And the other one in Aruba."

Holy shit, this was spinning out of control. Obviously Weston had anticipated this, because the bastard sat there with a smirk on his arrogant face. Seth was going to owe me more than a damned iced coffee for stepping into this snake pit.

"Please, both of you. This hostility is getting us nowhere. Why don't I talk for a moment with my client?" I tipped my head to the door and led Rodney and his father outside. "Is this true?" I asked when they were seated in my office. "Do you have offshore accounts you haven't disclosed?"

A guilty Rodney darted a glance to his father. Rodney might be twenty-seven, but I knew who called the shots.

"Please tell me the truth."

Jonathan Fuller glared at me. "We hired your firm to represent our interests, not that greedy whore's."

"Whoa. Okay, Mr. Fuller. Be angry, but I don't allow language like that. I understand divorce is contentious, but this is why people who don't really know each other and don't have prenups get into trouble. How much is in those accounts in total assets?"

Rodney bowed his head. "About three million dollars."

Jesus. This twerp was going to learn a lesson. "And how much was acquired during the marriage? That makes all the difference."

Rodney met my eyes. "About four hundred thousand. But doesn't the fact that she was cheating on me from the beginning mean anything?"

"Not for distribution of marital assets. Under the law, she's entitled to half of what you acquired while you were married." Rodney's face drained of color while his father's turned beet red. "I'll need your tax returns, and we'll have to include this in distribution. What we will negotiate on is alimony." I watched the anger rise in the senior Fuller's eyes. "How do you know she was cheating?"

"I hired a private detective. Every Wednesday she met with a man—the same man—at his house for an hour." Jonathan Fuller speared me with an angry look. "What the hell do you think she was doing?"

"I have no idea. Did you ask her?"

Rodney snorted. "My father said she wouldn't tell the truth, so why should I bother?"

Oh, for fuck's sake. This kid was being led by his balls. "This is the best I can tell you right now. Let's go back inside."

When we returned, Jill was pale and looked as though she'd been crying. Her mother sat with a pinched face, as if she'd sucked on an entire lemon. Weston had left his clients sitting, and his long frame leaned against the edge of the conference table. I caught a whiff of his cologne and damned myself for my traitorous body's response. I stepped away and set my jaw.

"Rodney, c-can I talk to you a minute?" Jill's mouth trembled, and her eyes grew shiny. "Please?"

"Don't listen to her," Jonathan warned, but Rodney bit his lip, the longing obvious in his eyes.

"What is it?" Rodney asked, and sensing hesitancy, I prodded him.

Jill left her seat, and Rodney met her halfway. "Can we talk alone for a second? Without my mother or your father?"

I beckoned them. "You can use my office."

"Jill, I don't advise—" Weston began, but she whirled around.

"But I want to do this." She and Rodney walked across the hall to the room, and I closed the door behind them and stood in front of it.

"Guard-dog duty, Brenner?" Weston sniped. "Is that your real job?"

"Don't try to interfere with them. I'm sure they'll pay your fee even if they do get back together." My lip curled in a sneer.

"I don't need some small-potato divorce case to make my bottom line." He paused. "Unlike some."

That insufferable, haughty gaze swept over the office. No, we weren't a hotshot international firm, and we didn't have a roster of multimillionaire clients like Walden, Booth, and Roth. *Obnoxious fucker.* Nothing had changed.

I brushed past him, but he grabbed my arm. "Don't touch me," I rasped, but he held on tighter.

"So you do remember." His fathomless eyes left me breathless.

"Fuck you," I grunted and pushed him off me, but he only laughed.

I stalked away to the restroom and shut the door behind me. My chest heaving, I braced my arms on the vanity. "I will not let him get to me," I muttered and closed my eyes, inhaling and exhaling at a steady pace to regain control. Why him? Of all the damn lawyers in the city, it had to be Weston Lively. The one man who, no matter how I tried, always managed to worm his way under my skin. The operative word being *worm.*

Since our first year of law school, Weston had been a scourge, a thorn I couldn't extract. A perennial frat boy who sailed through life on his family's name and wealth. At our first meeting, I'd thought he was another pretty face and was shocked that he was as brilliant as he was arrogant. No matter how hard I tried to beat him, he almost always came out one better than me.

When had he moved to New York? Last I'd heard, he'd been at his firm's Boston office.

Last time.

Without much success, I'd tried to block out that wild night on the dance floor and my hotel room. A night that had released a side of me I'd never known existed. From the moment his arms came around my waist on the dance floor, I was lost. It was as if I'd been hypnotized and bound to his will.

Contrary to what Seth imagined, I did go out, more so this past year than any other, in an attempt to exorcise Weston from my system. I'd thrown myself into the dating pool, hoping to meet a woman who could make me forget a wicked grin, gleaming eyes, and the rasp of scruff on my cheek.

I'd failed miserably.

Seeing him today only steeled my resolve to push harder to find a woman and rid myself of furtive dreams I allowed only in the dark. No more. I was sober and smarter. I'd never put myself in that position again.

With a tug to my cuffs and a snap of my shoulders, I strode out of the bathroom. Of course, Weston was waiting for me, shoulder propped on the wall opposite the bathroom door.

"Got yourself together?" That smirk infuriated me, and I tried to brush past him, but he stood in my way.

Outwardly I remained a frozen statue, but inside I was a needy mess of swirling, hot emotions, my blood boiling through my veins. Hating myself for my one weakness, I drew from my inner strength and said, "Let me pass. We're opposing counsel, and I'm here to represent my client, nothing more."

To my complete surprise, Weston didn't try and use further tactics and moved aside. I sucked in a deep breath, filling my lungs with much-needed oxygen.

"Very well, Mr. Fleming. I'll await our clients' return." He left me shaken but whole.

I leaned against the wall opposite the office where Rodney and Jill were conferring, and as the minutes slipped by, I came to the conclusion that there might be a reconciliation in the works. That made me happy—contrary to belief, divorce lawyers didn't want to see marriages dissolved. And while I might not believe in love and forever, I would never stand in the way of a client trying to work out their marital problems.

So when Jill and Rodney came out from the office, eyes glittering, cheeks flushed, and mouths kiss-swollen, I didn't need to ask.

"We're...not going to go forward with the divorce at this time." Rodney held Jill's hand. "We have a lot to talk about. Just the two of us."

For whatever reason, my eyes smarted, and I nodded. I might be jaded and despair of ever finding love, but I could still believe in it for others. "That's terrific. Take your time and see if it's what you want or what others are pushing you to do."

"Thank you, Mr. Fleming."

Weston didn't appear to share my view, and with a frown, waved Jill to him. "I think we need to talk. Jill, why don't you come with me?" She hesitated, and with a whisper in Rodney's ear first, left him to follow Weston into the conference room. The door shut behind them, and immediately raised voices could be heard.

"She swore she wasn't having an affair. The meeting with that guy every Wednesday after work was tutoring him in English." Rodney winced at the high-pitched yelling.

"She's an English teacher," he explained. "Her mother hates me because of the things I said about her."

"It's hard to control our temper and our words sometimes. We say things we later regret, but if you're truly intent on making the marriage work, I'd seek out a good therapist and not let anyone else influence you."

Of course that brought a growl from Jonathan Fuller. "Is that what you think? That I'm the one who encouraged this divorce?"

Was he kidding? He'd done nothing but stoke the fire. "I read the notes, and it seemed that from the first you were against the marriage. You didn't think Jill was good enough for your son? Why is that?" I could predict the answer, but I was curious to hear Fuller's excuse.

He looked me directly in the eye. "I know what you're thinking. That it has to do with money. But it's not only that. She's never tried to become part of the family—she's kept Rodney away from us. She wouldn't let him visit unless she was with him, yet her mother is always there. And yes, she started spending as soon as they got married—ripping apart their apartment, which was brand-new, to make it 'her own.'" The angry glare intensified. "So how would you feel? I shouldn't have a right to express my opinion? And when I did, she would yell and accuse me of trying to break them up and withhold Rodney's trust fund, which I have no right to do, if she had any brains."

"Dad, please." Looking uncomfortable, Rodney took his arm. "Can we not right now? Maybe we jumped into marriage, but I do love her. And I think getting divorced would be a mistake." He chewed on his lip. "I'm twenty-seven, and I have a right to make my own decisions. Please let me."

"We just don't want you to get hurt. It's not the first time you've been taken in, only this is the most serious since you married her."

This was getting extremely personal, and I had little desire to be in the center of a messy family debate. "Let's see what's going on in there." I knocked and opened the door. Tears streaked Jill's face, and Weston, intent and serious, sat across from her and her mother.

"What?" he snapped at me. "We're in the middle of discussing things."

"And I need to know if anything further will be accomplished today. My clients are ready to leave." It was nice to see the great Weston Lively lose his cool, but as if the bastard had read my mind, he shut his file and showed that sarcastic twist of his lips that had always made me want to punch his face.

"We're done. Ladies?" They filed out ahead of him, walking down the hall to the waiting room. Jill and Rodney spoke in low tones to each other, while the in-laws ignored each other's existence.

"Rodney? We'll be in touch." I shook his hand. When it came to his father, I tried to reason with him. "Let your son live his life. It's hard to see them make mistakes, but it's worse to lose them."

His hard jaw worked, but he gave me a curt nod. They left, and I said my farewells to Jill and her mother. Hands in his pockets, Weston stood by, a silent figure but looming in my mind. I turned my back on him and walked away.

"Brenner." He caught up to me easily. "No good-bye for me?" he teased. I could almost feel his mouth on my skin and his hot breath on my lips.

I stopped at the door to my office. "Good-bye." I stepped inside and shut the door in his face. After several minutes passed without him entering, I blew out a sigh of relief. I was safe, for now.

CHAPTER TWO
WESTON

Well, damn. I'd expected another boring Monday, made worse by a bitter divorce fight in a case I'd taken over for a colleague with the flu. Instead, I'd gotten lucky. In a manner of speaking.

Brenner Fleming.

I hadn't seen him since that frantic, mind-blowing jerk-off in his hotel room, and all it had taken was one of his growls of annoyance to get my stuck-in-neutral motor revved and running. It might've been a drunken romp neither of us would ever admit to, yet it had become the gold standard I'd judged all my other bed partners against. And they'd come up lacking every single time.

Back at my office, I should've been writing up my notes for the case, but instead I sat, remembering that night where I'd completely lost control for the first time. Who knew under that buttoned-up, tight-assed, prickly-as-shit jerk, a wildcat lay in wait?

And why the hell would it be Brenner Fleming to turn me on?

I'd chalked it all up to a night where we'd both let alcohol drive away our inhibitions, because no man before or after had drawn my attention. Yet here I was, thinking about him, and my dick twitched. This wasn't me. I didn't let my libido run my life in the office. Plus, I wasn't into men.

After that encounter, I'd filled my nights with women, eager to erase the echoes of Fleming's gasps and groans. I sure as hell didn't want another man, but my brain wouldn't give up the taste of Fleming's hot kiss, nor the sound of his sexy growl. Curious as to what he'd been up to, I googled him. My intercom buzzed.

"Yes, Daniel?"

"Come on by, West. I'd like to hear how it went this morning."

I'd only recently moved to the New York City offices of Walden, Booth, and Roth, one of the top firms in the country. They'd hired me straight out of law school, and after a week of fun in the sunny Med, I'd joined them and stayed in Boston. But after all the years of living in New England, I'd been ready for a change, and when an opening had popped up in their New York City office, I'd jumped at the chance for a transfer.

"Sure thing. Be there in two."

I exited out of my looky-loo of Brenner, picked up my coffee, and headed over. As a founding partner, Daniel Roth had one of the best offices in the building, his double-exposure windows overlooking a stretch of midtown all the way to the East River. I admired the view as I settled into a chair.

"Thanks for handling the Swanson mess this morning. Normally I wouldn't send in someone at your level, but all our associates were handling other matters." Daniel had been the main cheerleader for me to join the New York branch. We'd worked on several cases together—ones where nasty custody battles had walked hand in hand with huge real-estate holdings. "How did it go?"

I relayed the sanitized version of the case. "It started out like any typical acrimonious divorce, but once the two ex-lovebirds sat across the table from each other, they decided maybe they did love each other, talked it out in private without Mommy and Daddy egging them on, and concluded that a reconciliation might actually work."

Daniel didn't register surprise. "Happens in about a third of the cases. Who was opposing counsel?" He again checked the screen. "Roman and White? They're good."

"Brenner Fleming handled the case."

Hearing that, Daniel removed his reading glasses. "Fleming? That's surprising."

Anxious to know more, I hitched my chair closer. "How come?"

"He's a partner." Amusement danced in his eyes. "Maybe they were also slammed and sent in their big guns."

The reasoning seemed solid. As I recalled, Brenner Fleming's gun was pretty big.

"I wouldn't know. We've never met across the table. Or in court."

"You two went to law school together, weren't you? Didn't you know each other?"

"Somewhat. Same section and fraternity, but we weren't friends."

But I do know what his dick looks like.

Somehow, I didn't get the feeling that Daniel Roth, almost fifty years married and grandfather of three, would appreciate that bit of information, so I kept it to myself.

"*Hmm-hmm.*"

In the year I'd been working in the New York office, I'd heard that *hmm-hmm* on numerous occasions, usually before delivering news that would levy a significant change for the firm. Minutes passed with Daniel clicking his mouse through whatever he had on his computer screen. Not that I didn't like spending time with the senior partner in his massive office, but I did have cases to get to. Still, I kept my butt in the chair and waited.

"We're looking to expand the family-law division. In our senior-partner meeting last month, we decided to make offers to several attorneys we've had our eye on. What would you say to Brenner Fleming joining the firm?"

That came out of nowhere. True, the office was very busy, and while I wouldn't mind help, more partners might not necessarily be a good thing. And having Brenner Fleming underfoot definitely wouldn't be a distraction I'd look forward to. That irritating scowl, the stiff, holier-than-thou expression...was that really something I wanted in my face every day? In law school, it had been fun to tease and poke him. Our competitiveness had driven us to be better, but I'd always had the option to walk away or ignore him. Here, in the real world, I wouldn't be able to.

"Why Fleming particularly? Not that he isn't a good attorney, I'll give him that, but there are probably a thousand Brenner Flemings in the city, or the country, for that matter, who'd be thrilled to work with this firm."

"We've been thinking about this for a while now, almost as long as when we brought you over last year from Boston. Prenuptial agreements are becoming more complicated, involving real-estate trusts, stocks, bonds, even pets. Custody battles are heating up, especially with same-sex marriage. Frozen embryos for IVF, adoptions, surrogacy...who knows what will come up in the future? But we need to be on top of it all."

"Yeah, a whole new aspect of the law has opened up."

"We've made some inquiries and narrowed it down to several likely candidates, but Fleming is my first choice. I like his backstory as well as his contacts—Fleming knows a lot of real-estate developers, and we think that could bolster our real-estate division."

Ahh. That made perfect sense. It was all about the bottom line. Now I understood.

"What contacts does Fleming have? And what about his backstory is appealing?"

Curious eyes met mine. "You don't know?"

My mind was a blank when I searched my memory banks, and I shook my head. "We didn't exactly run in the same circles in law school."

"Not surprising. I didn't think Senator Preston Lively would welcome a foster kid to his house for Christmas."

Shock waves rippled through me. "Foster kid?" The news was stunning, to say the least. There'd never been a hint of Fleming's background. He'd come and gone at the holidays like everyone else, but then, we'd never made small talk about presents received or trips taken. I sure as hell wasn't going to spill the beans about my dear old dad and let everyone think my life as a senator's son was anything short of glamorous. Aloof and quiet, Fleming hadn't had many friends, aside from Bailey and a couple of library nerds. Most of his time had been spent trying to top me. "I-I had no idea. Like I said, we were more classmates than friends. Rivals, to tell the truth."

A lineup of family photos sat on Daniel's credenza. I'd met his wife, Rachel, and his oldest son, Lev, who worked in the real-estate division of the firm. They hosted monthly dinners in their Upper West Side apartment, with Daniel strongly encouraging attendance. For a large firm, it boasted a family atmosphere.

"There's no room for that in the here and now." Why did that simple statement sound like a reprimand? "Whatever was in the past between you two, it's long ago. I'm sure if he does come on board, you'll show him the ropes and work together amicably."

"Of course. I'm all about being a team player."

Rah fucking rah.

"I'll keep you updated as to our search and its success."

That was my cue for being dismissed, and I rose to leave, but couldn't keep from asking, "So you're ready to extend an offer to Fleming? And whomever else you've decided on?" Not that I cared about anyone other than Brenner.

"Close to it."

Back in my office, I had to forgo my research project on Brenner Fleming to do my actual work. I reviewed two prenuptial agreements from my junior associates, three divorce decrees ready for filing, and instructed my paralegal, Delia, to set up mediation sessions. There were four new clients to meet and interoffice meetings with our real-estate and estates-and-trust divisions. Delia waited for my okay on the dates for all, and I watched my calendar fill up for the rest of the month.

"Jesus, I'm tired just looking at this schedule," I grumbled, and from the doorway, Miranda Holt, a third-year associate, laughed.

"Come on, Weston. You're sounding like an old man." She licked her full, glossy lips. "And I know you're anything but."

My exterior remained calm, but inwardly I seethed. Miranda had been present that night when Brenner and I had hooked up—God, I hated that phrase—and had been at the bar when I'd returned. She'd spent the rest of the evening questioning me on where I'd disappeared to, had asked if I'd wanted to leave for someplace quieter, and what I thought of interoffice romances.

"Can I help you with anything? I'm kind of busy." I waved a legal pad at her. "Monday and all that."

"I'm busy too. SEC filings to go over *and all that*," she mimicked. "Just wondering if you've heard the rumors."

"No, and I'm not interested. I deal in facts. And I would hope you and everyone else do as well."

She made a *moue*. "Be nice. It's just that if they bring in more partners, what does that say for us grunts working up the ladder, hoping to get an offer? It doesn't seem fair." Without an invitation, she entered my office and sat, her tight sheath dress hiking above the knees, revealing smooth, tanned thighs.

"I guess that's a question you should be asking the senior partners. Now, please excuse me. I have a meeting to prepare for."

She flounced away, giving me a view of a round butt that should have caused heart palpitations. Instead, all I wondered was how she breathed in something so tight.

"Maybe I really am getting old," I mused and, shaking my head, went to work.

**

Friday evening, and there I sat at another boring bar dinner—no Brenner Fleming this time. I'd admit to looking. When Isobel Morton sat next to me, I'd hoped she'd relight my fire. We'd had a casual affair in Boston before she'd accepted a position at a firm out west. It had been fun and easy. No strings. Exactly what I'd always liked. And Isobel had turned into someone more than a bed partner. She'd become a friend.

"Let's blow this place. Come home with me? My bar is better," I murmured, and she ran a foot up my leg.

"I thought you'd never ask."

We made out like kids in the back of the car, then entered my dark apartment, hands all over each other. I didn't bother to turn on the lights as I led her to the sectional couch in my living room. Lips locked, we lowered ourselves to the cushions.

"Come on, West." Isobel straddled me. Long, slender fingers glided down my tie and plucked open several shirt buttons before continuing their southern progress. "It's been ages, and seeing you tonight..." Her tongue slipped out to lick a path across her lower lip, then dipped into my ear. "I haven't forgotten how good it was the last time."

Isobel had nice, juicy curves, and our mouths met in a lingering kiss. I cupped her plump ass, giving her the green light. She slid to her knees, and I closed my eyes, waiting for the magic.

Her skilled tongue tried its best, but when minutes passed with only a halfhearted sign of life, I gave her a gentle push. Eyes brimming with questions, she got to her feet. I smiled weakly as I zipped up and stood.

"It's been a bitch of a week. I guess the late nights caught up with me." I slipped an arm around her waist. "Come to bed. Let me take care of you."

She patted my cheek and flipped her shining hair. "Honey, I've been taking care of myself for years. I don't need a man to give me an orgasm. What's going on?"

"I don't know. It's never happened before. Must be all the work. Maybe Daniel's right, and we do need to take on more partners."

Lies. All lies. Sure, I'd had sex and it was satisfying, but not the same after that night. With Brenner. It was getting off to get off. This night was the first time I'd been unable to get it up, though.

Shrewd brown eyes met mine. "I love you, West, but you lie like a dog. What's really wrong?"

"Damned if I know."

"Is it another woman? You're not a cheater."

"No way. I've seen enough in my life to know that's not how I want to live."

Case in point: Dear old Dad. Master philanderer. And Mom had never suspected, too wrapped up in her illness. Until the day she'd died, she'd believed in the fairy tale, but for the illustrious Senator Preston Lively, he could finally carry on his flings in public without repercussions.

Except for my utter contempt, but then again, why should his son's emotional state of mind matter to him?

My hand in hers, we returned to the couch. "So? What's the deal? Are you unhappy with the move? Or maybe you left someone behind. Someone you want but can't have?"

Isobel was way too insightful. I let my head fall to the cushion and stared at the ceiling, still not ready to confess what I wasn't sure of, but maybe if I talked about it out loud, it would make sense.

"No. The job's great, and I love living here. You know I was happy to move to the city."

"But?" Her fingers stroked my arm, nonsexual and comforting.

"But you're right. I *was* with someone last year. And it left an impression I haven't been able to get out of my mind. No matter how hard I try."

"I'll bet. You can't fuck someone out of your system. I've tried."

A chilling thought ran through me. *Shit.* I'd never imagined she'd fallen for me. "Isobel, I—"

A snort of laughter escaped, and her eyes danced. "Don't flatter yourself. I'm not talking about you, even though you're hot as hell. When I moved to Denver, I met someone and thought he was the one. Turns out, I was his one of many. It's been about a year, and I can't stop thinking of him, no matter how hard I've tried. I thought tonight would help, but looks like we're both suffering from the same problem."

"Maybe so."

It wasn't that I feared Isobel's reaction, but I hesitated to explain that my attraction was to a man. Mainly because I wasn't sure what the hell was going on in my head. Until I worked out the strange predicament I found myself in, I planned to say nothing.

Besides, Brenner and I couldn't stand each other. It had been a one-time thing. A mistake neither of us planned to repeat.

CHAPTER THREE
BRENNER

A call came through on my personal phone, from the firm of Walden, Booth, and Roth. For one wild moment, I thought it might be Weston, and I alternated between thrills and fear before deciding I was behaving like an idiot and answered it.

"Hello? Brenner Fleming."

"Mr. Fleming, this is Joanne Wilcox calling for Daniel Roth of Walden, Booth, and Roth. Mr. Roth would like to know your availability for lunch this week."

Instantly on alert once I heard who was calling, my brow furrowed. "I'm sorry? Lunch?"

"Yes. He said it's your choice of days."

"Uh, well," I fumbled, a bit shaken by this out-of-the-blue invitation. "My time is limited for the remainder of the week, but I'm free today if he's available."

"He is. Twelve thirty?"

A quick check of my calendar showed my next meeting to be at three. Could this concern the Fuller-Swanson meeting? It wouldn't surprise me if Weston had whispered something derogatory in his senior partner's ear. Why that would necessitate a meeting with his senior partner was beyond me, but I would put nothing past Weston Lively when it came to making himself look better at my expense.

"That sounds good."

"I'll make a reservation at The Bar Room at The Modern on Fifty-third. Does that work for you?" I admired her brisk efficiency.

"Yes, I'll be there. Thank you."

"You're welcome. Have a nice day."

I had a meeting in half an hour I should have been preparing for, but instead I read up on Daniel Roth and the firm. Impressive was an understatement—offices all over the country, with top-tier attorneys. Superstar clients. The senior partners were all on the boards of numerous bar associations and authors of leading articles quoted in legal publications. Their winning cases set precedents.

Of course this would be Weston's firm.

Annoyed, I clicked out of the multiple screens and tackled the work I had in front of me. There was no reason to be jealous—we might not be top tier, but our firm was well respected, and we didn't lack for our own well-known clientele. My phone buzzed.

"Your ten thirty is here, Brenner."

"Thanks, Donna. I'll be right there."

My clients deserved the best, and that was me. I'd never give them anything less than one hundred percent.

**

It almost felt like I was playing hooky by leaving the office in the middle of the day. Lunch for me was most often a sandwich or salad at my desk while I read files or caught up on emails.

The Bar Room was adjacent to the Museum of Modern Art and overlooked the outdoor sculpture garden. I hadn't been inside a museum in years and vowed this would be the year I kicked my cultural ass in gear. If I could find the time.

The hostess led me to the table where Daniel Roth awaited. I'd never personally met the man, but I'd seen him lecture and I'd read his articles. He was brilliant at both. At my approach, he rose and smiled.

"Thank you, Brenner, for meeting me on such short notice. I appreciate it."

We shook hands, and I sat opposite him. A server approached, and Roth and I chose sparkling water. Then I waited.

"I'm sure you're wondering why I've invited you here."

"The thought did cross my mind, yes," I joked. "I don't believe we've ever had a conversation before."

"No, but that doesn't mean I'm not aware of the bright stars in our ranks."

I might be closing in on forty, but it still gave my heart a happy bounce to hear a compliment from one of the giants in the profession. "Thank you. That's very kind of you to say and nice to hear."

At the server's interruption, we ordered lunch. We each wanted the pea soup, Roth ordered the beef, and I chose the lobster pasta. He clasped his hands, and I girded myself, but for what, I wasn't sure.

"We've decided to expand our family-law division. Our clientele and caseload are growing, and we've had our eye on you for a while as someone we feel would fit in perfectly with our mission and goals." He took a sip of water. "Thoughts?"

Stunned, I sat speechless.

Behind silver-rimmed glasses, Roth's eyes twinkled. "I see I've surprised you."

A weak smile curved my lips. "To say the least. I'm extremely flattered."

"I hope there's not a 'but' at the end of that statement." Knowing Roth's reputation, I gathered he didn't hear the word "no" often.

"I'm not saying that. Of course, I'd need to know more about what you have in mind."

"Of course." He proceeded to outline an offer, after which I needed a moment to recover before I responded.

"I don't know if you're aware that I grew up in foster care—it's why I chose to practice family law. I never knew my parents and had no desire to find them. After several attempts at placement, I found wonderful foster parents, who told me to dream big and never stop reaching for the top." My entwined fingers trembled, and I hid them in my lap. "I'm overwhelmed, to be honest. Walden, Booth, and Roth is the apex of the mountain, and to receive an offer of partnership is beyond my wildest dreams."

"You understand the way we're structured—and your compensation? I'm not asking what you make at Roman and White, but I have a good idea. I hope you think this is a worthwhile move for you."

"I understand." Unprepared as I was for this offer, I knew enough of the procedure to ask pertinent questions, and by the time our food arrived, I had a good idea of my workload, how much my buy-in would be, and my compensation.

If I were interested, of course.

We tabled the business discussion, and Roth spoke of his family, particularly his grandchildren. I listened and waited for the inevitable question.

"Are you married or do you have a significant someone?"

"No. Just me, myself, and I."

Roth laughed. "Sometimes that's the best company one could wish for."

"It wasn't easy being a foster child. Other kids kept away from me, either by choice or due to parental wishes. I was bounced around until I reached the Dunns, who loved me as if I'd been born to them. My foster parents were my best and, for the most part, only friends."

Frown lines bisected Roth's brow. "That's a sad way to live, but I can understand why you feel that way."

Somehow I doubted that Daniel Roth, founding partner of his law firm, board member of MOMA, and grandfather, could relate.

"In a way it helped me in my career. They pushed me to rely on myself and trust my instincts."

"I think you'll find that our firm is different. Yes, we're a large firm, but we know each and every person who works for us. In many ways we're like a family." That charming smile tugged at his lips. "Sometimes we disagree and shout. We can be annoying and occasionally dysfunctional, but deep down we work for the good of the people we represent and the firm itself."

"I don't think I've ever heard a law firm describe itself like that."

With the dishes cleared and the bill paid, it was time to go.

"Brenner, I truly think you'd fit in with both the work ethic and the personal dynamic of our firm. I hope you seriously consider our offer."

"I will. Again, I'm thrilled to be considered for partnership. I have a lot to think about, as you can imagine. And thank you very much for the delicious lunch."

We shook hands and parted ways. I chose to walk the ten blocks downtown to run the information through my head. It hadn't crossed my mind that a partnership offer would be the reason for our meeting, and shockwaves still rumbled through me. Me, a foster kid who used to cry himself to sleep at night after finding out he wasn't invited to the Friday night movies, Saturday night sleep-overs, or Sunday video game get-togethers. Pearl and Bill Dunn, my foster parents, had done all they could—rented the newest movies, got all the best snacks and candy I could eat—but it didn't matter Monday morning, hearing everyone at school laughing and talking about their fun weekends.

As I grew older, I took Pearl and Bill's positive words about me to heart and used my time to study. I'd gone to a specialized high school, gotten a scholarship to college, and graduated in the top one percent of my class. Bill and Pearl had urged me to go away for university, spread my wings, but Pearl couldn't keep her illness a secret any longer, and I chose to stay home and help. A perfect LSAT score, recommendations, and being valedictorian of my college class garnered me a full ride to law school. When it was obvious Pearl wasn't going to make it through my winter vacation, we had Christmas at her hospital bedside and buried her right after the new year. She made me promise to keep reaching for the stars. To come out on top.

My three p.m. client was delayed, so I picked up my phone and called Bill in Pompano Beach, Florida, where he'd moved three years earlier.

"How's my hotshot doin'?" He cackled.

"I don't know about that, but I'm doing well. That's why I'm calling. I need your advice."

"Lay it on me, kiddo."

Bill had been a New York City bus driver for thirty years. He'd let me wear his uniform cap and would bring me down to the depot, where I'd get to sit in his lap in the driver's seat and pretend to drive the bus. He'd tell everyone I was his son and bragged about how I was going to be the first in his family to go to college and be a doctor or a lawyer.

We'd gotten even closer since Pearl died. And I missed him terribly.

"I've had a partnership offer."

"You're already a partner, I thought?"

"I am. But this is with another firm. A bigger, much more established firm. It would be a huge step-up career-wise."

"What's to think about?" I heard him shake the ice in his cup and couldn't resist a smile. Pearl had made him kick the soda habit, and Bill always carried a big cup of ice with sparkling water.

"It'd be a bit of a drain financially in the beginning with the buy-in." I chewed on my bottom lip. Without revealing what had happened between Weston and me, I could fall back on our law-school rivalry. "But also, there's this guy, another lawyer. He and I butted heads, always trying to outdo each other. Could be awkward."

"So? You ain't joining the firm to make friends. You're there for business. It's a large firm. You ain't gonna have to see him if you don't wanna. And you know how to act if you do come face-to-face. Just like how I told you about those snooty kids when you were growin' up. Shoulders up, head high, and look 'em straight in the eye. You got nothin' to be ashamed of."

God, I missed him.

"You're right, I know. Just sometimes I forget."

"Well, kiddo, that's why you got me around to remind you." He snickered, and I laughed along with him. "I thought maybe you was callin' me to say you found a nice girl and was gonna get married. That'd be the only way you'd get me to come up there again."

"No. Nobody yet."

He grunted. "I ain't gettin' any younger, you know. Wouldn't mind seein' a coupla grandkids."

"I'll see what I can do about it. I have a date tonight." In the excitement over lunch and the offer, I'd almost forgotten.

"Listen. You've worked your ass off your whole life to prove you weren't the names those kids called you. Don't think we didn't know. You deserve to be happy and have a family of your own."

My face burned. "I tried to keep it from you. I didn't want to be trouble. I didn't want you to send me away."

"We neva woulda. Your mother loved you as if you were born to her. And you were my son. Those kids' parents were lucky your mother held me back, 'cause I mighta done somethin' stupid to them."

Tears burned, and my throat tightened. "Thanks. I guess no matter what, when you're a foster kid, the fear never leaves that you don't belong and it can all disappear in a flash."

"Thirty years ago, it was almost impossible for an over-forty couple to adopt. But when you came to us, all scared and skinny, we knew you belonged with us. And I woulda gone to the mat for that."

"I know. And I'm glad families these days don't have to jump through all the hoops we did." By the time things had changed enough that Bill and Pearl could adopt me legally, I'd been past eighteen. It hadn't made sense for them to adopt me as an adult, but they were my parents in every sense of the word.

"Now tell me about your date. Who's the lucky lady?"

My lips twitched. "I met her online. We're having drinks, and we'll see how it progresses. She's a stockbroker—I haven't had much luck with lawyers, so I'm branching out."

"Good," Bill agreed. "Maybe she can give us some tips. Ha-ha."

I joined him in his laughter. "I'll wait for the second date, if you don't mind."

Talking to Bill always put me in a better mood, and after we said good-bye, I dove into my cases for the day with little chance to think of the lunch with Daniel Roth or the offer. It wasn't until I was walking into Cipriani Downtown to meet my date that I realized I should've sent a thank-you to Roth. I made a note on my phone to send one that evening.

"May I help you?" The hostess awaited at the entrance.

"I have a reservation—Brenner Fleming. I'm expecting someone to join me."

"I'm here, Brenner." A husky voice had me spinning on my heel. "Lydia Grant."

"Nice to meet you." She was beautiful, and her cheek was smooth and cool when she leaned in for a welcome kiss. A delicious scent wove around me, and my pulse quickened. A good sign—great, in fact. I hadn't had this kind of reaction to a woman in a year.

"This way, please." We were led to a table tucked away in the corner and presented with menus.

"Do you feel like having food, or should we start with just drinks?" Lydia met my eyes over the cocktail listing.

"I'm easy."

"Good to know."

Her brown eyes danced, and my cheeks burned. Not that I was a prude, but I'd never been the kind of person to enjoy sexual banter. Some things were better off left in private.

We ordered drinks and some appetizers to share, and she asked me about my job and where I worked.

"I'm not familiar with that firm."

"We're a boutique firm. I like it that way." Her frown surprised me. "What's wrong?"

"Nothing...just that I'd think you'd want to be in a more well-known practice. It'll make you a lot of money and give you exposure."

I wasn't liking where this was heading, but I figured that was why there were first dates. To find out these little quirks.

"Not everything is about making the most money. I deal with a lot of emotional issues with my clients. They're not simply another file to me. Keeping it smaller enables me to give my clients more personalized service." Daniel's reference to the firm being like a family was a reason I'd consider moving to them.

"My father is a doctor, and the first thing he taught me was never to get emotionally attached to my clients at work. I can't think about the people behind the companies I trade or invest my clients in." She lifted an elegant, silk-clad shoulder and accepted her drink from the server. "If I short them and they go bankrupt, it's not my fault."

Technically she was correct, but that didn't mean I had to like it. I was no Boy Scout, but there were certain things that would keep me up at night.

We ate our appetizers and chatted about plays and books—safe things we'd discussed online and agreed upon. When the server appeared and asked if we were interested in dinner, I opened my mouth to say yes, but Lydia answered for us.

"No, we'll take the check, please."

The server withdrew, and Lydia directed her forthright gaze to me. "You're a nice guy, Brenner, but there's no spark, and no reason to force it."

A bit hurt, I kept my opinions to myself. "Not a problem." I reached for the check, and Lydia slid four twenties across the table.

"Here's my share."

She snapped her purse shut and stood. I got to my feet, gave her a perfunctory kiss on the cheek, and watched her walk away. I paid the bill, got into my car, and within half an hour was in my apartment, writing that thank-you email to Daniel Roth.

Was I selling out if I moved to Walden, Booth, and Roth? My conversation with Lydia made me sound like a virtuous do-gooder, but in truth, receiving an offer like that made me feel damn good about myself.

After puttering around my apartment, I sat with a cup of tea and practiced a bit of meditation to wind down for bed. Of course that was the moment my phone buzzed, and figuring it was Daniel Roth, I decided to peek.

I was wrong.

> *Heard you had a nice meet and greet with Daniel. Are you going to say yes? Don't worry. I'll teach you the ropes.* ~W

And a fucking winky emoji.

All my inner peace vanished. How the hell could I work with Weston Lively? *Pompous ass.* The intervening years hadn't dulled his shine, and he'd only grown into the role as a wealthy and privileged senator's son who'd had everything handed to him without needing to ask.

"Bastard."

Ignoring the message, I went to bed, but Weston remained on my mind. The next morning, I woke up from a dream of the two of us that was so filthy, I couldn't catch my breath. Before I could think of moving, I had to get off. I palmed my dick, sliding my grip the same way Weston had touched me that night, and all I could think of was his hot, wet mouth on mine, the rasp of a scratchy late-night scruff, and hard muscles pressing me into the bureau. My body pulsed and throbbed with need.

"Oh, fuck."

I arched off the bed and came, shooting a hot stream over my hand. Guilty, I glanced around, as if someone had watched me pleasure myself, thinking of a man. But not just any man.

Weston.

In the shower, I argued with myself that I'd be foolish to allow that jerk to influence a major life decision. If I thought the move would benefit me more than staying where I was, Weston Lively would never keep me from my goal.

I deleted his message and headed to the subway.

CHAPTER FOUR
WESTON

Even though it had taken me more than an hour of searching through old alumni directories to find Brenner's number, there'd been no doubt in my mind when I texted him that he'd ignore it. I'd done it simply to get under his skin. Childish? Probably. But I'd wanted him to know that our steamy hookup the year before meant nothing and I was still in charge.

There'd been little time in the past month to casually drop in on Daniel to ask if Brenner had accepted the offer—I'd had to fly out to the West Coast to meet with a client, then to Florida for depositions. Upon my return, I'd had a mountain of paperwork to handle and emails to answer, not to mention a nasty custody battle. All this hostility from people who'd once promised to love each other for the rest of their lives saddened me. I might think that fidelity and the institution of marriage were a farce, but these people didn't, and I had to carefully navigate their fragile emotional state.

Today was the perfect example. A gay couple and their adopted child and dog: Randy, the Broadway star. His husband, Steven, a reality-TV celebrity. A fifteen-year age difference but they'd laughed at people's negativity. A giant, expensive wedding at the Met. Picture-perfect life on social media, until Randy had been caught with his tongue down a top model's throat and her hands in his pants. An explosion of photos of the infidelity came to light, and the marriage imploded.

Hand on the doorknob, I hesitated. Raised voices bled through the door, and I winced at the vitriol I heard. I pushed it open and decided I needed to set the tone from the outset.

"Good morning, everyone." My client, Steven Culver-Hobbs, and his soon-to-be ex, Randy Hobbs, glared at each other across the table. With a sigh and roll of his eyes, Randy's attorney greeted me, and I took a seat.

"It would be a great morning if we could get this done with." Randy's deep baritone swelled in the room. He was clearly playing a part, and Steven crossed his arms and said nothing.

"Well, a seven-year marriage, with a child and substantial assets, isn't something you merely get over. Plus." I put a hand on Steven's arm. "Steven is still suffering from your adultery. He's the aggrieved party here."

"You cheated," Steven burst out. "I gave up a career to stay home to take care of Forrest like we agreed, and you took that as a green light to stick your dick in someone else."

Unconcerned, Randy yawned. "You see the histrionics I've had to put up with? It's every day with these outbursts.

That doesn't make for a stable environment for a child. That's why I want full custody. Your career, such as it is," he sneered, "doesn't amount to crap compared to mine. Now that my current play is closing, I'm taking a few years off from acting to concentrate on Forrest and make sure he gets what he needs."

"What he needs is both his parents, but you ruined that."

Dammit, I needed to muzzle Steven. "Okay. So what are we looking at? There is a prenup, so the assets are taken care of, and you each can buy the other out of your current residence." I checked my list. "Bruno is going to stay with Steven."

"Yes. The dog was Steven's before our marriage."

"And you're not willing to share custody with Steven regarding Forrest?" I made a mental note to never see a play this dickhead was performing in. "That seems harsh."

"He's my son. I love him." Steven wept, and heartstrings I didn't know existed in my chest tugged hard.

"Steven's only thirty. I'm not sure he's emotionally ready for raising a child. I already have children and know what to expect." Randy lifted a shoulder, and I narrowed my eyes. I sensed a mix of cruelty and indifference, which pissed me off. Randy had checked out of the relationship and simply didn't care. He'd been married previously, and his ex-wife had their two children in California. Maybe this was his MO.

"Please don't take Forrest away from me." Tears rolled down Steven's cheeks. "You can have everything else, but not my child. If he stays with me, you can see him whenever you want, but you know he and I have bonded while you were performing. His therapist thinks it's for the best too. You loved me once, I know. Please, Randy."

Two grueling hours later, we had a tentative custody agreement hammered out. Steven would have custody during the school year, with weekend visits and summer vacation to Randy. They'd split major holidays.

"Goddamn, I need a drink," I muttered, walking into my office. There were several messages waiting for me, but I needed to decompress. Steven had hugged me after Randy left with his attorney.

"You have no idea how much getting custody means to me. I was kicked out by my parents when I told them I was gay. Forrest was our foster kid, and we decided to adopt him. He's had some trust issues because he was bounced around a lot as a young child, didn't even speak for the first year we had him. But I always wanted to be a parent, and I would never give up on him. Thank you."

Was that how Brenner Fleming had grown up? A different home every month or year? Abuse? God, what a nightmare. At the thought, I shuddered and dropped my head in my hands.

"Tough one, huh? I walked by and heard crying." Grady Allen stood in my doorway, and I met his eyes and nodded with relief. Grady was of counsel to the firm, our resident expert on adoption law, and I'd been planning on running the agreement past him before sending the final to my client and opposing counsel. He'd helped me on numerous cases since my transfer to the New York office, and we'd become friends. Grady was a psychologist as well as an attorney. Pretty damn impressive credentials.

"Awful. Come on in, and I'll tell you all about it and show you the agreement." I laid out the facts and what had transpired. Grady made a few corrections and additions to the agreement. "That boy is lucky he has a parent like Steven Culver to champion him."

"You're right about that." Harsh lines scored Grady's face, but his eyes were kind. The hint of several tattoos peeked out from beneath his collar and cuffs. He most definitely didn't fit with the white-bread corporate image of the firm. "Most foster children never get adopted, and many—especially if they're LGBTQ—end up in homes where they're sexually abused, so they often run away."

"Is that what happened to you?" On a hunch, I put the question out there. "I'm not looking to out you or anything. But I know how personally you take these cases."

"When it comes to children, I do. They're our most vulnerable." A rare grin tugged his lips upward. "And no, you're not outing me. I'm not gay, but I have a brother who is. We were separated and put into the foster care system and only found each other about ten years ago. So yeah. I guess to me, every child is a personal battle."

"Daniel knows your backstory?"

"Yes. He's invested in having people in the firm who can truly empathize and understand what their clients have gone through." His brown eyes crinkled shut with laughter. "Isn't your father a senator? Guess I can figure out where you fit in with all this."

Oh, I bet you have no idea. An absent father who cared more about his image than spending time with a son who'd discovered what an adulterous bastard he was. A mother who'd put herself second and had ignored taking care of herself until it was too late. I prided myself on never allowing my personal life to bleed into the professional, so much so that when my father had been reelected to the Senate the first time, I'd made sure to schedule depositions across the country to avoid having to attend his oh-so-incredible victory party.

And now that he had his little girl and young wife, I doubted he even noticed I was missing. I'd had to find out from a press release that I had a half sister, as he'd never bothered to let me know. At the moment, however, he was on track to be his party's nominee for president—something I had yet to deal with—and was trying to reconnect and get me involved, but I ignored his emails and texts. I didn't give a damn about him and his career, and I sure as hell wasn't going to meet my little sister on a stage in front of the cameras so he could get his photo op.

"I guess I bring the fun. And the dashing good looks."

Laughter burst from Grady. "Along with a massive ego."

I grinned. "I have no complaints."

Grady hitched his chair closer. "Lemme ask you something."

"About?" I wasn't against a little office gossip. It broke up the monotony of staring at papers and filings all day.

"Miranda Holt. You two a thing?"

I put up my hands. "Nope. No. Is that what she's saying?"

"No, I just think she's hot as fuck, and I want to ask her out, but wouldn't if you two were dating."

"Go for it."

He studied me, and I could see the wheels turning. "You have someone else?"

"No. And yes, she's beautiful and brainy. I just don't date other lawyers, especially in the same firm. I know others have made it work, but I've heard horror stories about how messy it can get. Even if we are in different divisions, it's best to steer clear."

"Good thing I'm not a partner, then."

That was something I'd always wondered about. "How come? I'm sure Daniel would snap you up in a second."

A twinkle lit Grady's eyes. "Maybe that's about to change as well." He got to his feet. "Gotta go."

"Wait." I sprang out of my seat. "What're you saying? Are they asking you as well?"

"As well as who?"

I made a face. "Brenner Fleming. Daniel's really high on him joining. Do you know him?"

"Yeah, sure. His firm is small but high quality." Grady shrugged. "He's a good attorney. I could work with Fleming—

why, you've got an issue with him? He's always seemed like a pretty solid guy. Knowledgeable and levelheaded. Plus, he's excellent in child custody cases."

"No, no issues. We knew each other in law school." I grimaced, and Grady laughed.

"So it was like that? Listen, law school isn't the real world. Besides, that was fifteen years ago—a lifetime. You're not the same person you were then, and I'll bet he isn't either. I'm sure if he comes over, you'll be able to work with him."

Once Grady left, I sent the file to my paralegal to be updated, and yawned. I hadn't had a moment to myself this past month. I sat in my chair, listening to blessed silence.

So of course the phone rang, and my secretary buzzed me.

"It's Daniel."

"Thanks." I waited for the *click*. "Hello? Daniel?"

"Weston. I'm heading back to the office. Are you going to be there in the next hour?"

I checked my calendar. "Yes. I have a phone conference on the Fuentes-Sterner case, but other than that, I'm free."

"Okay. See you then."

"Uh, can—"

But the phone went dead, and I had little time to ruminate, as my paralegal entered with the file for my phone conference and I had to prep. Luckily, it was a mediation, and both sides agreed to be...agreeable. Cases like this put me in a better mood, and afterward I strolled into Daniel's office. He pointed to the chair in front of his desk.

"Sit, sit."

I could tell something was up, but I kept my thoughts to myself.

"We've made some decisions, and Brenner Fleming and Grady Allen will be coming on board as partners. You and

Brenner have each indicated that there's a bit of a history between you, but Brenner has assured me that it's all in the past and will have no bearing on your ability to work together." Stern-faced, he removed his glasses. "I'm certain you can give me the same guarantee?"

"Of course." Recalling my earlier conversation with Grady, I realized he was right. "Too many years have passed to keep up a silly rivalry that has no meaning in the real world. We're adults, and our main concern is serving our clients."

I could play nice in the sandbox.

Daniel chuckled. "Good to hear that my words have had the desired effect on you. As I mentioned, we're also beefing up our real-estate and estates-and-trust divisions. We're looking to increase our billings significantly with all these additions."

"More money is always a good thing." Maybe it was crass to say out loud, but I always spoke my mind. "I know what Grady brings to the firm, but how is Fleming a rain-maker for us? I'm not questioning you, obviously. Just curious."

"It's convoluted, but Brenner is friends with restaurant owner Tony Gigante."

"I see." Something niggled in my brain. "Isn't Gigante related to the mob?"

Daniel sighed. "I've yet to see any proof, and believe me, I've looked. But aside from Gigante's restaurant connections, and his wife's beauty business, Brenner is friendly with Gigante's wife, Christine. And she comes with a very big fish—Madden Steele."

I whistled. "Now that's a name I recognize. Very big fish indeed. I'm sure he has his own attorneys, though."

"With the money Steele Industries has, they have their businesses spread around. We'd be handling some of the corporate tax work." Darkness settled over Daniel's face.

"Brenner mentioned that Christine Gigante has quite a few friends who are contemplating divorce. Sad, isn't it? It's the one part of the job I've never liked—benefiting off someone else's misery." He pinched his eyes shut for a moment. "But then again, I guess we're also helping people start new lives."

"And escape from terrible situations. Although some don't know when to give up and walk away. They keep holding on to something that died."

Perhaps something in my voice caught Daniel's attention because he said, "Anything you want to talk about, Weston? You know my door is always open."

But mine wasn't. I'd slammed it shut, locked it up tight, and thrown away the key.

"No, just ruminating on the past month of cases I've seen."

"Such as? Care to share with me? Perhaps I could help."

A dispirited sigh escaped me. "Do you ever get tired seeing the breakdown of a marriage? All the hate that was once love? I know you and Rachel have been married for almost half a century, but sometimes I wonder if that's a thing of the past."

"And you reaffirmed exactly why I campaigned to have you come to New York and work with me. It's not despair you feel. It's your heart aching." I watched as Daniel left his chair to come sit by my side. "I know your father wasn't the best role model. But you believe in fidelity. Love."

"Whoa." I held up a hand. "I don't know how you ended up there, but that's not where I was heading. And as far as Brenner Fleming and what he can bring to the firm, sounds good. If you're happy, so am I." The last thing I needed was to unburden my sad self to my senior partner.

Daniel studied my face. "Good. He'll be here tomorrow. I'll bring him by to say hello."

I nodded. "I'll see you then. I'd better get back to my office. I have a client who's unhappy with the custody arrangement her husband is looking for, and I'm afraid it could get ugly."

"Okay. Good luck."

My upcoming call would be miserable, but I couldn't help the smile on my face at the thought of seeing Brenner in the morning. I might've told Daniel that our rivalry was silly, but sparring with him had always put me in a good mood, and I relished the opportunity to flex those muscles. I returned to my office, but before I called the client, I made an appointment for a haircut.

Had to look my best when I came face-to-face with the enemy.

CHAPTER FIVE
BRENNER

There was no reason to be nervous. I'd spoken to the senior partners at my firm, and though they were sad to see me go, they didn't make a counteroffer. I hadn't expected them to. It was hard to compete with the best. After that, it was easy.

At nine thirty I arrived at the offices of Walden, Booth, and Roth and was escorted to Daniel Roth's office, where he greeted me with a handshake.

"Brenner. Good to see you. I can't tell you how thrilled we all are that you've decided to join us."

Highly doubtful, as Weston Lively's name was still on the masthead, but I refrained from pettiness. "It's great to be here. I'm looking forward to jumping in, feet first."

"As soon as all the legalities are straightened out and the paperwork is signed, sealed, and delivered." A tall man stopped at the doorway, and Roth's eyes lit up. "Grady, come in, please. Have you met previously? Grady Allen, Brenner Fleming."

Grady approached with an outstretched hand, and I stood to greet him. "No, I haven't worked with you personally, Grady, but I've heard of you. I do some 18b cases. I see we're going to be the newbies in the division."

A surprisingly charming smile brightened Grady's face. "Looking forward to working with you as well. There's a good team in place here." His gaze sharpened. "I hear you know another colleague, Weston Lively."

"Law school classmates," I responded dryly. "But we've been out of touch since we graduated."

Except when he touched my dick last year.

Roth—*Daniel*—joined us at the door. "Let's go say hi to Weston, and then I'll introduce you to everyone else."

Coming from a small, four-partner, twenty-person attorney firm, I'd expected to be a bit overwhelmed, but I passed more people in the one floor of the office here than I normally saw in a week at my old firm. I'd have to adjust, but I'd deal with it. The bump in my partnership draw and the prestige of working at the firm would make that easy. Even with the prospect of working with Weston, I was feeling pretty good about all of it.

"West. It's official," Daniel announced. "Grady is a partner, and here's Brenner Fleming. We're about to sign off on his partnership, so it made sense to bring them on together."

I braced myself, and with a grin on my face, stepped forward. "Hello, Weston. Good to see you again."

"I'm glad to see you too." His hand clasped mine, and it was as if we were back in that room at the Marriott. My throat dried, and sweat broke out over my body. But it wasn't only me affected. I could see West's green-gold eyes widen and his lips press tight. He jerked away and stuffed his hands into the pockets of his slacks.

Daniel said, "Obviously Grady knows his way around, but he stopped by when I was talking to Brenner, so he's tagging along for the unofficial meet and greet. I'm going to finish introducing Brenner, then show him his office and let him read through the mountain of material."

"All the fun stuff," Weston teased, but his face was strained. I caught Grady's odd look but chose to ignore it and nodded at Weston. I followed Daniel to meet the other attorneys, then he brought me to an office two doors down from Weston's. Guess I couldn't request to sit on the opposite side of the floor.

"Here it is. We've had our IT department prioritize you, so I don't anticipate it should take longer than a week for you to be fully on board. Your attorney has sent the partnership agreement for us to review. We'll get that done and have you part of the family." Daniel put a hand on my arm. "I'm serious when I say that we might be a large firm, but we're not that big that we treat everyone like numbers, easily replaced. Walden, Booth, and Roth works because we are collaborative. Anyone in your division is available for you to bounce ideas off of should you need it. Though it often seems that all we deal with is the wreckage of families, I chose family law because we have the ability to fit the broken pieces together. I'll leave you to get the lay of the land."

For someone who didn't like change, this was all happening pretty damn fast. A bit overcome, I nodded, walked into the office, and sat behind the desk. I had a nice view of midtown, and the space was painted in a soothing pale green. The gleaming black conference table was surrounded by gray padded chairs. Bookcases filled with the New York State CPLR as well as McKinney's, and legal treatises lined the wall. It was twice the size of my office at Roman and White, and I snapped a few pictures and sent them to Bill, with the tag "movin' on up." A call from my attorney popped up on my phone.

"Laz? How the hell are you?"

"Not as good as you, I'm thinking." He chuckled. "I cc'd you a copy of the partnership agreement I returned to them. Big shot."

"Very funny. And you should talk. How's your client, Madden Steele? I see he's got another complex going up, this time in Long Island City."

"He's good, and I'm not involved with the company, only his personal business. Seriously, though, from the agreement, this looks like a great move for you."

"Yeah. I think it could be. Still can't believe it. It happened so fast." I ran a hand over the clean, smooth surface of my desk, as if touching it made it more real. "Not too bad for a foster kid."

"You did good. And you deserve good things."

When I'd first been admitted to the bar, Laz and I had met handling 18b criminal court cases—assigned counsel for people who couldn't afford a lawyer and for which Legal Aid representation would be a conflict. I was intrigued by the attorney who came to court in jeans and sneakers, tattoos up and down his arms. I'd found myself involved in pro bono immigration cases involving separating children from their parents, and Laz and I had worked together and become friends. I admired his dedication and passion.

"Thanks, Laz. I'm not sure anyone deserves anything, but I'll take it."

"Heard Grady Allen is joining with you."

The legal grapevine ran as hot and fast as any Hollywood gossip. "Yeah, my first time meeting him in person, but I've heard his reputation. I just met him for a hot second when Daniel was bringing me around."

"He's good people."

"I'll keep that in mind."

"You should," Laz stated, and his insistence had me laughing.

"Someone's got opinions."

"Look, Brenner. We've known each other for close to fifteen years. You can lose yourself in a case, giving your all to your clients."

"Someone has to look out for the kids. Too often the parents are more interested in hurting each other and using their children as pawns than doing what's right. I have to make sure they're taken care of."

"You've got a soul, Brenner. You're climbing higher on the ladder of success with clients who don't have to worry about how to pay your fee, but I know you won't lose track of the people who can't."

I winced, knowing that lately I'd neglected the pro bono side of the profession, and I vowed to become more active once I'd settled into the partnership.

After the call ended, I sat staring off into space, until fingers snapping in front of my face brought me around.

"Slacking off already, and you're not even on board yet." Weston's laughing face drove away all my good vibes.

"What do you want?" I pushed his hand out of my line of vision.

"Is that any way to treat your new fellow partner?"

God, I wanted to smack that smug grin off his face. "Actually, I was thinking about how I need to start doing pro bono work again. I'm sure that's high on your list, isn't it? Helping the less fortunate?"

There was no time for him to answer, as Daniel passed by in the hallway, then backtracked and stopped. "Oh, good, just the two I wanted to see." He joined us. "Saves me the trouble of calling a meeting."

Puzzled, I glanced at Weston, who seemed as lost as I was. "Is something wrong?"

"Not at all. I'm having HR schedule you, Brenner, for all the usual workplace training. But our director of human resources reminded me that with the influx of new partners and hiring additional associates, now would be the perfect time for team-building exercises."

To be expected, but I didn't like where my thoughts were heading, and from Weston's tight-lipped expression, I surmised he was thinking the same thing.

"Every two years we do a day of team building. The firm rents a hotel in the area solely for the partners. We hire a company to run the exercises during the day where you're assigned partners, but you can sit with whomever you want for dinner." He chuckled. "Hopefully by that time, you won't be sick of each other."

Weston grimaced, and Daniel frowned.

"Is there a problem, Weston?"

"No, not at all. Sounds like a great idea," he rushed to assure Daniel, whose troubled face smoothed to an approving one.

"Good. You'll both be expected to attend."

"Great," I said with a nod.

Daniel walked out, and Weston snorted. "*Great*," he mimicked. "I'm sure you're thrilled about these ridiculous scenarios they'll put us through. You don't have to suck up to Daniel."

"What the hell are you talking about?" My temper, always on edge with Weston, flared hotter. "I'm being polite."

A sneer tugged at a corner of his mouth. "I remember how eagerly you used to raise your hand in class, so anxious to show the professor how well you briefed the case and knew all the talking points."

"Oh, give it a rest. You wouldn't know hard work if it bit you in the ass."

A thunderous expression darkened his face, and he leaned closer. "What the hell is that supposed to mean?"

Unwilling to be at a disadvantage and have him loom over me, I got to my feet, coming nose to nose with him.

"I thought I spoke pretty clearly and simply with no big words to confuse you." A muscle in his jaw ticked. "Everything you've accomplished in life, you got handed to you because of your father."

Sparks flew from those furious eyes before they narrowed to slits. His nostrils flared. "You don't know what the fuck you're talking about."

It was fun to poke the bear, and obviously mentioning his senator father got under his skin. "Don't I? Daddy must've paid a lot to help you get where you are."

Weston paled. "Go to hell," he snarled and stalked away.

A twinge of regret twisted in my chest. Had I gone too far? Or was I too close to the truth? Weston was extremely bright, of course—he'd beaten me in class rank at almost every turn in the three years we spent at school—but I'd heard mutterings from other students about his family connections.

It was probably best to leave for the day. I had an office to pack up at Roman and White, plus a million little things to work on, such as acquiring a new paralegal. When I passed by Weston's office, he slammed the door in my face.

So much for mutual goodwill.

** **

"We're here by the beautiful Long Island Sound to work on team building." The speaker, Mitch Carlson, a midfifties man dressed in a polo and khakis, stood at the lectern in the front of the ballroom. About forty people filled the space. Most knew each other, but there were about five or six of us—the new partners I'd met earlier in the month at orientation—who, like me, sat alone without anyone to chat with.

Carlson continued. "All of you will meet tonight at dinner and fill out strengths quizzes, and then tomorrow morning, right after breakfast, we'll match you up with another person we've deemed your opposite and start to work. The purpose will be to gain trust and learn from each other."

Out of the corner of my eye, I spotted Weston slipping in the back and taking a seat in the last row. Grady Allen walked past him and chose the chair next to mine.

"Did I miss anything?"

"Just opening remarks. We fill out a questionnaire at dinner, and tomorrow they pair us up with our opposite to begin trust-building exercises."

A groan escaped him. "Damn. Now I remember why I had no desire to be part of a firm." Laughing eyes met mine. "All this stuff gives me hives. I'm better working alone. But I do like the benefits."

"Maybe we'll get lucky and they'll put us together. We're pretty opposite."

A knowing smile tugged at the corner of Grady's lips. "You think so?"

I wasn't sure what to make of that remark, but I had no time to ask questions or speculate further as we were called in to dinner and I was seated by another new partner from Contracts. We talked about our first jobs out of school and interesting cases we'd handled. I was feeling better about the move to the firm, and Weston and I had each managed to keep out of the other's way—I'd barely seen him all evening. He and Grady had found a way to sit together, and as I hadn't seen Weston fill out his test, I would lay bets he'd manage to get out of doing the exercises. From his reaction when I mentioned his father, I concluded that I'd hit a nerve and maybe the truth. People who grew up like Weston Lively were used to having a smooth path with no cracks, causing them to stumble and fall.

I filled out the test and handed it in. After the dinner was finished, most people headed to the hotel bar, but recalling what had happened last time, I chose to turn in early. On my way out, Grady waved me over, but as Weston stood by his side, I shook my head and walked toward the elevator.

The bed was surprisingly comfortable, and as soon as my head hit the pillow, I fell into a deep, dreamless sleep. At nine the next morning, I found my way to the room where breakfast was being served, but all I needed was coffee and lots of it. I finished my second cup and felt a hand on my shoulder.

"How come you didn't want to join us last night?" Eyes slightly red-rimmed, Grady held his own mug.

My lips twitched. "Maybe because of how you look. What time did you fall asleep?"

His eyes danced. "Who said I slept?" He knocked my shoulder. "Just kidding. But you know how it goes. These weekends away are for people to let their hair down."

"Not me. I fell asleep at ten and woke up at eight. Best night's sleep I've had in weeks." I glanced around. "Do you know when we're going to get the test results and see whom we're paired up with?" I didn't see Weston approach and couldn't spare a dig. "Is your partner in crime here, or did he sneak away already?"

"I don't sneak, Fleming. I have nothing to be ashamed of." Scorn dripped from his eyes. "Or hide."

My stomach dove into free fall, and I turned away, pretending to be interested in the display of breakfast foods and pastries. My third cup of coffee in hand, I ignored Weston's smirking face and addressed Grady directly. "I'm going to go wait for the test results. I'll see you later."

Seats were filling up, and I took a chair on the aisle. Mitch, the facilitator, iPad in hand, waited until everyone was seated. "All right, everyone. We've got our results. I'll read them in no particular order, and then the two partners will meet up here and be given your materials."

Minutes passed, and I watched people pair off, including Grady, who gave me a salute as he sauntered past to join Maryann Evens, an older woman of about sixty, wearing a strict, conservative suit. Large round glasses perched on her nose, and her silver hair was pulled into a tight bun. I'd seen her in orientation, studying every pamphlet and resource guide they'd given out. She was a real-estate attorney, and I didn't think I'd heard her utter anything other than hello. They'd definitely chosen their partnership correctly, as the contrast between her and the tattooed, jeans-and-T-shirt-wearing Grady Allen was striking.

The two of them began chatting like old friends, but that shouldn't surprise me—Grady had that enviable quality of making people feel comfortable. Maryann took their packet, and the two of them walked away. A swift appraisal of the room showed about ten of us left, including Weston, who sat with his legs stretched out and—unsurprisingly—was on his phone. I doubted Weston took anything seriously.

"Weston Lively." At the sound of his name, Weston slipped the phone into his suit pocket and strolled to the front.

"Jerk," I muttered to myself. He behaved as though he were accepting an Academy Award.

"Who's the lucky person who gets to spend the whole day with me?"

Mitch squinted at the screen. "Brenner Fleming."

Well, shit.

CHAPTER SIX
WESTON

Now that the teams were chosen, they'd separated us into two rooms, and we were at assigned tables. Brenner and I sat several seats apart. He hadn't looked at me once, and I wasn't about to be the first one to speak. Not after that nasty crack about how I'd used my father to get where I am today.

Bastard knew nothing. I hadn't seen the man in years.

Matter of fact, only this morning, my dear old dad had emailed me with an invitation to his primary election night party, a week and a half from now. Me and his closest thousand friends. I'd deleted it.

A different facilitator, a young woman in a bright-green dress and purple-rimmed glasses, waited for everyone to finish getting settled. They'd provided coffee and pastries for us, and I made sure to take an extra-large cup. Black. The night before, Grady and I had gotten a little deep into the Grey Goose, and my head was still feeling the effects.

"Good morning, everyone. I'm Sara Lindstrom, your facilitator for the day. I hope we're all ready for a day of exploration and trust-building. The purpose of this exercise is to allow you to open up and see the world not only from your point of view, but from others' as well, something we all need, I think, don't you?"

She nodded at the murmurs of agreement. I heard a huff from the side and cut a glance at Brenner, who sat stone-faced. His usual piss-ass expression. Suddenly, I wanted to annoy the shit out of him, and I forgot about my headache.

"She's right, don't you think, Brenner?" I put on my most winning smile.

The full force of his withering stare pierced through me, and then he faced the front of the room again. Of course, I wouldn't let that stop me. There was no denying—especially to myself—that I could be an annoying bastard at times, and this was going to be one of them.

"You're going to have to talk to me at some point. Like it or not, we're partners for the day."

"Did you rig this deliberately to try and piss me off?"

I took a moment to answer and sipped my coffee, sensing it would be a minimum three-cup morning to deal with all the bullshit. "I'm glad you think I have so much power, Brenner, but the truth is, I'm a mere mortal." I smirked. "Though many have called out to God when they were with me." Damn, I was good.

"Unreal," he muttered. "I'm sure they have. But hell is another dimension of the afterlife."

I couldn't help it and busted out laughing. Sara stopped speaking about partnerships, and the entire room turned to look at us. While Brenner's face flamed, I shrugged. "Sorry."

"Care to share what was so funny?" Sara encouraged.

I smirked at Brenner. "No. Sorry. It was personal. I don't think Brenner would appreciate it."

A multitude of brows rose high, and Brenner glared blue daggers at me before a wicked grin kicked up his lips. "Oh, I don't mind. To paraphrase, Weston insinuated that being with him is out of this world, and I said hell is also."

Snickers and laughter abounded, and I didn't like how Brenner had turned the narrative around. "All right, can we return to the tasks at hand?" I called out. "I'm sure we have a lot of work for the morning."

"Suck-up," Brenner whispered.

A bit disconcerted by our interruption, Sara placed the perky smile back on her lips and picked up her script. "Our first assignment is for each of you to face each other and give five strengths and five weaknesses about yourselves. Your partner will write them down, and at the end of the weekend, we'll revisit them and see if you have a change of heart about any or all of them. You will have thirty minutes to complete this."

Chairs squealed and shifted as people began the task. I followed suit, but Brenner remained frozen, staring at the tabletop.

"Is there a problem?" I asked.

"This isn't going to work. We should be reassigned to different people."

"The hell we are," I growled. "And be the only ones who can't do the assignment? You know they'll report that to the senior partners. I'm willing if you are."

It was the truth. Maybe Brenner would stop being the uptight dick I knew in law school, and we could start acting like adults. Not that I didn't like to push his buttons, but I was curious to see what his answers would be.

That annoyed face reappeared. "I guess you're right."

"How much did it hurt you to have to say that?" I joked.

To my surprise, Brenner laughed, and an unexpected and shocking wave of heat rolled through me. My breath caught, and I grabbed my almost empty cup of coffee and finished it. What the fuck was that? I could barely get it up for Isobel, but Brenner laughing set my balls on fire.

"I, uh, need another cup of coffee." Without waiting for him to respond, I jumped out of my seat and ran to the back of the room, where the machines were. I took a second to settle my racing nerves. Obviously, I was still worked up from the previous night and the two women Grady and I had been talking to. Either that or the hangover I was fighting.

Brenner's dark head was bent over the table as he wrote. He hadn't shaved this morning, and a rough stubble covered his jaw...and why the fuck was I noticing that? *Jesus. Now my libido woke up to make an entrance?*

My hand shook, and I drank some of the new coffee I'd poured and refilled it. In a goodwill gesture, I decided to bring some to Brenner. Not knowing how he took his, I brought it to him undoctored.

"Here." I slid the cup to him. "I figured we could both use some fortitude."

"Thanks." He peered inside the cup. "How did you know I took it black?"

"I didn't. I drink it that way." My grin was halfhearted. "I'm sure if you didn't like it, you'd let me know."

He rubbed his chin. "We only have around twenty minutes left. I've started my list. Better move on it."

"You got it, boss." I took up the pen provided. It wasn't hard to list my strong points. As for the weaknesses? *Hmm...*might take a while. I gnawed on the end of the pen before scribbling out some things.

"Finished? I don't want to run out of time."

Of course not. Brenner wasn't a rule-breaker. Some things never changed. "Yep. Let's go."

Brenner folded his arms. "Since you always claim number one, you go first. Besides, I know you love talking about yourself."

I grimaced. "Funny. All right. My strengths: I'm a fast learner, I'm organized. I'm loyal, and I don't stop until I win."

"That's four."

I winked. "I'm a great lover."

Brenner flushed, and his eyes shifted side to side. "What the fuck does that have to do with work?"

"Nothing. I just figured it'd get a rise. I like annoying you." Cackling, I waved a hand. "Number five: I don't lie, and I always say what I mean. It goes hand in hand with always being able to spot a bullshitter. It works in depositions or if I think people—including clients—are lying to me or trying to fudge the truth."

Brenner nodded, writing on his pad. "And your faults?"

I nibbled on my bottom lip. "Of course, that was harder. But I can be quick to judge, a bit of a wise-ass—"

"A bit?" Brenner snorted.

"Hey." I jabbed my pen in his direction. "This is my self-assessment, not yours. To continue...I have a hard time letting go, and I tend to think I'm always right. Plus, if you hurt me or someone I care about, you're dead to me."

"So no forgiveness?"

"Forgiveness is easy if the person means nothing. But if you're supposed to care...no. I don't give a shit about explanations."

All I could think of was when I'd been fifteen and on a class trip to Dallas. I'd wanted to surprise my father, who'd also been there for a conference, so I'd sneaked out of our hotel to visit the one my father was staying at. I'd stepped out of the elevator and turned the corner...and my whole world blew apart, seeing him kissing a woman in the doorway of her hotel room before rubbing her ass and following her inside. Meanwhile my mother had sat at home, sick and unsuspecting.

"That's pretty harsh."

"I don't care. Some people don't deserve a second chance if they abused their first."

Brenner blinked, and his hand stilled. He lifted his head and met my eyes, and I almost flinched. The intensity of his gaze penetrated my soul, as if he were tearing apart the surface and digging beneath my skin. I had to switch up the mood.

"All right, I bared my guts. Your turn." Pen poised to paper, I was truly curious.

Brenner clasped his hands. "Strengths: I'm tenacious, punctual, honest, hard-working, and compassionate."

"Hard-working and passionate." I spoke aloud as I wrote, waiting for him to respond. I wasn't disappointed.

"I said *compassionate*," he snapped, a flush rising over his face. "Stop that."

I grinned. "Wise-ass, remember?"

Brenner rolled his eyes. "My weaknesses: I hold grudges, have a tendency to make snap judgments, not into socializing, don't trust easily, let work dominate my life."

From where I sat, knowing what I did of Brenner, it was all true.

"Well, all this makes us a messy couple." I slipped the page into my folder as Sara called out time.

"I hope you've finished and gained a little insight into yourselves. We're going to take a ten-minute break, and when we return, we'll do a trust-building exercise."

Half the people left their seats to get snacks, stretch, use the facilities, or do whatever. I checked my phone for any texts or emails. Grady had texted:

Dude, you surviving?

About to answer, my grin faded, replaced by the hot flush of anger at another text from my father.

> *The least you could do is respond. Paige and Emily will be at my side a week from Tuesday. I expect you to show your face and stop acting like a spoiled brat. Be a man.*

My vision blurred, and I shoved away from the table. I had to get out of the room. I needed air and ran for the nearest exit. Once outside, I dragged in deep breaths, but the shaking didn't stop.

Fuck him. Who the hell did he think he was to talk to me like that? He'd treated my mother like crap and only cared about me now for his photo op. For years I'd waited for an invitation to meet my sister, but none had come. Knowing my mother would want me to step up and be a big brother, I'd bitten the bullet and called their house and left messages, but they'd never been returned. Her first birthday had come and gone, and now she was almost four and I still hadn't met her. I leaned my hot cheek against the cool windowpane.

"West?"

Fuck. I closed my burning eyes for a second before facing Brenner with a forced smile. "Is it time already?"

"We still have a few minutes. Are you all right?"

"Yeah, of course." I brushed the hair off my sweaty brow. "Why do you ask?"

"I don't know, maybe because you look like you're about to throw up? Plus, you ran out of the room like a bat out of hell after checking your phone. Did you get bad news?"

"No." I pressed my lips together, but I wasn't sure if it was to stop myself from spilling my guts or busting out crying. Neither of which I cared to do with Brenner.

Not that he believed me, as the expression on his face indicated. "Uh-huh." He waited, and I collected myself as best I could.

"Aw, you want to walk in together, like we're friends?"

Side by side, we headed into the conference room.

"You're acting like more of an ass than usual," he murmured. "And I don't care what you say. I know you're lying. I've seen prisoners looking happier than you."

Ignoring him, I strode ahead and sat in my chair. With everyone in place, Sara once again stood up in front.

"This next exercise is one that many of you might be familiar with. We ask one of you to stand in front of the other and allow yourself to fall backward. The objective is to have trust in your partner to catch you. Both of you will do the falling and the catching, so no one gets an advantage over the other. And for those who don't feel they can catch their partner, you can improvise by placing a chair under them as they lower themselves to sit. The premise remains the same."

Brenner and I shared a glance, and neither of us appeared happy about this test.

"Well? You want to catch me or have me catch you first?" Putting on my most innocent face, I held my hands up. "I'll let you choose."

From the stupendous frown and deep furrows in his brow, I could only imagine the thoughts running through Brenner's brain.

"You'll *let* me. How magnanimous of you," he sniped, but then his face cleared. "My decision is you make the choice. Why should you get to decide who decides?"

"Do you hear how ridiculous that sounds—even for you?"

That jab settled it, and Brenner straightened up. "If that's how it's going to be, I'll catch you."

I took off my suit jacket, rolled up my sleeves, and held my arms out. "Come and get me."

CHAPTER SEVEN
BRENNER

Maybe Weston Lively could fool most people, but I wasn't one of them. Whatever he'd read on his phone had triggered him and sent him running. For the first time, the mask was off—that arrogant, devil-may-care facade I'd always hated had slipped, revealing unexpected emotional turmoil living inside him.

But if he refused to talk about it, I wouldn't push. He wasn't required to divulge his innermost feelings to me. I copied him and stood in my shirtsleeves. Other partners had already started, and I watched for a moment to see their techniques. Some caught the other person almost right away, but most waited until they were off-balance.

"Ready?"

Weston peered over his shoulder. "When you are." He winked. "Be prepared. I'm heavier than I look. All the weights I lift." He flexed his biceps, and I rolled my eyes.

"More like the weight of your ego."

He turned and began to tip toward me. I let him go a little past vertical, then caught him under his arms. *Damn.* He was right. He was pure solid muscle.

"*Oof.*" I grasped him tighter. Heat poured off him, transferring to me. His hair tickled my nose, and the curve of his ass pressed into my hips. He wore a light cologne that shouldn't have affected my breathing.

But it did.

We stood frozen for a second. Could he feel the rapid thump of my heart? I needed him off me and pushed him away.

"Nice catch," he murmured, but he didn't meet my eyes. "My turn."

"Give me a second."

"Take all the time you need."

Other teams had finished, and I didn't want to be the last one on display, with everyone watching.

"Okay."

I stood and fell. I expected Weston to catch me almost immediately like I had with him, but he let me lean and lean. I lost my balance and fell into his arms and chest with a loud grunt as he staggered several steps. We ended up with his arms holding me, his face buried in my neck. Again, like before, we remained rooted in place, only this time Weston's lips on my neck elicited an unwanted reaction from us both. His semi-hard dick pushed against my ass, and a throb of something unexpected curled low and deep in my belly. Cold, then heat, rushed through me, and my vision swam.

"Jesus, West." I sprang away from him. "What the hell was that about?" I snapped.

Looking almost as shaken as I felt, Weston pushed the hair off his brow. A flush stained his face. "I-I don't know what you mean. I caught you."

"You waited and almost let me fall on my ass. I should've known better than to trust you."

Confusion clouded his eyes. "Wasn't that the point? To let you know I'd catch you even if you tipped far past midpoint? If I did it right away, the exercise would prove nothing."

I stormed away from him, heading for the bathroom. God knew, I needed a minute to get my shit together. I splashed cold water on my overheated face and braced my hands on the sink. The door slammed open.

"What's wrong with you?" Weston approached me.

"Me? What's wrong with me?" My stomach churned at how turned-on I'd gotten from West's arms around me. It kept happening, and I didn't like it, didn't want it, yet I couldn't seem to stop it. And since there was no way in hell I'd let him know, I deflected with anger. "I'm the one who should be asking that question. You waited until the last second."

"No, I didn't. I was in complete control. I knew what I was doing."

"That's bullshit. Everyone else did it before their partner got too close to falling but you."

"I was following the directive. It's a trust exercise. I wanted you to feel like you could fall and be off-balance and I'd be there to catch you. Anything else you're thinking is your imagination."

"No, it's not." I wanted to say, *And neither was that hard-on in your pants*, but that would be starting something without knowing how to finish. "And while we're at it, stop standing so close to me." I scowled.

"I'm not. It's all in your mind. Like everything else you think about me."

"I don't think about you at all. You mean nothing to me."

He blinked, and I wondered if I'd gone too far. His lip curled, and he splayed his fingers over his chest. "I'm heartbroken."

"Another lie. You have to have a heart to have it broken."

He paled, and his lips tightened. "You know, Fleming? I used to think you were a nice guy. Now I see you're just a bastard."

Was that a slap in my face about where I came from? That I was a foster child with no idea who my parents were? Anger choked me, and I struck, wanting...needing to hurt him. Like he'd hurt me.

"I see nothing's changed since we left law school. You're still the same pretentious, spoiled brat you always were. Money can buy you an education and nice things, but it can't buy you decency. Something you clearly lack. Now move."

I pushed past him, and shaking, I stalked down the hall, but footsteps pounded after me. I quickened my pace, but he caught up with me.

"Brenner, wait."

"Why?" I stood stiff, my body rigid, cold through and through. "So you can insult me further? Does that make you feel better about yourself?"

"I'm sorry. I-I didn't mean it."

"Wasn't that one of your strengths? I *don't lie, and I always say what I mean?*" I mimicked him. "Good for you, Mr. Truth-teller. You know what? It's one of my strengths as well. So go to hell, Weston. And I mean it."

I left him standing there and returned to my chair. Thank God these exercises were almost finished. I checked through the handout and saw there was only one more: the memory game.

Weston slid into his seat a few seconds before Sara took to the podium again. Neither of us looked at the other.

"You all did so well with that last exercise. We have one last task, and then the lunch break. For this, you'll be required to sit with your partner and learn more about each other."

Great. I sighed and shifted in my chair. Weston didn't look to happy, either.

"This exercise is called The Memory Game. You and your partner will face each other and share at least two separate memories you feel have shaped you into the person you are today. It can be whatever you choose, but the premise behind it is that the more we discover about each other, the more we learn that we share more similarities than differences."

"Jesus, could this get any worse?" I heard Weston mutter to himself.

"Don't worry, I'm not jealous about your European vacations or the sports car you got for your high-school graduation."

Red-faced, his jaw worked hard, but he remained silent.

"After lunch, we have one final team-builder that will take up a good portion of the afternoon. We will split into four teams, and you'll have a scavenger hunt. We've found that teamwork really does make the dreamwork, and this will help you forge good working relationships. You won't be with the same partner you've had for these exercises."

"Thank God." It had only been a couple of hours, but it felt like an eternity.

"Oh, you'll miss me when I'm gone," Weston smirked.

Ignoring him, I pushed my chair away from the table. "Let's get this done with. Two memories that shaped my life." Defiant, I glared at him. "The first was hearing the stories about how when I was eighteen months old, I was taken from my mother in a drug raid and put in foster care." There was so much more to that, but I'd choke rather than reveal my most intimate secrets.

Weston's eyes blew wide with shock but, refusing to allow him to speak, I continued.

"The second was when my foster mother died in my first year of law school. It was just my father and me after that. I never knew what a family was until them."

I couldn't deny my curiosity and waited for Weston. He shrugged. "I mean, you already said. My European vacation where I got laid for the first time, and my car–a Mercedes coupe." He winked. "Got all the hottest girls at school." He rose to his feet. "I'll be right back."

Without waiting for me to answer, he left me sitting there, weighing the word salad he'd tossed at me. "That was a load of crap," I mused as a phone vibrated on the table. Not mine–it was Weston's. The screen lit up with a text message. Was it wrong of me to read it? Absolutely. But he'd left it face up and it wasn't locked.

The text was from his father.

> *Listen, you ungrateful, worthless prick. I'm tired of putting up with your shit. You'd better show up primary night or we're done.*

"Is that my phone?"

I jerked around to see a furious Weston standing behind me. "Yes, I–"

"You what? Decided to read my personal messages because I said something shitty to you and hurt your feelings? Tit for tat?" Visibly shaking, he grabbed the phone out of my hands. "This is low even for you, Brenner. Fuck off. I'm done." And he left.

It was lunchtime, and the group from my room joined the others for the lunch buffet the hotel had set up for us. I waited a few moments to gather my racing thoughts. Did that perfect life I'd imagined Weston sailing through, untouched by any nasty reality, actually not exist? Maybe

Weston had constructed a fairy tale because the truth was too ugly. I might not have grown up in a typical family, but I did know that no loving father would ever talk that way to their child. A quick search on my phone brought up all the pertinent information.

The senator had remarried the same year Weston's mother passed away, hence Weston's likely resentment toward his father. Preston Lively and his wife, a very young woman, had a little girl. Scanning the videos, I saw no sign of Weston at Senator Lively's victory parties at either his first, second, or third senatorial wins. In his last acceptance speech he only mentioned the support from his wife and how much he loved being a father to his daughter. No mention of Weston at all.

Looks like we both have things we'd rather bury than talk about.

People milled about the room set up for our lunch, talking in small groups or waiting in line to get their food. I made no attempt to find Weston, but after choosing a sandwich and taking some salad, I caught sight of him sitting with Grady and several other people. Many of the seats were filled, and I was never the type to insert myself in conversations, so I found a table with only two other people and sat.

"Ralph Bennett." A moon-faced older man nodded to me. "Mergers and Acquisitions." He took a bite of his food and chewed with gusto. "At least the food is good."

"Not a fan of team building?" I asked with a grin. "Brenner Fleming, Family Law."

"Never seen much point to it. People like who they like." He shrugged and kept eating. "But they're the experts. What do I know?"

The other man smiled. He was about my age, slim, with a head of dark curls and bright-brown eyes. "Manuel Ortega, Real Estate. Call me Manny. We did a lot of these at my old firm. I don't mind them. Sometimes people surprise you. And you discover things about yourself."

"I think you're right. It's good to learn about people and not make snap judgments." I sipped my water. "How long have you each been with the firm?"

Ralph, who'd finished his food, wiped his mouth. "Four months. Came from the SEC. My wife's been pushing me for years to go to the private sector and make some real money." He chuckled. "She's a partner at Sullivan and White and says she's tired of being the breadwinner."

They all laughed, and Manny seemed to hesitate before saying, "I've been here almost two months. My husband is a cardiology resident at New York Hospital. We're working hard right now, trying to save up as much as we can to buy a house and then to have a baby. We weren't sure if it was the right thing for me to buy into the partnership, but Johnny and I decided you never know if an opportunity to join a firm like this will come again. I was a fourth-year associate at Sheffield Brown, but they weren't moving ahead to make me a partner. So I took the leap. How about you?"

"I'm pretty boring. I've been here about a month, and came from a boutique firm specializing in divorce, custody arrangements, and adoptions. I was a partner there, but when Daniel Roth approached me, the opportunity—both prestige and earnings-wise—was too good to pass up. That's about it for me."

"Wife? Kids?" Manny's eyes lit up. "Girlfriend? Boyfriend? I can hook you up with either. I have three bright and beautiful cousins—Rita's a lawyer, Marina's a real-estate broker, and Esther is a stockbroker. And Johnny's got a cute resident, Evan, who's looking for a boyfriend."

"Are you sure my father didn't send you here to match me up? He's been nagging me for years to get married." Stalling, I ate some of my sandwich. "I guess I'm a confirmed bachelor. I've never found the right woman."

"You're young. You've got lots of time. Trust me," Ralph insisted. "I've got plenty of years on you, and there's lots of living to be done. My wife and I are married close to thirty years, and we're still not sick of each other. Excuse me a minute. I'm going to grab a few of those cookies. I'm not allowed to have dessert at home, so I want to get my happiness while I can."

Manny and I laughed as Ralph hurried off. "And that's why you want to hook me up with someone?"

Manny waved a hand in the air. "Nah. He's kidding. If they're married for so long, I'm sure they love each other."

I was happy for Ralph, who sounded like he had a good, solid marriage. But I also knew the other, ugly side. So many people started off with forever in their eyes, yet only a few years later sat across the table, snarling with hatred. Betrayal, money problems, lack of trust...so many pitfalls could cause a marriage to fail and love to die.

Maybe I'd shied away from commitment because I'd seen too much ugliness and didn't want to fall victim to it all. I'd rather keep it light and easy than open myself up to hurt.

A burst of laughter caught my attention from Weston's table, and when I looked in that direction, I found his eyes on me. My heart slammed at the mix of fury and pain in his face.

"What's with that guy?" Manny asked. "He looks like he wants to bite your head off. You know him?"

"No. Just same section in law school."

"Maybe he wants to step it up a notch." Manny leaned close. " 'Cause he looks like he's jealous we're talking to each other."

I sputtered with laughter even as hot and cold simultaneously washed over me. "Don't be ridiculous. West is straight, and so am I. We've never gotten along. It sounds silly, but any time we're together, we spend it trying to top one another."

Manny's eyes twinkled. "I'll bet."

Somehow, I had a feeling we weren't talking about the same thing.

CHAPTER EIGHT
WESTON

Who the hell is Brenner talking to?

The man murmured something in Brenner's ear that had him laughing out loud. Brenner. The perpetual scowler. I watched as they whispered to each other. He squeezed Brenner's shoulder and I caught sight of the light picking up the gleam of a wedding band. He walked away, leaving Brenner alone, and that made me feel better, though I couldn't understand why.

"What're you staring at?" Grady murmured. "Or should I say whom?" His voice held an undertone of amusement I didn't appreciate. As if he were looking inside my head and seeing the mishmash of twisted emotions.

"Nothing. Just seeing who's here."

"*Mmmhmm.*"

I set my coffee cup on the table and shifted to face him. "Okay, what?"

A lazy grin ticked up Grady's lips. "What, what?"

"Come on. I'm in no mood for games. You clearly have something to say. So go ahead, spit it out."

Maddeningly slow, Grady finished his coffee. "You're awfully jumpy. And all throughout lunch, you kept glaring at Brenner."

"Glaring? Better get your eyes checked, my man." I'd always prided myself on my poker face and made good use of it while talking to Grady, who was a master at digging beneath the surface. "I don't know what you're talking about. I was seeing if there was anyone I hadn't yet met and wondering who'd be at the bar later."

"Classic denial," Grady said.

"Meaning what? You're talking in riddles."

Grady shifted his chair closer. "If I didn't know better, I'd think there was something going on between you two."

"Are you fucking crazy?"

Unfortunately, at that moment there was a lull in conversation, so the entire room heard me go off. Heads swiveled to gape at me, but I brushed them off with a shake of my head. "Nothing to see here, folks. Just two friends having a bit of fun." Waiting for everyone to return to their conversations, I leaned over and hissed, "I meant that, by the way. What the hell are you talking about, 'something going on'?"

Grady merely smirked. "I said what I said. You know what the words mean. And I'm not only talking about today. There've been times since he joined the firm when I've seen you watching him."

"Yeah, hoping he didn't screw up." A blatant lie, as Brenner was as sharp an attorney as they came.

"Yeah, okay, West." Grady cackled. "That's the most bullshit thing you've said all day."

"I am not into him," I gritted out. "I like women."

His smile beamed bright. "If you say so."

"You're just being a dick. You think you're funny."

Grady popped a cookie into his mouth. "I am?"

It was true—I liked women. And over the past year since Brenner and I'd had our...encounter, I hadn't had a single sexual thought of another man. It must've been a deadly combination of pent-up sexual frustration and too much alcohol that had twisted my libido for that one night. If I really was into guys, I'd want to have sex with other men, not only Brenner.

Not that I wanted to have sex with Brenner. One drunken hand job didn't make me bisexual. Neither did constantly thinking about it a year later...did it? *Dammit.* I was confusing myself.

Trying to remain calm, I blew out a frustrated breath. "Fleming means nothing to me. He's a pain in the ass, is all. Do you know what he did? He read a text on my phone."

Grady's brows shot up. "What? That doesn't sound like him. How did that happen?"

"Well, I, uh...I left my phone on the table earlier when we were doing the exercises, and the screen lit up with a message. But he shouldn't have read it."

"I agree, but if the same thing happened and it was sitting right in front of me, I doubt I'd have been able to ignore it." Eyes narrowed, Grady peered at me. "You're upset, and I don't think it has anything to do with Brenner reading your text. I think it's the text itself."

Heat rose to my face. "It's nothing," I mumbled. "I'm fine. How's that adoption case going?"

"Don't make me use that psych degree on you, man. What's wrong? You haven't been yourself all day."

"No? Who have I been?"

This was Grady I was talking to, not some first-year associate who wouldn't challenge me. Plus, that psych degree meant it was almost impossible to bullshit the man.

"West, come on. I thought we were friends. I confided in you when I got shot down by Miranda." His lips twitched. "Did I tell you that the day after they announced the new partners, she came by my office to say she'd like to take me out for a celebratory drink?"

"Not surprised in the least. She's only interested in seeing whoever can help her up the ladder."

"Yeah, you were right. And man, it was painful to have to say no. She wore a tight little dress…damn. I didn't know I had that much willpower."

"Your restraint is admirable." I snickered. "I know how she can be when she wants something."

Twin brows shot high. "I'm all for an ambitious woman, don't get me wrong, 'cause confidence is sexy as hell, but they have to like something about me other than my partnership in the firm."

"Are you looking for a girlfriend?" While Grady and I were pretty friendly, we'd never delved much into our personal lives, preferring to take in ball games or go clubbing, where one or both of us would inevitably leave with a lady. I had no intention to let him into the fucked-up dynamics of the Lively family. This, however, was the first time he'd ever mentioned wanting a relationship, and I wondered what had changed.

"I might be. I feel like I'm too old for the scene, and to tell you the truth, I'm tired by the end of the day. Who wants to be 'on' all day at the office and then have to stand around and be impressive all night? Maybe it's clichéd, but I'm thinking it's not so bad to come home to someone who actually cares about me. Someone I want to know better and be with all the time. Being in foster care meant never knowing if a home was your forever place or one where you'd pack up and leave. I want a family. Permanence."

"Wow." I guess it had never occurred to me to put myself in his shoes, but what Grady said made sense. What

I didn't tell him was that you could have that home, have everything you could want, and still be the loneliest person in the world.

But I didn't need anyone's pity.

"So what is it? Something's bothering you."

I drummed my fingers on the tabletop. "Maybe...I don't..." It made no sense to deny it. Grady was my friend. "It's my father."

"What about him?"

"Here. See for yourself." I shoved the phone at him, and he picked it up. Darkness clouded his eyes when he handed it back to me.

"You're not going, I presume?"

"No. I never have." The room started clearing out. I could see Brenner by himself at the table.

"Any particular reason?"

With Grady, I knew I had to choose my words carefully. "We don't get along. As you might've figured out from his message. Anyway, we'd better get going."

"You're not going to tell me, are you?" My steady gaze was all the answer he needed, and he shook his head. "Fine. But you know I'm here for you if you need to vent."

The last thing I wanted was to dive into the rot of the relationship between my father and me. It was deep and ugly and would send me into a dark place I had no desire to revisit. My smile was tight. "Thanks. It's not a big deal, so please, let's drop it."

Grady looked unconvinced, but I wasn't about to cave and he knew it. "I think your partner might be waiting for you. What're you going to do about him?"

"Nothing. Hopefully with the scavenger hunt, we can ignore each other. I'll catch you later at dinner." We parted ways, and I passed by Brenner, who scrambled up from his chair and followed me.

"West, wait up, please."

I kept going. Brenner caught me by the arm and held me with a firm grip. I could feel the heat of his hand through my shirtsleeve and whipped around.

"I think it's pretty obvious I don't want to talk."

"So let me. I want to apologize. I was wrong to read your text, and I'm sorry."

If I refused to accept his apology, I'd look petty. "Forget about it. No big deal."

"Are you sure?"

I neither needed nor wanted Brenner Fleming to feel sorry for me. "I said it and meant it, remember?"

"Yeah, I remember, but–"

"No buts," I snapped and ran a hand through my hair. "Look, just drop it. Consider it one of the things you didn't know about me."

"Is there more? I still don't know anything other than what you used to talk about in the frat house. Girls, vacations, and partying."

Two could play this game, and I cocked a brow. "Does that mean you're willing to talk as well?"

Brenner's eyes widened; then he pressed his lips tight.

"I didn't think so."

We stood in the middle of the hall with people walking on either side, but our gazes clashed. I recognized that expression from years ago. Lockdown. Fifteen years ago I would've believed it was typical Brenner Fleming disapproval based on a combination of jealousy and annoyance. Now I wasn't so sure.

Hmm. Maybe there was something to be said about this exercise I'd dismissed as nonsense. Despite how angry I'd gotten earlier with Brenner, I itched to know more about his past. What the hell had happened to him as a child? The tidbits he'd dropped so casually in passing sounded horrifying and explained so much about his personality. Brenner was as cagey about his past as I was, though for different reasons.

With the room filling up, I wanted time to sit and check my messages before the afternoon session began. "We only have one more thing to do today, so let's get it over with."

"Guess that explains how you feel about the whole weekend."

"What, that it's a waste of time?" An inelegant snort escaped me. "All this forcing people together to play nice. If we don't like each other, we should still be able to get along like adults." I took my seat and scanned my phone. Nothing from dear old Dad. Hopefully he got the message and fucked off. For good this time.

Brenner's brows skimmed his hairline. "That's funny."

My attention shifted to the man at my side, and I bristled. "Why?"

With a face filled with skepticism, Brenner rolled his eyes. "Are you seriously asking me that? I think it's pretty obvious you and I aren't ever going to get along. We can barely sit next to each other."

"Were we supposed to be friends after this? That's not what this weekend was about. It's trust building." Curious to hear his answer, I continued to push him. "Do you trust me more than you did before this weekend?"

"Considering my baseline was zero, anything should be considered a win, don't you think?"

I grinned at his smirk. Maybe if we hadn't disliked each other from fifteen years ago, we could've become friendly. That wild drunken night flashed through my mind, and as my stare intensified, Brenner's eyes darkened and his lips parted.

Is he thinking about it too? Does he want a repeat?

Do I? What the fuck?

Grady's words came back to haunt me. Bastard had put these ideas in my head. And yet, I had unanswered questions. I couldn't help but get in a dig and at the same time try and find out some information. "I see you made a friend at lunch."

A stare of genuine confusion met mine. "Who? The two men I sat with? Manny's in Real Estate and Ralph's in M and A. They were very nice."

"Most people in the firm are. Even me." I could turn on the charm, even with Brenner Fleming.

"Jury's still out on that one."

For some reason that hurt. "You can't let go. Or won't."

"We spent three years in law school together, and we never knew anything about each other. Why do you think that is?"

"I knew you always wanted to beat me and come out on top. But rarely did."

That familiar sour expression made its reappearance. "Forget I said anything."

Sara took to the podium, and everyone quieted down. "We know you're tired of being cooped up, so the scavenger hunt we've arranged will take place all over town."

Murmurs of approval rose in the room. Sitting all day in one room, the walls had begun to close in on me, and judging by the smiles on everyone else's faces, they felt the same.

"As I said earlier, we made sure the partner you have now won't be in the same group for the scavenger hunt. I hope you found the morning session helpful and that you learned something new about your coworkers. We'll be passing out sheets with the new teams and what you need to find for the hunt. One in particular will be something everyone has to get, but other than that, you all have differ-ent items of equal ease or difficulty to find."

Brenner and I exchanged a quick glance before facing front again.

"It's good they're switching it up so we don't get stuck with each other for the whole time." I crossed my arms and leaned back in my chair. "I'm sure you'll be glad to get rid of me."

"As much as you're ready to say good-bye to me."

We each took a sheet, and I saw Grady was with me. Brenner was with his new lunch friend Manny. "Well, it's been real, but can't say it's been fun. I'll see you tonight at dinner."

Anxious to leave Brenner's surly presence, I hustled away from him without waiting for a reply. Out in the hall, I met up with Grady and the other members of our group. We scanned the sheet and saw the items we needed to find—a T-shirt from the local high school and a picture of their mascot, a takeout menu from Elm Street Diner, a picture of the memorial plaque at Fort Stamford, a playbill from Curtain Call, and a coaster or cocktail napkin from Bar None.

"So whoever returns first with all these things wins?"

Eyes on the paper in his hand, Grady answered, "Looks like it. There're six of us per team. How about we split into groups of two and divide up the stuff to get?"

A serious-looking woman with a pointy chin and a prominent widow's peak of dark hair gave a firm nod. "Sounds good. I'm from around here, so I can do the memorial plaque and get the T-shirt and the picture of the husky. The plaque is not that easy to find." A smile lightened her stern face. "But I know where it is. Who wants to come with me?"

A tall, thin, Black man raised his hand. "Me, Amanda. We can catch up on the way. Amanda and I went to high school together," he explained. "I'm Darrell Johnson. Tax and Finance."

They all shook hands, and I shuddered. "Taxes. I give you credit. But you guys definitely help us out when we're doing alimony and monetary settlements in our divorce cases. Grady and I can take the playbill and the bar. Is that okay with you two?" My question was directed to the two remaining men, who'd introduced themselves as Fernando Ortiz from M&A and Stuart Roberts from Real Estate. Fernando was slim and slight, with a neatly trimmed beard, while Stuart was stocky and barrel-chested, with a freckled face and fiery red hair.

They glanced at each other and shrugged. "Sure," Fernando said. "I could go for a snack anyway. We'll take the diner."

Stuart rubbed his hands together. "Now you're talking. Let's get popping."

"Let's all exchange numbers so we can keep in touch with each other. And don't get too hungry. We want to be the first to win."

Stuart's light-blue eyes twinkled. "No worries. I'll get my food to go."

They all laughed, and Grady checked his watch. "They say to meet at the hotel bar. See you all later."

We waved off the four, who set off in the direction of the front door. I took out my car keys. "Ready to go? I figured the playbill first and the bar second?"

Before Grady could answer, Brenner walked out with his partner, Manny. The guy he was with at lunch. My eyes narrowed at the light, easy laughter between them. I remembered Brenner used to be the same around Bailey Marks. Why the hell was Brenner such a grouch with me? All I ever saw was a perpetual scowl.

"Stop staring," Grady murmured.

"You're being ridiculous. Let's go. I want to win this thing." I strode away, walking past Brenner and his friend. "Just like old times, right, Brenner?" I gave him my sunniest smile and watched the lines of anger cut a deeper groove in his face.

Was I being childish? Yep.

Did I care? Nope.

I had no idea why, but I was going to make sure I came out on top.

CHAPTER NINE
BRENNER

It wasn't until we were in the car, on the way to the high school, that Manny started questioning me.

"So what's with that guy?"

Of course I knew whom he meant, but I feigned ignorance. "What guy? There were more than thirty people in there."

"The one who almost knocked into you and said something about old times."

"Weston. I told you about him at lunch, remember?"

"Yeah, but he's deliberately baiting you." Manny's brows drew together. "I thought you didn't know him well, but he acts like you do."

If knowing him well meant touching his dick and watching him come all over my hand—then, yeah. We were fucking besties.

"We never liked each other. He's one of those silver-spoon kids—you know, rich family, prep schools. The attitude grated on me. Plus, we were always rivals for first in class, *Law Review.*" Thinking back, it all seemed so silly, especially now that we were working for the same firm.

"Ah. I get it now. And he would come out on top?"

"Put it this way: Weston Lively doesn't like to lose."

Manny's smile flashed big and bright. "Then he's gonna be real mad when we beat the pants off him."

"Yeah," I responded, sounding weak as hell.

All I could think of was Weston's pants around his ankles. The burn of his hot, throbbing dick in my hand. Lips on mine, demanding and hard. *Fuck.* Why did this keep happening? As if I could push the memory out of my head, I rubbed my face.

"You okay?" Manny peered at me.

"Yeah. I'm good. Maybe when we go to the bar to get our item, we can grab something to eat."

"Sounds like a plan. I wouldn't mind a quick beer."

Once we left the corporate park where the hotel was located, the car took us through a pretty town. We were headed to the high school to try and find a football T-shirt, which we assumed would be sold in the school itself. But when we arrived and tried to open the door, we discovered it was locked.

"Damn." Annoyed that our plan was stymied, I scanned the grounds and spotted the football team practicing on the field and pointed. "Look. They must have a spare shirt, and if not, maybe we can pay them to give us one of their extras."

"Good idea," Manny agreed. "Like a donation to the team. Schools are always looking for money."

We jogged across the grass to the field. At our entrance, one of the coaches ran to us. "Can I help you?"

"Yeah, we were wondering if you have any spare team shirts you can give us."

"For?"

"A corporate scavenger hunt." I decided to throw out my idea whether they asked us or not. "We're happy to make a donation to the team fund."

He lifted a shoulder. "Don't see why not. Any size?"

"Doesn't matter." I extracted two twenties from my wallet and handed them to him. "Is this okay?"

"Sure thing. Hang on a sec. I have an extra in my bag." He left us, and we watched him rummage in his bag and pull one out.

Shirt in hand, the coach returned. "Here ya go."

Manny took it and handed the coach some more bills. "Add that to our contribution."

"Thanks." He pocketed the money, returned to his players, and we trudged through the grass to the front of the school and the street.

"I wonder what the other teams have to get," Manny said. "Hopefully it won't be easy for them." At my surprised face, he grinned. "Johnny says I'm too competitive." He shrugged. "But you know how it goes. Being gay and Hispanic puts me behind the eight ball. I have to work twice as hard to even get noticed."

It shamed me that I hadn't really given it much thought. Manny just seemed like a nice, fun man. I hadn't considered his struggles. "Has it been hard at the firm?"

"No. One of the reasons I was eager to join was the diversity in the makeup of attorneys." He pulled out his phone and punched in the address for the bar, which was, according to the app, almost ten miles away. A grunt escaped him. "It's not like the city here for sure. The car won't be here for at least ten minutes."

We sat on the steps of the school, a warm breeze playing across our faces. Listening to the birds singing and the rustle of leaves on the trees, I realized I rarely took the time to sit and enjoy the quiet surrounding me.

"Maybe that's a good thing. I can't remember the last time I simply sat and did nothing."

Beside me, Manny stared straight out. "We're kinda always in a rush, huh? Guess it's the way we live—crowds and competition forcing us to be a step ahead."

"You grew up in the city?"

"Yeah. Sunset Park. My old man washed dishes in a Mexican restaurant, and my mother was a school lunch lady." His smile held a combination of pride and sadness. "First in my family to graduate from high school. When I got into Pace, my *mami* cried and showed everyone in the neighborhood my acceptance letter."

"What did she do when you graduated law school?"

"She was in line at five in the morning to make sure she got a prime seat to see me walk across the stage." Deep brown eyes met mine. "The owner of the restaurant my father worked at closed it down and threw me a party. He said I was the future." Tears sparkled on his lashes. "I came out to my parents that night, and for a month my father didn't talk to me. When I'd enter the room, he'd walk out."

I'd heard similar stories from some of my clients, but it never failed to upset me. "And now?" Almost afraid to ask, I had to know.

"It took a while. Thankfully, he never called me names or anything like that. He's old-school and doesn't get it, but he's trying. When Johnny and I decided to get married, we just had a small ceremony, and they came. My *mami*, she's been cool all along. Loves Johnny and tells everyone her son-in-law is a doctor." He chuckled. "Brags to all her girlfriends how good Johnny is to her—and he is. Brings her flowers, and she's taught him to cook some of my favorite foods. My father and Johnny bonded over sports. Johnny'll watch anything—soccer, football, baseball...if there are men running around on a court or a field, he's there. They go to the games and leave me at home."

The car pulled up, and I squeezed his shoulder. "I'm glad."

On the drive, Manny got a call, and his face lit up. "It's Johnny. Excuse me. *Mi corazon*. How are you?"

Shutting out Manny's conversation with his husband, I checked my phone to find it depressingly empty. I sent Bill a message to say hi. I thought about the text Weston had received from his father and how much animosity there was behind the words. Despite myself, I googled the senator to see what else I could find.

Senator Preston Lively was without a doubt a good-looking man, but there was a cruel tilt to his lips and no hint of kindness in his icy gaze. Recalling how Bill would take me to the park on the weekends to play ball, or how every Sunday night was pizza and a movie, I doubted Weston had that kind of relationship with his father. I read on.

Weston's father's family had been in politics for decades. Was his father angry at Weston for not following his path? Could that be the reason for their estrangement? I scrolled farther and found a gossip piece, more than twenty years old, which insinuated that the then-councilman Lively had been seen in the company of other women. I couldn't find another article. Someone with Preston Lively's power and position could easily have a story like that buried. Infidelity was a more likely culprit than Weston failing to enter politics and would explain the ugly vitriol between them.

"Whatcha looking at? Must be pretty intense." Manny cocked a brow.

No way would I reveal I'd been digging into Weston's past. "Nah, just reading the headlines. Nothing good." I huffed out a laugh.

"Well, forget it." Their phones buzzed in unison. "That's Boris. He said the theater is closed, so they can't get the playbill." His lips twitched, and a cackle burst from him. "They ended up searching the dumpster to find one. Remind me not to shake his hand."

Laughing, I bumped Manny's fist. "You got it."

Traffic held us up, so it was close to five by the time we walked inside the bar. After Manny ordered himself a beer and me a Tito's and soda, we took a seat in a booth. I scanned the sticky plastic menu. "I wouldn't mind a snack."

"Johnny's always lecturing me on eating healthy, so I want to get my junk-food fix while I can." There weren't many customers yet—a couple of older men sitting in a corner, eating burgers, and a bunch of twentysomethings at the bar, drinking drafts and doing shots. I winced, remembering how out of control the guys in the frat house would get at that combination. One of the guys caught me staring, and I quickly looked away, but not before I saw him elbowing his friends.

The bartender came over to us. "You want food?"

Charming personality he was not, but I was hungry. Behind him, several of the guys at the bar whispered and snickered.

Oblivious, Manny scanned the menu. "Should we do the appy platter?"

"Sounds good to me."

"Thanks. That's it, I think." Manny returned the laminated card to its holder.

"Okay. It'll be about ten minutes."

"No problem." Keeping an eye on the guys at the bar, I sipped my drink.

"You seem distracted. Don't let those jerks bug you."

Surprised, I set my glass on the coaster. "You saw them?"

Resignation deepened Manny's eyes to a rich, dark brown. "I'm used to it. In a place like this, where I'm not sure if I'll be safe, I always check out my surroundings."

"Jesus," I muttered. "I'm sorry. It shouldn't be that way." I wondered if this was how it was for Bailey too. He was such a good guy—like Manny.

"Maybe one day it won't. I try and be optimistic."

Our food came, and it was decent pub fare. As he ate, Manny's mood lightened. "So tell me more about you, aside from the fact that you're not married, not looking, and don't like Weston Lively." His white teeth flashed bright in his handsome face.

I licked my fingers free of the sticky wing sauce and wiped them on the napkin. For a moment, I watched him eat. He'd chosen to be vulnerable with me, so I decided it was only fair I did the same.

"I grew up in foster care. From what I was told, there was a drug raid at our house, and my mother ran out with her boyfriend, leaving me behind. I was asleep in a playpen. They took me to ACS, and when I was given a medical exam, they found remnants of weed and some other drugs in my system. Maybe I'd gotten into whatever was passed around in the house. Who knows?"

As I spoke, Manny stopped eating the wing he'd picked up, his eyes never leaving my face. There was more to tell him, but I couldn't. The words stuck in my throat, their ugliness coating my insides with the pain I'd grown up with.

"And look what you made of yourself. You ended up with good foster parents, I hope?"

A smile tugged at my lips. "It took a few tries, but yeah. My mom died first year of law school, but my dad, Bill, is in Florida now. They were the best. Never let me think I wasn't good enough because of where I came from. They told me I could do whatever I wanted and encouraged me to work hard and to not pay attention to kids who made fun of me because I didn't have 'real parents.' "

"Kids can be cruel. And I'm sure your dad is very proud of you. Look how far you've come."

We resumed eating and finished off the food, leaving nothing but bones and crumbs behind. I remembered why we were there and stuck one of the coasters into my pocket. A quick check of my phone showed me that the rest of our team had completed their tasks and were returning to home base. "Now that we have the things off our list, I guess we should be getting back. We do want to win. Everyone else is ready."

"Hey, Brenner?" I met Manny's eyes and saw the sympathy in them but no pity. Still, it was like a fist squeezing my heart to give away the pieces of myself. "Thanks for sharing that part of your life. I know it's not easy. When I was in law school, I volunteered at several youth shelters, and I know how kids get caught up in the foster-care system. You're a success story."

"I think we both are."

Manny's hand covered mine and squeezed. Hard. We stayed that way for several moments, and then I raised my hand to the bartender. "Can we get the check, please?"

He brought it to us, and I set my credit card on the tray. "I'll pay the tip in cash."

"I'll get your receipt." The unsmiling man walked away.

Manny reached for his wallet, but I waved him off. "It's not a big deal. Buy me a couple of drinks at the bar tonight, and we'll call it even."

"All right, then. I'll call for the car."

I signed the receipt, put the cash down, and we left. The sun had yet to set, but the heat of the day had vanished. The leaves of the old oak trees arching over the streets would soon turn orange and crimson with the coming autumn, and I could picture the bright-orange pumpkins at each door and storefront. This town was so pretty, like a storybook.

"Well, look who we got here. A coupla queers."

I stiffened, but Manny leaned in. "Ignore them. They'll go away if we don't respond. The car'll be here in two minutes."

"What's that, sweetheart?" One of the punks strode to him. "You talkin' to me?" Jaw flexing, Manny stared straight ahead. The guy wasn't satisfied and knocked Manny's shoulder. "Answer me."

For the first time fear slammed through me. I couldn't believe this was actually happening, out in the open. The four men, all bigger and taller than I recalled, surrounded us. Why the hell I'd thought I could reason with them, I had no idea, but I guess I'd hoped that if they talked longer, there'd be less of a chance they'd get physical, so I said, "Look, we're attorneys here for a weekend business retreat. We're not here to make trouble. We just want to leave."

Beer breath assailed my nostrils as one of the Neanderthals stuck his face into mine. "Lawyers? I don't like lawyers. Especially queer ones." He shoved me into one of the huge old trees lining the sidewalk. My head hit the trunk. It hurt, and I grunted in pain.

"Please, stop—"

"Shut up. You think you're better than us?" Another hard thrust, and my head snapped back hard, sending a white-hot bolt of pain through me. Stars danced in front of my eyes. The others were pushing Manny around as well. Where the fuck was the car?

A fist to my stomach left me gasping for air. Another to my head sent me to my knees. A kick to the ribs had me crying out in pain. They kept kicking me. And then blackness.

CHAPTER TEN
WESTON

Grady lifted his glass. "To the winning team."

"As predicted."

The rest of our team laughed along with me, and we toasted each other. To my shock, the second team after us wasn't Brenner's but another group. Not that I'd been watching, but I hadn't seen him or anyone from his group at the bar. Fernando searched the room. "Some of the teams haven't even returned yet. I don't see Manny."

My antenna buzzed. "Oh? Are you two friendly?"

Fernando inclined his head. "We know each other from the Hispanic National Bar Association, and I've met him and his husband at events. Manny's a great guy—smart and friendly and a great lawyer. He helped my wife and me close on our house last year."

"I'm sure they'll be back soon. There are still people trickling in." I tipped my half-empty glass at the door. Here comes their team." The members of Brenner and Manny's group walked in, frowning.

Fernando waved to them. "Hey, guys, what's wrong?"

A heavyset older man spoke up. "We haven't heard from Manny or Brenner. They texted us after they picked up the T-shirt and said they were off to the bar."

"Maybe they're eating and lost track of time." The excuse I offered was met with shrugs and uncertainty. And knowing Brenner and how...anal he was, for lack of a better word, I couldn't imagine that occurring. One of his strengths was punctuality. Plus, as foolish as our silly rivalry was, I knew he'd want to come in first. A knot of concern formed in my stomach.

"Maybe," a woman from his team said, chewing her lip. "But that doesn't explain their lack of response. We were all in constant contact until about two hours ago, and then nothing."

"Text them again," Grady urged.

She picked up her phone, and her fingers flew over the screen. After a moment, she shook her head. "Still unread. Like all my other messages."

By now it was close to an hour since we'd come in from our trek around town, and everyone else had returned and were telling stories of their afternoon. Fernando's phone rang.

"It's Manny. Dude, where are you?" The color drained from his face. "Shit. I'll be right there. He okay?"

My stomach dropped. He? Brenner? "What happened?" I set my glass on the bar top, and Grady did the same.

Fernando shoved the phone into his pocket. "They're in the hospital. They got jumped by a bunch of homophobes outside the bar."

"Let's go. I've got a car." I sprinted to the garage as the others followed, and we got into the car. I gunned the engine, barely waiting for everyone to close their doors. Anxiety ate at my insides, and none of us spoke on the ten-minute drive. I parked, and we raced into the emergency room.

"Brenner Fleming and Manuel—" I turned to Fernando. "I don't know his last name."

"Ortega," he supplied. "They came in about an hour ago."

The clerk checked the screen. "Yes. They're in bays three and four but you all can't go in there. Only one person per patient."

"I'll go for Manny," Fernando said.

"I'm with Brenner." There wasn't even a question. The two of us pushed open the door to the chaos of a typical emergency room—gurneys everywhere with patients lying on them in various stages of distress. Doctors, nurses, and EMTs all hustling around while the overhead speakers blatted out calls and codes.

I paid attention to none of it, my sole concern finding Brenner. "There." I pointed. "Three and four."

Pulling back the curtain, I saw Brenner sitting on the examination table, head propped in his hands. Something in my stomach twisted, sending a knife's edge of pain straight to my heart.

"You'll do anything for attention, won't you?" The curtain fell behind me as I stepped inside. With some difficulty, Brenner raised his gaze to meet mine, and my breath caught. He sported numerous cuts to his cheeks, a busted lip, and the bruising suggested he'd have at least one black eye. "Jesus, Brenner. What the hell?"

"Bastards came after Manny and me. They thought we were a couple. Seems the combination of gay and lawyer set them off. Do you know how he's doing?"

"No idea. Fernando is with him, but he called to let us know."

"And you came…why?" Brenner winced as he shifted position.

"Seriously?" That hurt. "Come on. Aside from what they did to your pretty face, what else is wrong?"

The curtain opened. "Mr. Fleming?" The doctor directed his sharp eyes to me. "You are?"

"A friend. We work at the same firm, and we're both here for a corporate team-building event."

He didn't answer me and addressed Brenner. "We're going to take you to X-ray for your ribs and have you checked out to make sure you don't have a concussion. Are you dizzy, nauseated, anything like that?"

"No. I'm fine, aside from the obvious." Brenner managed a wan smile that was more like a grimace.

Anger swelled inside me at whoever had done this to him and Manny. I'd never had a violent urge in my body, but I wanted to hunt down those punks and beat them senseless.

"I'll wait until all your tests are done."

If I'd stood naked in front of him, Brenner couldn't have looked more surprised. "What? No, go back. I'll be fine."

I didn't get a chance to argue because the orderly came to take him, and they left without another word. Without Brenner, it made no sense to remain in the examination bay, so I left, but peeked into the next room where I'd seen Fernando disappear to check on Manny. The room was empty. Out in the waiting area, Fernando and Grady waited for me, along with the other members of Brenner's team.

"Where's Manny? How is he?" I questioned Fernando.

"He's all right. Shaken up and a few bruises and scrapes, but they're releasing him. He said Brenner took the brunt of the attack. Maybe because he tried to reason with them. Who knows?"

"He should know better. You don't argue with idiots."

Manny appeared in the doorway to the waiting room, complete with bruises on his face and a scrape on his chin. He joined our group, and I waited for him to greet the other members of his team and then introduced myself.

"Hi, I'm Weston Lively, a friend of Brenner's."

"Hey. Where's Brenner?" I found his abruptness odd but ignored it. The man had been through enough. He didn't need me judging him.

"They took him to X-ray for his ribs, and they may keep him overnight to see if he has a concussion, but he said he has no symptoms," I explained.

"What happened?" Grady asked Manny. Other people from the firm had come as well, and we made a crowd in the small waiting area.

"We were in the bar and had a drink and some food. These punks were drinking beer and doing shots. Definitely got an anti-gay vibe from them—they kept staring at us, like they thought we were a couple. We got the bill and went out to wait for the car to take us to the hotel, but they followed us, and that's when the harassment started. I warned Brenner to ignore them, but he thought he could talk his way out of it." For the first time, Manny met my eyes. "He's never had to deal with this before, and it's hard to imagine so much hate until it's directed your way."

"How did you get away?" Instinctively, my hands had curled into fists. "They could've killed you."

"The car we ordered arrived, and they ran when the driver got out of the car and screamed at them. He took us here."

"Thank God for that," I muttered.

Grady put a hand on my shoulder and leaned in close. "You're gonna stay to make sure he's okay, aren't you?"

"I want to, but Brenner said I shouldn't."

Grady tightened his grip. "Since when do you listen to what other people say?" He didn't wait for my smartass answer, and I wasn't sure I had one. I was too scared. Grady pinned me with a frown. "You know Brenner's wrong. You're the one he's known the longest. Things like that matter when you've been hurt."

All of a sudden, nerves kicked up. "I-I don't want him to get angry."

The harsh lines of Grady's face softened. "I am one hundred percent sure he won't. I'm going to head back to the hotel and grab something to eat. I can call Daniel and let him know—I'm sure he'll want to hear that both Manny and Brenner will be okay."

"Yeah, thanks. I forgot all about that. You're right." The image of Brenner's battered and bruised face took up every bit of real estate in my head.

"Make sure you keep me in the loop." Grady gave my shoulder another squeeze, and then he made the rounds to try and convince the others to return with him. They all departed, except for Manny. He remained behind, his expression guarded, as it had been all evening.

Several of the uncomfortable plastic chairs in the waiting room sat empty. I took one, stretched out my legs, and waited.

Manny gave me a face full of puzzlement. "You don't have to stay. I'm not going anywhere."

I laced my fingers over my stomach. "Neither am I." Manny sat, choosing to leave an empty seat between us. Debating whether to go there, I decided to hell with it. "What's your problem with me?"

It didn't really matter much, but I wondered if Brenner had said something to him. If he had, it was sure to be negative, which probably accounted for Manny's attitude.

Hmm. Maybe I did care. As much as I didn't think I minded people disliking me, I wanted to know why.

"I don't know you. We've never spoken."

"Exactly."

"My only problem is Brenner lying in a hospital bed." Manny shrugged.

Why I was on the defensive, I couldn't say, but I was too wound up and stopped speaking. A check of my watch showed it had been more than an hour since Brenner was taken to X-ray, and I approached the clerk at the desk.

"Can you tell me if Brenner Fleming is back from X-ray?"

Bright-tipped fingers flew over the keyboard. "Yes, he's in room 803."

Fear exploded inside me. "They admitted him? Did they find something wrong? Do—"

"I'm sorry, sir, but I can't tell you anything else."

Of course she couldn't. I forced a smile and left the emergency room, heading for the elevators in the main building. Footsteps pounded after me, but I didn't stop.

"Weston, please wait," Manny called after me.

I didn't wait and followed the overhead signs to the elevator and jabbed the button. Manny caught up with me.

"Why didn't you stop?"

"Why should I?" I snapped, unconcerned about his opinions, too scared at what I might find upstairs. The doors opened, and I entered and pushed the eighth-floor button.

"I'm sorry—"

"I don't care. Looks like they may have found something wrong, because Brenner's been admitted. So excuse me, but that's my focus."

We waited in toe-tapping frustration as the elevator stopped several times in between. When we finally reached the eighth floor, I hurried out and down the hall to the room the clerk had given me, to find a weary-looking Brenner lying in bed, staring at the ceiling.

"You just couldn't stand not coming in first, is that it, Brenner?" I strolled in, attempting to act casual, but the fact was, he looked like hell. Black-and-blue marks had blossomed over his body, and pain lines were etched into his too-pale face. Anger mixed with fear twisted inside my chest at how close he'd come to being seriously injured.

"I thought I told you to go home," he muttered.

"Yeah, but you know I don't listen to what you say." I pushed a chair to the side of his bed and sat. Manny walked in and winced.

"God, Brenner."

"Hey. I'm okay." He tried to sit up but couldn't mask the pain and groaned. "Ow, shit. That hurts."

A nurse walked in. "I'm sure it does. You have four severely bruised ribs, a sprained ankle, and a mild concussion. You're going to hurt for quite some time."

That sounded as bad as Brenner looked. Without thinking, I put my hand on his arm and patted it. "Don't worry. I'll stay here with you."

Apparently, Brenner wasn't impressed. "Don't be ridiculous." His growl had little effect on me, and I didn't respond. "I don't need a babysitter, and I'm in the hospital, where they can look after me." To Manny, he softened his tone. "Thanks for stopping by. I'll be out in the morning and touch base when I get home. How're you feeling?"

Whatever I had to say to Brenner would be between the two of us, so I stayed silent.

Frowning at me, Manny answered, "I'm okay, just some bumps and bruises. I'm sorry you took the brunt of it."

"Are you going to talk to the police?" I asked. "I'm sure they can be identified by the bartender or someone else."

Manny nodded. "I plan to stop by the station before heading back to the hotel."

For the first time, I smiled. "Good idea. You should get a move on it so the bozos don't get a head start, in case they make a run for it."

Manny's eyes narrowed, but I kept up that fake-ass grin. I wanted him to leave, and the sooner the better.

"I'll check in with you in the morning. I'm really sorry this happened, Brenner."

Brenner dismissed him with a wave of his hand. "Not your fault. I'm sure I'll be out of here tomorrow. I should've listened to you and not opened my mouth to those idiots."

True, but I decided to keep *my* mouth shut. I didn't need that famous Brenner Fleming scowl. Manny looked to me as if expecting me to come with him, but I kept my ass in the chair.

With a huff, Manny said, "Now I see why you're friends. You're both grouches," then left us.

"I thought you were leaving too."

"I don't think you should be alone. And yes, there are nurses, but you don't have someone personal to watch over you. What happens if you start to feel sick and no one's around?"

Dubious blue eyes met mine. "And you're going to be here to take care of that? You expect me to believe you care?"

"Ouch. That hurt. Come on, Brenner. Enough already."

Brenner turned his head to face me, and it must've been too quick for his pounded-upon brain to catch up. Whatever he'd been about to unleash on me faded to the wayside. He paled, and beads of sweat glistened on his face.

"Shit, I'm gonna be sick."

I grabbed the plastic bowl from the table and held it under his head while he puked up his guts. After he was finished, I poured him a cup of water, and he swished out his mouth. I set it aside and waited for him to thank me.

"Get out."

Shocked, I blinked. "What?"

"Get the hell out of here." He shut his eyes.

Recognizing defeat, I walked out of the room. I should let Brenner Fleming sit with it, but I couldn't, in case something was seriously wrong. I stopped by the nurse's station to tell them he'd gotten sick.

"You're a good friend," one of them said, and I forced a smile.

Too bad Brenner didn't think so.

CHAPTER ELEVEN
BRENNER

I slept poorly that night. Between the pain in my ribs, the pounding in my head, and the swollen ankle, I couldn't get comfortable. Nausea came and went, and true to their word, every couple of hours a nurse or aide would come into my room to make sure I was lucid.

"I swear I'd get more rest at a baseball game than here," I complained to the resident who'd come to check my vitals for what seemed like the four hundred and fifty-eighth time.

"You might at that," she laughed. "But the good news is, you're going to be discharged. Just let me run through some tests first."

After twenty minutes of counting and moving my head–which, although it still ached somewhat, no longer sent shooting spikes of pain through my skull—she declared me ready to go. My ankle throbbed in the brace they'd put on it.

"There you go!" she said, way too cheerfully for my liking. "I'll forward the discharge paperwork, and they'll come and tell you when you can leave, but it'll be a little while. It's barely nine a.m."

"Thank God." At her departure, I decided I should get up and use the bathroom to try and get ready. Moving gingerly, I swung my legs over the side of the bed. A bit lightheaded, I waited several moments for my vision to clear before attempting to stand. When I was fully upright, I faced the bed and put half my weight on the injured ankle. It buckled, so I returned to my previous stance as a flamingo, perched on one leg. I needed those crutches and fast. No way I could walk on this ankle yet.

"Fuck," I swore, pain radiating up my calf. How the hell was I supposed to walk or do anything? Every part of me ached.

"Tsk, tsk. Didn't anyone ever tell you not to swear in public? So low class."

At Weston's mocking voice, my head snapped up, and my vision swam. I forgot and leaned my weight fully onto my injured leg, which sent me off-balance. To my horror, I started to fall.

Strong arms wrapped around me, and a raspy cheek pressed to mine. Weston's lips found my ear. "I've got you. Don't worry."

Those words sent a shocking wave of heat through me that even the painful state of my body couldn't shrug off and deny. I wanted to push him away and tell him to let go, but the truth was, I hurt so bad, I couldn't afford to, so I allowed myself to sink into his chest. I'd never known how good being held could feel. And the fact that Weston was doing the holding only made it better. I turned halfway, and our eyes met. I wasn't expecting Weston's face to mirror my emotions—uncertainty, fear, and desire.

"I'm okay. You can let go." I hopped on my good leg.

"Let me help you to the bed." I allowed him to steady me as I lowered onto the mattress. Frustrated by my body's inability to do what I wanted, and a bit disturbed by my reaction to Weston, I rubbed my face.

"I can't believe this."

"What were you trying to do?" Weston looked at me, arms crossed.

"Go to the bathroom and get dressed. They're discharging me. I can't go out in a hospital gown." My legs stuck out from beneath the thin fabric, and Weston's lips kicked up.

"No, you wouldn't want to give anyone a show."

Something about how Weston's gaze traveled up and down my body left me breathless, and my natural reaction to him kicked in.

"What're you doing here?"

He sat in the chair he'd occupied yesterday. "When I called this morning to find out how you were, they told me you were going to be discharged, so I figured I'd come over and help you."

My brow furrowed. "Why?"

"Why, what?"

"Why do you want to help me?" I pinned him with a frown. "I mean, it's nice that you're trying, but we're not friends. We barely tolerate each other, so I don't understand this sudden desire to insert yourself in my life. In law school—"

"Oh, cut the shit with law school already," he snapped, surprising me with his vehemence. "Fifteen years have passed, for Christ's sake. Do we really need to keep doing this? Maybe I've changed. Haven't you?"

I blinked, the shock of his words sinking in. "I-I don't know."

The air between us crackled with awareness, and I wondered if he was thinking about that night. The pain in my ribs faded, replaced by a different kind of ache. I licked my lips, and the golden glints in the depths of his green eyes burned bright. Was Weston into men? Into *me*?

Was I into him?

Shit, I was getting hard under the gown, and I couldn't let him see it happening.

An aide bustled into the room. "Mr. Fleming, I'm here to get you ready for discharge." Oblivious to the tension between Weston and me, she kept up a rapid-fire stream of talk, even as he and I continued to stare at each other. It was as if a spell had been cast over me and I couldn't look away.

"Mr. Fleming?"

I jerked my attention away from Weston's face. "Oh, yeah, sorry. Thank you."

She held out an arm for me to take, and with her help, I hobbled to the bathroom. She handed me my clothes and waited outside the door. "Do you need me to help you?"

"Yes, please." My hands gripping the sink, the aide helped slip on my briefs and removed the brace before pulling my jeans up. The shirt was another matter. Lifting my arms with my ribs so sore hurt like a bitch, and I had no idea how I'd be able to put it on. Weston had remained in the chair, but his penetrating gaze reached across the room. I could almost feel his hands on me again.

I wanted it.

"I-I can't do this."

"It would've been better if you didn't have a pullover," she agreed. "But we'll make do."

"We could trade." With his fingers already flying down the buttons, Weston took off his shirt. "We're the same size, I think. Here." His nearness in his half-undressed state sent a throb low in my belly, and though I tried not to gawk,

I couldn't help noticing the swirls of golden-brown chest hair. We hadn't gotten naked that night—only our dicks had made an appearance—and I had no idea why the sight of Weston without his shirt tied me up in knots and made me alternately hot and cold and decidedly uncomfortable. I sneaked a glance at Weston, and his face reflected the same turmoil boiling inside me.

The aide's eyes widened, and she laughed. "Now that's being a good friend."

"Why, thank you. I try."

One thing Weston knew was how to turn on the charm. In that respect, he was a true politician.

"You're lucky, Mr. Fleming," she said as she assisted me in slipping an arm into the sleeve.

I met Weston's smirk with a slight shake of my head yet couldn't help my lips from twitching. He was annoying as hell, but helpful all the same, and I couldn't get mad at him. The shirt did fit, and the subtle scent of Weston's cologne clung to it, invading my senses.

"There you go." She finished buttoning it.

Finally, I was dressed. I shoved my good foot into my sneaker without bothering to put on socks. I knew I had to say something to Weston, who'd sat watching me struggle.

"All set?" he asked.

I chewed my bottom lip. "Yeah. Uh, thanks for giving me your shirt. It made it a lot easier."

"At your service." That cocky grin I'd always hated appeared, but for some odd reason, it didn't bother me now. Maybe Weston was growing on me. "As a matter of fact, I'm going to take you back to the hotel and then drive you home to the city."

"What?" The ride would take well over an hour, and I couldn't imagine sitting in a car with Weston for that long. "Absolutely not. You don't have to do that. I can manage."

He snorted. "Yeah, okay, Mr. I-Can't-Put-My-Pants-On-By-Myself. Are you kidding? You came by train, right?"

I nodded.

His usual devil-may-care expression softened. "Come on, Brenner. Can you picture yourself dragging a suitcase behind you and sitting squashed next to someone who might've eaten tons of Taco Bell for lunch and now has regrets?"

I couldn't help it and busted out laughing. Which hurt like fucking hell, bringing tears to my eyes and spiraling me into intense pain. "Oh fuck, don't do that again," I gasped, holding my sides.

"Case closed. After you're discharged, we'll check out of the hotel, and I'll take you home." Eyes twinkling, he twirled the car keys around his finger.

My head and ankle throbbed in unison, and I had little desire to fight with him. "Fine, fine. Whatever."

The wheelchair came along with my crutches, and after they adjusted them to my height, I was brought down-stairs. It felt damn good to be out of the medicinal hospital air, even if I was sitting in a parking lot. Weston pressed a bill into the orderly's hand, then moved me farther away from the curb.

"I'll just be a minute. Going to get the car."

I gave a slow nod, my head still throbbing. As I waited, I mulled the odd turn of events. How and when had Weston become—I hesitated to say it—my friend? I'd hold off judgment. A car pulled up—a Mercedes, of course—and Weston hopped out and attempted to take my arm.

"Lean on me."

I shook him off. "I have the crutches, and I need to learn to use them." After only five steps, my breath came in short pants and my shirt—well, Weston's—was soaked through with sweat. "This looks a lot easier than it is." I gritted my teeth but again refused Weston's help. To say he was frustrated with me was an understatement.

"Let me help you."

"No."

That earned me a frown. "Why are you torturing yourself?"

Because I was a stubborn, determined asshole, unwilling to accept Weston's gesture of goodwill. In my mind I still had reasons to be mistrustful and clung to the past, though I was finding that increasingly difficult to justify. After what seemed like hours, I reached the car door and leaned against it. I hated to admit it, but Weston was right. I could never have made it home on my own. I opened the door and carefully lowered myself into the passenger seat. The pain in my ribs made it impossible to twist and put the crutches in the back seat of the two-door coupe. Unasked, Weston handled it without a word.

He slid behind the wheel and leaned over me. I stiffened, frighteningly aware of his nearness. His eyes widened. That previous crackling intensity grew between us in the deafening silence.

"I have to put your seat belt on." His husky voice shot a bolt of electricity straight to my dick.

"Oh, uh, yeah. I can—"

"No, Brenner. You can't. Let me."

My throat dried as his hand grazed my lap. There was nothing to indicate that Weston was being anything other than helpful, yet my body's confusing reaction put me on edge and made me snappish. He clicked the belt into the slot and withdrew.

"Ready?"

Was I mistaking the strain in his voice? A quick glance revealed his lips pressed in a tight line.

"Yeah."

The drive to the hotel was silent. He parked and got out of the car, took my crutches, and opened the door. It hurt like a bitch, but I eased out of the car and stood. My head took a second to catch up to the rest of me, and I swayed, my vision blurring at the edges. Weston grabbed me around the waist.

"I have you."

His lips were close to mine, and I had a sudden, shocking urge to feel them. I blinked. "West," I murmured, and his fingers tightened their grip as his breath hitched. I liked that he was just as off-balance. That cocky smile had vanished, replaced by smoldering heat.

Babbling voices broke the spell.

"Brenner, how are you?"

"Oh God, are you okay?"

A swarm of people surrounded us, but Weston—who I'd assumed would step away—kept a steadying hand on me, and I found myself leaning on him.

"Give the guy a little room. He just got out of the hospital."

Grady and Manny appeared, along with the rest of my scavenger-hunt team, all with the same concerned expression.

"You feeling any better?" Manny asked.

I forgot and nodded, which sent a shard of pain through my skull, and I groaned. "Shit. Uh, yeah?" I mustered an answer. "But it hurts. A lot. I can't lie."

"Yet he still thought he could take the train home, lugging a suitcase." Weston shook with laughter. "That half-assed idea went out the window when he tried to walk to the car."

I glared at him. "I thought I could. Don't be a jerk about it."

Weston smirked. "I call it as I see it."

Despite the pain it caused in my head, I rolled my eyes. "If you don't shut up, I'll find someone else to take me home."

"I think it's a great idea to have Weston take you," Grady interjected. "If you want, we can help you pack. Are you hungry? The restaurant is open for lunch."

My stomach lurched at the thought of food, and I took a few shallow breaths. "N-no. But I could use some coffee."

"Let's settle you inside and get you what you need." Without me even realizing it, Weston took control, and I found myself attached to his side as we walked into the hotel and were seated. He ordered a pot of coffee and held out his hand.

"If you want to give me your room key, I can get your stuff together and bring your suitcase downstairs. Checkout is in less than half an hour."

The coffee tasted like hot perfection. "No. I'll do it. I didn't bring much." The last thing I needed was Weston touching my things.

"Then I'll help."

I opened my mouth to protest, but Manny said, "Let them do it, Brenner," surprising me. His gaze was so focused and direct, I sensed he wanted to be alone with me, that there was something he wanted to discuss.

"Fine," I grumbled, pretending to concede, curious to hear what he had to say. "Can you please get my wallet out of my back pocket?" I asked Manny. "It hurts to twist around."

He did as I requested and handed the key card to a grinning Weston, who plucked it out of his hand, and along with Grady, left us. I waited until they were out of earshot.

"Okay. What do you want to say that you didn't want Weston to hear?"

That inscrutable expression returned. "What's going on between the two of you?"

Heat swept through me. "Going on? What the hell does that mean?" But I knew. Damn Weston, and damn my stupidity for getting myself into this predicament.

"He seemed awfully protective when you were getting tests."

"Protective?" I sputtered. Heat burned my cheeks, and I hated how my emotions lay so close to the surface. "You're ridiculous."

"I don't think so."

The conversation needed to be quashed. Immediately. "Weston is being nice because he probably feels guilty for saying some shitty things to me yesterday. Nothing more. Okay?"

"Maybe so."

But Manny's skeptical face reflected my growing uncertainty. Was there something brewing between us that neither Weston nor I understood?

CHAPTER TWELVE
WESTON

"That's the last of it." I slammed the drawer shut after checking it was empty. "Brenner wasn't kidding when he said there wasn't much. I tend to overpack, but he brought the mere essentials and nothing more."

It hadn't taken us very long to clear out Brenner's things—the man was as neat and organized as I remembered from our time in the frat house. Grady pulled the rolling weekender bag to the door.

"When you're a foster kid, you learn to travel light. And to keep your things together so you can pack them away in case they move you without warning."

That had never occurred to me, and I now saw how that might account for Brenner's animosity toward me. To him, I represented a life he wanted—a home and parents.

Little did he know: a house didn't make a home, and parents could be a curse as well as a blessing.

"That's rough. Is that how it was for you?"

"Let's just say I wasn't the model foster kid. But I eventually decided to stop being a little shit, and it all worked out. I had good foster parents who were patient and gave a damn. Many kids don't."

"I'm guessing Brenner was one of those?" Curious to hear more, I wasn't in a rush to get downstairs.

"Possibly. Or living with unresolved trauma from being in the system or from growing up in a hostile environment." Grady's smile was thin. "Kids aren't always the nicest to other kids who aren't like them."

So many clashes between Brenner and myself spun through my mind. I dropped onto the bed. "Now it makes sense. Brenner was biased against me from the start, and I played into it, times a hundred. I was everything he disliked."

"You're not that kind of guy, West. Not anymore. Maybe in school you were, but everyone acts like a bit of a dick then. None of us knew who we were." From across the room, his eyes met mine. "Some still don't, but it's okay. We're all just here, figuring shit out as we go along."

"Maybe," I hedged, certain he was trying to tell me something, but I wasn't ready to get into a heavy discussion. "You're pretty grounded."

"I have a couple of rules I live by: Don't fuck up a good thing. Be kind. Don't fight the inevitable."

On the way down to pick up Brenner, I contemplated Grady's words. I tried to be kind, but I could probably improve— I lost my temper too easily and grew impatient. I didn't fuck up good things because I rarely had anything worth celebrating in my personal life. My hard-partying days had given way to mostly solitary nights, peppered with the occasional hookup with someone I'd never see again. I supposed I could thank my father for crushing any dreams of a relationship. He'd lied to my face and everyone else's so convincingly, how could I ever trust anyone? The good in my life came from positive settlements for my clients.

Exiting the elevator, we split up—Grady to settle Brenner's bill and me to find Brenner in the restaurant. Brenner and Manny were in a deep conversation, which I had no qualms about interrupting. With a smile on my face, I pulled out the chair next to Brenner.

"All set. Grady's gone to check you out, and we have all your stuff here."

Brenner couldn't meet my eyes. "Thanks, West. I do appreciate it. And everything you've done."

The snarky response I had prepared died, and I found myself hesitating. I remembered Grady's words. Be kind. "Uh, you're welcome. I'll go put the suitcase in the car and bring it to the front of the hotel to make it easier for you to get to."

He finally met my gaze. "That would be great."

"I'll help him while you do that," Manny offered.

"Perfect." All right. Being nice to Manny wasn't so hard. I could do it. "Thank you."

Grady walked with me to the garage. "It's really nice of you to take him home. What made you offer?"

I raised a shoulder. "I have a car, so why not? It's only right." I chafed a bit under Grady's relentless stare, which penetrated right through my bullshit shield. "And I guess I didn't like the way we left it with each other after we split up into teams. I might've overreacted to him looking at my phone, said some shit, and figured I should make it up to him. This seems like the perfect opportunity."

We reached the car, and after turning off the alarm, Grady and I took off. I swung around the circular drive to where Brenner waited with Manny, but before I cut the engine, Grady put a hand on my arm.

"Don't take this the wrong way, but I think you and Brenner have some unresolved personal issues you should explore."

Puzzled, I put the car in park and faced him. "What're you talking about? I already said—"

"I'm not talking about the text message."

"What the hell are you saying, then?"

Through the windshield, I watched Manny hover by Brenner as he limped along on his crutches. Brenner stopped for a breather, and he and Manny exchanged some words. With a grin, Manny took the crutches, and Brenner leaned into him as he slowly tried to walk.

Grady said, "You know what? Forget it. I'm talking out of my ass."

My attention remained riveted on Manny and Brenner. "I have no idea what you're talking about." I unclipped the seat belt and opened the door. "I'd better help them. Brenner's pushing himself too hard."

I strode over to Brenner's side. "Ready?" Manny handed me the crutches. "I can take it from here. Thanks for the help."

Manny's lips twitched. "Yes, boss."

Ignoring him, I steered Brenner toward the passenger side, where Grady had vacated, and stood waiting.

"Your chariot awaits."

By this time Brenner's face was a bit pale, and I made sure he took his time getting comfortable.

"You okay?" I asked as he wiped the sweat off his brow. "You don't look well."

A quicksilver smile came and went. "Always with the compliments. Depends on what you consider okay. My head hurts, my ribs hurt, and my ankle hurts. But I'll be all right." He raised a hand. "Thanks, Grady, for your help."

"Don't thank me. It was all Weston. Take it easy, and don't come to work until you're ready." He handed Brenner a bottle of water.

"Thanks. Yeah, I spoke to Daniel. He told me to take the week off, but sitting in my apartment will drive me nuts. I need to keep busy."

"You need to recuperate," I answered, sliding behind the wheel.

Blue eyes glinted at me beneath thick lashes, but Brenner remained silent, and we were off. Around ten minutes passed before he spoke.

"Why are you doing this?"

"Maybe I'm a nice guy? Could that possibly be the reason?" I teased, but Brenner's expression remained thoughtful, almost grim.

"I'm serious, West. This is a complete one-eighty for you. I don't understand it."

"I already told you. I'm thinking it's time to put the past behind us. If you're willing, that is. We're working together now, and it just seems stupid."

If I thought he'd be thrilled at the prospect, I was wrong.

"Is this because you found out I was a foster kid and you feel sorry for me? Because I don't need anyone's pity."

That was when I understood that Brenner still held a ton of hurt and pain from a past he'd had no control over, and I needed to be careful with my words. Joking about it wouldn't help.

"I don't pity you," I said softly. "Yeah, I was shocked and surprised to find out about your past because you were always so strong and determined in everything you did. I figured you were one of those overachievers who had parents pushing you to be the best."

"Like yours did?"

My chest hurt. "No. My mother, as much as I loved her, was a quiet, meek woman, raised to listen and not make waves. Her wants and needs came second. She existed to please my father, and he didn't give a damn about anyone but himself."

"So you really don't get along?"

I was unable to hide my sarcasm. "Pretty obvious from that loving text, huh?" I sighed. "Sorry. My father has been angry with me since I decided not to attend his alma mater and go it my own way." Not exactly the truth. The day I confronted him about his affair was the day our relationship died, but I wasn't ready to spew all the ugly from my guts.

"Why? You're a huge success—valedictorian of our class, *Law Review*, a partnership at one of the top firms in the country." His brow wrinkled. "How could he be mad just because you didn't go to his school?"

How to explain? "That was only the start of our downfall. My father wanted to have me under his thumb. He's a controlling, manipulative person who thinks only of his image. He took my action as a personal slight. His dream was to create a political dynasty—senator and eventually president. I would come up behind him in the ranks, mirroring him step by step."

"And you don't want that."

The Triborough Bridge—now the RFK, but no real New Yorker called it that—loomed ahead of us as we sat in traffic. I could simply answer no and be done with it, but to hell with hiding it.

"I'd never want to be anything like Preston Lively. I hate him," I spat out. "I hate everything he stands for, everything he is. He's no father of mine. As far as I'm concerned, I'm an orphan."

Brenner flinched, and recalling his history, I instantly regretted my words.

"Shit. I'm sorry. That was so wrong of me. I just meant—"

"I know what you meant. Some people should never have children."

I wondered if Brenner had ever tried to locate his biological parents but decided not to push it. We'd had enough soul-baring for the day.

For the remainder of the trip, Brenner didn't ask any more questions and remained silent. I figured I'd shocked him with my vitriol, but fuck it. If he wanted the truth, he was going to get it, warts and all.

"Who's going to help you when you get home?" I hadn't thought about it as we approached the city. "I'll get you upstairs, but who'll be there to make sure you don't fall and hurt yourself worse?"

"I'll be fine."

Typical Brenner answer that didn't tell me anything. "You're not going to call anyone, are you? You're a tough guy."

"Please be quiet. I have a headache, and I just want to get home and go to bed."

About to snap at him that of course he had a headache—he'd had a goddamn concussion—I darted a quick glance to see him wince and bite his lip, in obvious pain but too much of a prideful jerk to admit it. That painful twist in my chest tightened, and I made a decision. One I knew Brenner wouldn't like, but I was used to his snarls and scowls by now. I exited the FDR at 72nd Street and headed toward Second Avenue.

"Where are you going?" Brenner's brow furrowed, and his eyes narrowed. "I told you I lived in Brooklyn, by the Bridge."

"Yep. But I live on Park, between Sixty-seventh and Sixty-eighth. Look. I know you're going to fight me on this, but I have a two-bedroom apartment—"

"No," Brenner cut me off.

"You're being ridiculous."

"And you're being presumptuous to think I'm going to be okay with staying with you."

I pulled into the No Standing zone on the side of my building and shut off the engine. "Give me one good reason why not."

"I'll give you more than one. I have my own place. All my things are there. I don't want to. That's three. How's that?"

"Not good enough. Who's going to be there if you fall? What if you need help or start feeling sick?" I shifted in my seat to face him, though he refused to meet my eyes. "Come on, Brenner. It's what a friend would do."

"Since when are we friends?" He met my eyes.

"Someone has to take the first step." I smirked. "Or hop, seeing as you're on crutches." He remained steadfast, and though this idea had popped into my head only as we'd entered the city, it made perfect sense. "For the third, fourth or tenth time, enough already with the bullshit of law school. Trust me when I say I'm not that guy anymore. And neither are you."

"I don't know why you say that. I'm not different, aside from a couple of gray hairs here and there."

"Sure you are. You've just got to let yourself accept that you're a success. I know how you feel."

At that, Brenner choked out a laugh. "Ow, my ribs. I can't believe you said something like that."

"What?" I was at a loss.

"You know how I feel. *You.* Weston fucking Lively, whose father is a US senator and running for president, knows how I feel—a foster kid who bounced around the system, who doesn't know who his mother was, and who lived in a tiny two-bedroom apartment in Brooklyn." His eyes crinkled shut. "You live on goddamn Park Avenue. I bet my parents' whole apartment is smaller than one of your bedrooms."

I worked my jaw. "I'm not apologizing for having money. I donate to charities and help where I can. Am I lucky? Fuck, yeah. Did I shove it in people's faces when I was younger? Also yes, but I don't anymore. Let me prove it to you. Come upstairs with me and stay until you feel better." At Brenner's skepticism, I rolled my eyes. "It's not forever. I'm not asking you to move in. I don't need a roommate."

"I'm sure you don't. But like I said. I have all my things at my apartment—my clothes, my work stuff…"

Seeing he was running out of excuses, I jumped. "We can go pick up what you'll need. I doubt you'll need to stay more than a week."

His brows raised. "A week? I was thinking a couple of days, max."

"Start with that and see how it goes."

"You're not going to take no for an answer, are you?" At my wide grin, Brenner scowled. "It's only because you have me trapped here that I'm agreeing to this. Plus, we'll probably end up not speaking to each other again. It's not as if we have anything in common."

CHAPTER THIRTEEN
BRENNER

"Yes, Christine, I'm fine. I'm going for a checkup in a few days." I had my phone to my ear as I opened the file of a new case.

My friend Christine, socialite, cosmetic mogul, married to successful restaurateur Tony Gigante, and self-appointed matchmaker had been horrified to hear what had happened to me. We'd met when my old firm had bought a table at her yearly benefit to support research for blood cancer. Her mother had passed away from the same disease as Pearl, and we'd bonded over our devastating losses.

"Sweetheart, they're paying for everything, I hope? It happened on their watch. You could get workers' comp and stay home to rest."

Wouldn't that look great? Only a month into my partnership, and I'd be after them for compensation and how to stay home and not work. It had been a week, and while my head was back to normal, my ribs and ankle still gave me trouble. Much as I wanted to dispute Weston's claim, I begrudgingly admitted it had been a hell of a lot easier staying with him.

"Not my thing. I'm doing better. Honest. How're you and Tony? And the little one?"

"We're great. Better than. Tony's stepping away a little to spend more time with us—we bought a place in Tuscany we're going to be at for several months a year in the summer. You should think of joining us." Laughter bubbled in my ear. "Lots of beautiful women to meet."

"I'll keep that in mind whenever I get the time. Being a new partner, the last thing I want is to ask for time off."

"How are you managing at home? Isn't it painful? Tony once got a broken rib in a football game with his brothers, and he could barely move. You have four bruised ones, plus everything else. Do you need me to get you some help?"

When it came to organization, Christine was a superstar, and I knew she was itching to do something for me. I shifted in my seat. "It's hard getting comfortable," I admitted. "But I'm, uh, staying with someone, and they've been helpful." I braced myself for the inquisition because I knew Christine would jump on my words. She did not disappoint.

"Someone? Who? A new girlfriend? Darling, have you kept me out of the loop? Naughty boy. Who is she?"

Even though it hurt to laugh, I chuckled. "No, it's nothing like that. A work colleague. He and I know each other from law school, and he offered to let me stay with him while I recuperate."

True to his word, Weston had helped me recuperate. I thought he'd be out most nights, but he'd stayed at home and ordered us dinner. It had been...nice.

"Ah. That's good. You shouldn't be alone. I'll have Tony send some food over tonight. Give me the address."

Knowing she wouldn't allow me to say no, I recited it, and she hummed her approval. "Park and Sixty-eighth? Now those are my kind of friends. Who is this person, and why have I never heard you mention him before?"

This was delving into territory the depths of which I wasn't willing to reveal. "Like I said, he's a law school fraternity brother and a partner at the firm I just joined. By the way, didn't you tell me you had some friends who might need my services?"

A sigh resonated. "Yes. My brother-in-law's cousin. He and his husband were as madly in love as my friend Archer and his husband, Madden, but something happened, and now they're barely speaking."

"Tell him to give me a call. And thanks for the offer of food. You know it's not necessary."

She laughed. "Of course it is, darling. *Ciao.*"

I wondered what she meant by that, but I didn't have much time to spend thinking about her. My interoffice line buzzed.

"Brenner, are you ready?" Dawson, my paralegal, asked. "Mrs. Hobson is here."

My first client of the day had arrived. A story as old as time, and a pattern that saw little chance of being broken—a wealthy couple, married for thirty-five years, until the husband decided to replace her with a younger version. He wanted the divorce as quickly as possible to "start his new family" with his twenty-two-year-old fiancée. It reminded me of the article I'd skimmed about Weston's father and his new wife.

"I'm coming."

I gathered up my crutches and hobbled out of the office. Weston and Grady were in Weston's doorway, and they rushed to my side.

"Let me help." Weston reached for my pad, sending me off-balance, and I slipped, putting my full weight on my bad leg.

"Ow, stop. I can do it. I just can't believe it still hurts after a week."

"Of course it does. Between that and your ribs, it's going to take time. Why are you being such a stubborn ass?" he complained. "Lean on me."

"I said I'm okay." I brushed him off. "My paralegal is coming." Thank fucking God Dawson appeared. "See? Thanks." I handed him my pad and pen. "I'm ready to go."

Weston scowled, but I didn't respond. I wasn't about to tell him that I enjoyed my evenings in his apartment. Contrary to what I'd anticipated, it was nice to have someone to come home to and eat dinner with. And true to what he'd insisted, Weston wasn't the sarcastic, showboating asshole he'd been in school. We shared similar tastes in television, sports teams, and movies. We were politically compatible and—although I hated to admit it—he was funny as hell. Every day, that wall of anger I'd built toward him tumbled down, brick by brick.

But the real reason was something I wasn't willing to think about. Especially moments before walking into a client meeting. Once I was off the damn crutches, I'd be able to go home and put this strange episode behind me.

The day passed fast and furious, at a different pace from my old firm. I found it interesting to see how a big firm handled family-law situations, as these were the cases that so often rested on emotions rather than numbers, charts, and cold facts.

At six thirty, Weston stood at my door. At the beginning of the day he was immaculate—shirt crisp, tie perfectly knotted, hair styled. End-of-day Weston had his tie undone, collar unbuttoned, and golden, sun-streaked hair falling over his brow. Less put together and more approachable. He yawned.

"Are you ready? I'm beat. Can't wait to go home, get out of this suit, and eat something. I had to skip lunch 'cause my meetings ran into each other, and I've only had a protein bar."

"I'm pretty hungry myself. My friend Christine said she was going to have her husband send some food from his restaurant, so we can have that for dinner. He owns Gigante's. I hope you like Italian."

"Oh God, Gigante's is amazing." His eyes rolled back in his head, and he licked his lips. Fascinated, I couldn't take my eyes off his tongue. Thank God I caught myself staring without him noticing. I rubbed my eyes.

"Yeah. The food is good."

"Good? Use your words, Fleming. It's way beyond that. Let's get going. I don't want anyone to steal it if it's left downstairs. I wouldn't put it past these people."

I hobbled toward him on my crutches. "Steal? Your fancy neighbors? They'd never do anything wrong." I snickered.

"Don't you believe it." Weston's face turned dark. "They'd be first in line to jump in a lifeboat if the ship was sinking, to hell with babies and children."

The drive to his place was only several blocks, but with rush-hour traffic it still took twenty minutes. By the time we entered the lobby after dropping the car off with the parking valet, it was after seven. Weston questioned the doorman, who insisted no food had been delivered.

"Let's go upstairs. We'll have to order something right away," Weston grumbled. "I had my heart set on chicken parm."

Why did I feel like I'd personally disappointed him? "I'm sorry. I assumed it was today. I didn't think to ask."

He let us into the apartment and tossed the keys onto the entry table. My energy had begun to flag, and I stood leaning on my crutches.

"No biggie. I'm gonna change first, and then we can decide." Concern creased his brow. "Here." He held out his arm. "You look exhausted. Let me help you to the couch."

With no strength to argue, I let him put his arm around my waist. I leaned on him, and together we moved in sync. The couch looked a long way off. My ribs hurt, and I needed to stop and catch my breath. Something I was finding hard to do with Weston so damn close. His chest rose and fell, and the scent of his cologne and sweat filled my senses. I met his eyes, shocked by their green-gold fire.

"Has it been so awful being here with me?" Weston murmured, his mouth almost near enough to touch my cheek and tingling lips.

"No. I like it." At my confession, his grip grew tighter. He pulled me close, and I didn't resist. I couldn't. I fucking ached to kiss him, but I didn't know how to make that first move. Weston, too, seemed caught off guard by this...this thing growing between us, and we stayed locked in a staring contest, the air alive and vibrating, ready to explode.

"Me too. You've been driving me crazy for weeks. I can't explain it. I don't understand it." His mouth hovered near mine, and I could barely hear his words over the thunderous pounding of my heart.

A powerful surge of lust rocketed through me, and like that night in the hotel, I was fast spinning out of control. "What's happening here?"

West cupped my cheek. "Maybe it's time to find out?" He leaned in to kiss me, and my eyes fluttered shut.

The buzzer sounded, and we sprang apart. The motion sent daggers of pain through my side.

"Ow, fuck, ow, ow." I clutched my side, and West, wild-eyed and flushed, raced to the door.

"What?" he snapped.

"Christine Gigante to see you."

"Uh, yeah, sure, send her up." He pinched the bridge of his nose for a second and smoothed down his hair. "Are you all right?" He returned to my side, and with a gentle hand, led me to the sofa and helped me get comfortable.

"Yeah, fine." I couldn't look at him.

The bell rang, and Weston left me to answer it. With her usual exuberance, Christine breezed in through the door.

"Hello, you must be Weston. I'm Christine Gigante. Thank you so much for taking care of Bren in his hour—or days as it looks—of need."

Following on her heels was a burly man in a dark suit, hair buzzed close to the scalp. He carried two very large shopping bags. He stayed silent and watchful by her side.

"I've brought some food that should last you for a while. Omar will put it away if you show him to your kitchen." She turned on her perfect smile.

"Oh, yeah, sure. This way." Weston waved at Omar, who still hadn't said a word but followed him.

I'd known Christine long enough to understand she wanted to be alone with me, and I attempted to unscramble my brain quickly enough to speak. She dropped her purse on the table in the entranceway, and her stilettos clicked fast and furious across the shining wooden floors as she hurried to my side.

"My poor baby. Look what those bastards did to you." She kissed me hello, and her gleaming red nails touched my cheek. Her eyes narrowed, and a devilish light brightened her eyes. "Are you feeling any better? It's so nice of your friend to help you out." She crossed her legs. "Tell me all about him."

"You're kidding. Don't tell me you didn't look him and his family up immediately when I told you I was staying with him."

Her laugh was merry. "It's like you know me, darling. Of course I did. A father who's a presidential candidate?" Red lips curved upward, and her eyes danced. "How deliciously juicy. He's gorgeous." She leaned in close. "Why didn't you ever tell me? You know I'm safe."

Fear shot through me. "Tell you what?"

Her finely arched brows rose high, and she studied my face. "I see. Well, I'm glad you have Weston to help you, but you know you could've asked me. I would've sent someone over to your apartment to look after you."

I imagined the hulking Omar, sitting silent in every corner, and I made a face. "Uh, thank you, but no thanks. I'm fine."

"I'm sure you are," she murmured.

Weston returned. "Christine, you do realize there are only two people here. You've brought enough food for a month."

"Darling, we're Italian. Food is love." She patted the space next to her. "Come sit and tell me about yourself. I had no idea you and Brenner were friends."

"I don't know if you'd call us friends." Savvy enough to understand what she was up to, Weston chose to sit across from us in the club chair. "We knew each other in law school, and now we work together. I have an extra bedroom, and I offered it to him to make it easier for him to get to work."

"That's awfully nice of you, considering you're not friends. Doesn't your girlfriend mind?"

"I wouldn't know, since I don't have one." Weston grinned. "Is that a subtle way of asking if I'm single? The answer is yes."

"Gorgeous and smart. What a stunning apartment. I wouldn't have expected a single man to live in such elegance."

The light dimmed in Weston's face. "It was my mother's. She grew up here in the city before she went away to school and met my father and got married. I inherited it when she passed."

"I'm so sorry for your loss. I know how devastating it is to lose your mother." Christine sympathized, and West ducked his head, obviously still in pain. My eyes burned, recalling my foster mother and how she never got to see her dream of me graduating law school. My heart hurt for the three of us.

I watched Weston and Christine, but my mind was on Christine's words. How the hell did she suspect something had happened between us? She'd always been way too insightful for me. I'd have to be extra careful around her.

"Are you with us?" She waved a hand in front of my face. "Or are you dreaming of something or someone else?" A knowing smile ticked up the corner of her mouth. "I have to get home to TJ, but it was wonderful to see you. Please take care of yourself."

"I will," I promised. "I see the doctor at the end of the week."

"Good, although I think you'll be fine in Weston's very capable hands," she purred. "Let me know if you need anything else. Weston, make sure he behaves. He can be very stubborn."

"Don't worry. I'll make sure he listens to me."

"I have no doubt. You look like a man who gets what he wants."

Heat washed over me, and I scowled. "Didn't you say you have a child to go home to?"

She picked up her purse. "Don't be such a bear." She leaned in to kiss me. "You smell nice. What a coincidence—

you and Weston wear the same cologne." Knowing eyes met mine, and my face burned. "We'll talk soon."

"I'll walk you out," Weston said, and Christine, followed by Omar, left the apartment.

Weston stood at the arched entrance to the living room. It was a beautiful classic six apartment, only seen in true prewar buildings. Although the kitchen and two bathrooms had been modernized, the interior architecture had been retained. Crown molding in every room, inlaid wooden floors, and ceiling medallions framed old-style chandeliers, all befitting the grandeur of the apartment. Exactly the kind of place I'd imagined he lived in, and one I'd never dreamed of being able to afford. With this partnership, one day, I could.

"Are you hungry?" he asked. "I wasn't kidding when I said Christine brought tons of food. We'll be eating this into next week."

I managed a faint smile. There was no way I'd be here, but I didn't want to sound ungrateful. "Yeah. I'm starving."

He crossed the room to where my crutches lay propped against the side of the couch. "Let's go to the kitchen." He held out his hand, and I simply looked at it.

"I can do it, thanks."

A faint red flush stained his cheeks. "Uh, yeah, okay."

I needed to get out of there before I did something stupid. Like let Weston kiss me. And kiss him back.

CHAPTER FOURTEEN
WESTON

I was so fucked.

Brenner had been right. I should've let him go home like he'd wanted to before the weekend, and this...this thing wouldn't have happened. I wouldn't have spent all these sleepless nights, thinking of him in the next room, naked in the shower. Every second of those few minutes in the living room replayed in my head. I'd been moments away from ripping his clothes off and finding out what his dick tasted like, what it felt like in my mouth.

These tangled emotions had never happened with any man. Except Brenner. Why him? I didn't look at Grady or anyone else and want to eat their face off. Brenner Fleming had unleashed something wild and primitive inside me that I had to be careful to control.

We'd spent the days after that almost-kiss circling each other, cautious and polite. I helped him but kept my distance, and he did the same. His doctor had advised him to take it easy, and Brenner had given in to my insistence that he stay with me for a few more days. I could admit—to no one but myself—that it was damn nice to have someone to come home to, even if it was confusing as hell why it was a man. Specifically, Brenner Fleming.

I rubbed my face and paced the office, avoiding the news of the day, which was the real reason for my foul mood. My father's primary tonight was splashed all over the news, as the race had proved tighter than initial polls had indicated. His challenger had been digging deep into our family history, and I'd gotten several calls, which I'd ignored. It wasn't about protecting my father—he could go to hell and stay there as far as I was concerned. But I'd be damned if I'd let them make a fool of my mother and paint her in a negative light.

"West?" Brenner stood at the door. "I, uh, knocked, but you didn't answer, and your secretary said you weren't on a call. Everything okay?" His brow furrowed, blue eyes wary as if he couldn't decide whether to stay or leave.

"Yeah, I'm all right. Just a lot of shit to deal with."

"Your father? I know the election is tonight. Are you—you're not going to his party, I assume?"

"To be with him? Hell, no." I forced a smirk. "I defrosted the last of the leftovers from the food Christine brought last week." Of course, Brenner didn't know the real reason the sight of Preston Lively sent my mood swinging wildly between uncaring and wanting to punch his face in.

"In that case, it's six o'clock. Do you have anything else to handle, or do you want to leave? I could take a cab if—"

"I'm ready. Just let me shut down a few things, and I'll meet you in reception."

Brenner left, and I powered off the computer and was about to shut off the television, when the station aired some reporter interviewing my father and his wife. Even though I said I didn't care, I couldn't turn off the broadcast. His arm was wrapped around her waist, and she held little Emily, who, as my father was making his talking points, held out her arms and babbled, "Daddy, Daddy."

"Oh, she's precious," the reporter gushed. "A real daddy's girl."

"There's my sweet baby." He took her in his arms and kissed her blond wispy curls. "Yes, she is. I spend all my free time with her. There's nothing like having a little girl. A true blessing."

"Oh, the cuteness," I snarled, my already crappy mood turning dark. No. It wasn't little Emily's fault. The blame rested totally on my father. Paige was nineteen when he'd hired her as his personal assistant, and after my mother died in the middle of my father's third term, she'd stepped right in her place. Nothing like having a stepmother younger than you.

"How does your son feel about his little sister? Of course, there's a huge age difference, but is he as doting as you?"

I stilled and held my breath, waiting to hear what my father would say.

"My son has a very busy life in New York City, and unfortunately, he hasn't had the time. But Emily is still young, and I'm sure they'll be close and Weston will be a big brother to her if she needs it."

Paige flipped the gleaming blond hair that hung well past her shoulders, sunlight catching the massive diamond on her finger. "We're hoping Weston will join us for a family celebration real soon." She flashed a perfect, camera-ready smile.

"Don't count on it," I muttered and stabbed at the remote to turn it off. I gathered my things and left, and found Brenner waiting for me. "Shit, I'm sorry. I didn't mean to make you stand for so long."

He shot me an odd look. "I wasn't. I just came out about a minute ago."

I could see Brenner was becoming more adept on the crutches, and his face was almost healed from the scrapes and bruises.

"How's the ankle doing?"

"Better. It's all different colors and still puffy, but not as much. Hopefully at my next appointment, my doctor'll say I can start putting some weight on it soon."

"Good. That'll be a relief. The black eye is fading too. It's now only a little green and yellow." Our conversation remained stilted. I helped him into the car, and he sat stiff when I leaned over him to click the seat belt in place. I had a crazy notion of kissing him, for no other reason than to see what he'd do. I always had been one to push the envelope. However, because we were in a public garage, I refrained.

At home we separated to change clothes, and I came out first and decided to get dinner ready. The night before, we'd had chicken parm and broccoli. The last tray was eggplant rollatini and chicken marsala, so I heated that up with pasta. It was plated and ready by the time Brenner joined me.

"This is domestic," I joked, pushing the plate to him.

"I'll probably be healed enough to go home this weekend. I'll see what the doctor says. I'm sure you'll be glad to have your apartment to yourself."

Brenner chewed his food, and I did the same, with less of an appetite than I'd had for the delicious food. I couldn't tell him I didn't mind. We chatted about our cases and other things that happened during the day, and though he'd only been here about a week, he fit right in.

With the meal finished and the dishwasher loaded, I stood in the kitchen, watching Brenner make his way to the living room. I had two devils on my shoulders—my father on one side and Brenner on the other.

My father I could deal with. I shut his lying, cheating ass out, and that was that. Brenner was a different matter. We were deliberately ignoring each other and what had happened—twice now—between us. I couldn't figure out if it was because he was too scared to continue or freaked out that he wanted to.

Me? I didn't know either, but something urged me to scratch that itch and see. The first time I could write off as a fluke—being drunk and horny led to many unintended consequences. But last week wasn't a mistake. I'd wanted to kiss him—hell, I'd been fucking hungry for him. So yeah, curiosity was definitely spurring me on.

Brenner turned on the television, and of course the stations were all carrying election news. It was primary day here in New York for city council seats as well as other positions, but not in my district, so I didn't care. The reporters, naturally, were concentrating on the presidential race.

"Sorry, I can turn it off." Brenner reached for the remote, but I snatched it away.

"No. It's fine," I reassured him. "I'm actually curious to see what happens. I'm going to get a snack and something to drink. What do you want?"

"Uh, it doesn't matter. Beer is fine."

I poured some chips into a bowl and put it on the table. To hell with beer—this was a job for vodka. I prepared two tumblers with ice, took the bottle from the refrigerator, and set everything on a tray. Laughing, Brenner took his.

"This is how I know we grew up differently. I would've shoved the bottle under my arm and carried the two glasses."

"I'm a classy guy, don't you know?" I sat and stretched out my legs. "Tell me about it. Growing up, I mean."

Brenner shut down. "I really don't–"

I decided enough was enough. Time to spill my guts.

"My father cheated on my dying mother with his personal assistant. But it didn't start with her. When I was fifteen and on a school trip, he was in the same city. I thought it would be fun to surprise him, so I sneaked out of my hotel to his. When I got off the elevator, I saw him with another woman. They were kissing at the door to her room before they went inside. His hand was on her ass. I turned around and left." That image remained seared in my brain. Forever. "I had to go back and pretend everything was okay to my mother because I couldn't tell her. She was going through treatment, and I'd be damned if I would tell her anything to upset her. She died in the middle of my father's third term, and he married Paige. They wanted me to come and be part of the wedding. It was too soon—not even a year since she'd passed, and I was still mourning her death, so I didn't go. But I was a nice fucking guy and sent a present. I received a formal thank-you and then nothing. I've never met Paige, and I wouldn't give a damn about them, except I have a four-year-old half sister." My voice cracked, and I gulped half my drink. "I had to find out from a press release that she was born—I wasn't invited to the christening or any of her birthday parties. And every picture I see of her kills me."

"West, I'm sorry. I–I never knew."

"No one does. And when that bastard is asked, *Where's your son? Where's Weston? How come he's not here?* he lies and says I'm too busy working in New York City. If he ever once let me know, I'd get on a fucking plane and be there for her. Not him." I laughed. "Because they've never invited me for Christmas, Thanksgiving, or any vacations they've taken. I've seen their holiday cards, and it's just the three of them. Like I don't exist."

Pale and stunned, Brenner touched my arm. "West, I'm—"

"Don't say it." I stared unseeing at the television screen. "Don't feel sorry for me. I don't want pity—yours or anyone's. I only told you so that you'll know why I am the way I am. After I caught him in his sleazy affair, I didn't give a damn about anything. The one thing I knew was that I'd never be anything like him—it's why I refused to go to his alma mater and chose a different school. He was furious, but that only made me happier and more driven. When we met in law school and you challenged me, I took out on you all the anger I'd bottled up over my father's infidelity and my mother's illness. I focused on one thing—being number one. I couldn't lose. It had nothing to do with you personally. It would've been anyone who stood in my way."

"Makes sense. I guess we both had secrets we weren't willing to share. I figured you were a rich, spoiled kid who had everything handed to him and never had to work for it."

My lips twitched. "I *was* a rich, spoiled kid who had everything handed to him. But that didn't mean I wasn't smart. Or didn't work hard. Playing tag team with you for best in class was a great incentive."

"Glad I could help."

"Was that a joke, Fleming? Don't tell me you have a sense of humor too."

"I'm here with you, aren't I?" he razzed, and I didn't understand why I noticed how his eyes crinkled shut when he laughed.

"Don't get too full of yourself, Fleming."

You're cute too, but I can't say that.

"Polls are closed. They're beginning to call races." The humor faded from Brenner's face as he glanced at me.

My lip curled in disdain as the networks called the primary for my father almost immediately. "Well, that's that. The great Preston wins again—this time by twenty points. That'll feed his ego."

"What about his opponent in November?"

I shrugged. "No idea. But you see the polls. He's leading. I may hate his guts, but the people love him."

A smiling news reporter advised us that my father was about to make his victory speech. Brenner picked up the remote. "I'll shut it off."

"No. I want to hear what he says. I love when the lying, cheating fucker talks about family values."

The set cut to the podium of the ballroom, where hundreds of supporters were packed in to hear him speak. They didn't have to wait long. He strode onto the stage, trim as ever in his navy suit and red-white-and-blue-striped tie, golden hair silvering at the temples. His skin was tanned, unlined, and glowing. Paige, with Emily in her arms, wore a red dress, her blond hair glittering under the lights.

"You don't look like him except for the hair," Brenner remarked.

"And thank God for that. I take after my mother's side of the family. I'm named after her—Weston is her maiden name."

"You're from Texas?"

"Yeah," I said warily, knowing exactly where this conversation was heading and hating it.

His jaw dropped. "Shit, are you...Weston Oil?"

I didn't want to meet his eyes. "That was my great-grandfather. I obviously have nothing to do with the company, but I won't deny that it's where my mother's family's money comes from. They bankrolled my father's career, never knowing he was cheating on her probably from the get-go."

My attention was drawn again to my father as he basked in his glory before the music lowered and the din of the crowd lessened.

"My fellow Americans, we did it. Thank you for this win as we march to take back the White House. We have so much work to do. I look forward to the upcoming races and being your party's nominee. I called my challengers and wished them well and hope they stand by my side. I want to thank you all for being here and all the hard work you've put in these past months. This victory is yours as much as it is mine." The crowd roared with approval.

"He sure knows how to work a crowd," Brenner remarked.

"A master."

The cheering stopped, and Preston cast loving eyes on Paige and Emily. "None of this would be possible without the support of my family. Paige has brought life into my heart. I didn't know what having the support of a loving wife meant until she showed me with her tireless campaigning. And my baby girl is the best thing to ever happen to me. I thank God every day for giving me the blessing of this child. She is the light of my life, and everything I do is to make the world a better place for her and all the children."

"Shut it off." Without waiting to hear what Brenner would have to say, I jumped up from the couch, headed for my bedroom, and slammed the door behind me. I'd had enough soul baring for the evening and had no desire to hear his pitying words.

I sat on the edge of my bed, hands clenched into fists, trembling down to my toes. My eyes stung with unshed tears. That bastard had wiped away his whole life with us.

A knock sounded, and I brushed at my face. "Not now." The door opened, and Brenner made his way into the room.

I hadn't turned on the lights, but the drapes were half-open, enough to illuminate Brenner's grave expression. I scowled. "I thought you were smart, Fleming. Those were two little words."

"And you should be smart enough to know I can see right through your bullshit." Using only one crutch now, he set it by the night table and joined me on the bed. "I'm sorry, West. That had to be hard to hear."

Unwilling to trust my voice, I lifted a shoulder. I wanted him to leave. I wanted him to stay.

I want him.

He sat silent. Waiting.

"It's like the first part of his life didn't exist. He doesn't care about me, fine, I don't give a damn. But to not even acknowledge my mom...she supported and helped him before she got sick. But it doesn't matter because she's gone." Bitterness rose in my chest.

"You matter too."

I shook my head and tried to stand, but Brenner put a hand on my arm, holding me still, his eyes wide and silently questioning.

"What?" I asked, my heart thundering.

Our eyes locked and I shivered but leaned in, and he met me halfway. Our lips brushed, hesitant, but after the first touch, the second and third bloomed with growing need. A switch flipped inside me, and everything I thought I knew about myself faded away as our breaths mingled. Brenner's lashes fluttered against my face, and I cupped his cheek, hungry for more.

"Don't leave."

He covered my hand with his. "I'm not."

When his tongue touched my lips, I opened and licked it with my own. Like a backdraft, fire exploded inside me, sending me spinning out of control. "Fuck," I groaned, and Brenner's hand curved around my nape, tangling in my hair, yanking me closer, pain mingling with pleasure. So much damn pleasure, I thought I might die from it.

"West—"

"Don't stop." I covered his mouth with mine, the kiss frantic and desperate. I reveled in the rasp of his late-night scruff. I wanted to drown in his sweat and heat. Our tongues slid together, rubbing softly, then hard, in a dance I'd never planned to learn but instinctively knew the steps to. Brenner increased the pressure of his mouth on mine, and our teeth clashed. I bit at his lips.

"More," he moaned. "West, please."

Mindful of his injuries, I laid him down, my attention focused on the thick bulge in his sweats. I rubbed him through the thin fabric, and he quivered violently. I did it again and again, until he lay gasping, his hips bucking up.

"You like it?"

"Feels so good, fuck, don't stop."

I bent closer, smelling his desire, which only fueled my own. We'd traveled this road already, and I needed to keep walking the path to see where it took me. I pulled off his pants and briefs, my gaze latched on his dick, rising stiff and red, the tip gleaming. His eyes met mine, and without thinking, I swiped my tongue over the wide head. It tasted bitter and salty, not unpleasant, and I wanted more.

"Oh Jesus, oh God, do it again," Brenner panted, and knowing I was giving him pleasure was the biggest fucking turn-on of my life.

Giving in to what we both wanted, I licked him, and recalling how I liked my dick sucked, I put my lips over the crown and slid down as far as I could. Velvety soft against my mouth, yet hard as stone when I pressed on it. Brenner's groans and sighs rose in the room, and his hands slapped the mattress.

"Gonna come, can't...stop..." He stiffened, and I tried to pull off, but I still caught some come in my mouth before it hit my lips, chin, and cheek. In wonder, I watched him shake and gasp through his orgasm.

Brenner opened his eyes. "I should've been making *you* feel better."

I pulled off my T-shirt and wiped my face. "The night is young."

A smile tugged up the corner of his mouth, and my heart tumbled.

We're just having fun here, aren't we?

CHAPTER FIFTEEN
BRENNER

Weston Lively sucked my dick.

Five words I would never have imagined uttering, yet here I was, half-naked in his bed, having exploded in his mouth. And all over his face.

Tension crackled between us as he crawled up to lie next to me. I reached out a hand and trailed a fingertip along the cut of his cheekbone, then traced the perfect outline of his lips. He teased it with his tongue, and incredibly, my dick twitched, still in recovery from my shocking orgasm only moments earlier. I slid my finger fully into his warm mouth, and he sucked, adding flicks of his agile tongue.

"Let me do for you," I whispered, still in disbelief that I was in bed with a man—with Weston—and he'd made me come. There was no denying it, or the fact that Weston was just as turned-on, evidenced by the thick cock outlined in his pants.

"What do you have in mind...uh...yeah...that," he grunted as I cupped his erection and squeezed it. "Do that."

My ribs prevented me from moving too swiftly, but Weston helped by wriggling out of his pants to lie fully naked. I stared at his body—the hard dips and cut of muscle, the golden hair on his chest and his strong thighs. All of which I'd seen in other men in locker rooms at the gym or on the beach. None of which had ever held my interest or turned me on.

Until now.

Weston's dick was hard and thick, with a pulsing vein running up the side, inviting me to touch. I wrapped my fingers around the thick length, and hearing a sigh of plea-sure escape Weston, I began to stroke him. I picked up some sticky precome to help lubricate, watching in fasci-nation as he writhed and thrust into my hand.

"Faster," he grunted, and I did as he asked, never taking my eyes off him. A curious ache stole through me, and a throb hit me low in my belly.

Damn, I wonder what he'd feel like in me.

I ached and, half-hard, I tried to shift closer, but it hurt, so I stayed in place, my hand working his shaft. When I jerked off, I liked it hard with a little twist on top, so I gave that same treatment to Weston, who hissed.

"Good or no?" I murmured, continuing to apply pressure.

"Yeah, do it, Bren, oh fuck." He arched off the bed, hips snapping, head flung back, giving me a vision of passion I'd never imagined. "Bren," he cried out and lost it, his hot come streaming through my fingers. The sight of Weston Lively coming undone sent me reeling, and I grabbed my cock. Another orgasm ripped through me, and I joined him on the bed, the two of us lying flat staring up at the ceiling, chests heaving.

"Are you okay?" I asked, curious if he'd try to downplay it. Prepared to accept it if he did.

"You're kidding, right?" he murmured, and rolled on his side. Even in the shadows of the bedroom, I could see the haze of lust in those incredible green-gold eyes. He ran his fingers along my leg, and I trembled. "It was fantastic. What we did that night when we were drunk rarely left my mind. Then last week, when we almost kissed..." He bit his lip. "I couldn't stop wondering what you'd taste like. I don't know what's happening here, but are you okay with it?"

I reached out to touch his hairy chest. Who could've guessed I'd like it? But I did, and Weston's hum of pleasure let me know he was into it as well. "I-I don't know either, but it's like you said. I haven't been able to stop thinking about you...and me. It's never been like this with any other man. Only you."

He winked. "I am one of a kind."

I rolled my eyes, enjoying the banter. "You, me, and your ego. Good thing you have a king-sized bed to fit us all." Realizing I might be getting ahead of myself, I bit my lip. "I didn't mean I'd be sleeping here with you. I don't want—"

"I do. Please stay."

My fingers curled over his heart, and I felt its rapid thumping. "Okay. I'd like that."

"Me too." He hesitated, then swooped in to kiss my cheek. "I'll get your pants for you." He pulled on his sweats, picked up mine, and helped me on with them. "Are you feeling any better with the ribs?"

"I think so. I haven't needed the painkillers since last week. They made me dopey." I pulled up the covers and watched Weston climb in on the other side. "Can I ask you something?"

"Yeah, sure."

"Do you have any regrets that this happened?"

Concern spread across his face, and a tiny line bisected his forehead. "Why are you asking? Is that how you feel?"

"No." I exhaled a relieved breath. "There's been something in the air between us for a while now."

"I never regret what I do." To my surprise, Weston snuggled closer. I hadn't counted on him being affectionate and sweet. "Or whom." He grinned, and ran a foot over mine. "But just so you know, I have no intention of this happening with anyone else. We might've started out hating each other, but somewhere, it got turned around, and now I can't stop thinking about you. I'm not looking to question or analyze it. I want to see where this takes us. If you're ready."

Stunned by his revelation, I licked my lips. "I-I think I am." Who was I kidding? "I definitely am. I think that's why I didn't fight you about going home after my first doctor's appointment." The heat of my secret truth warmed my cheeks. "Maybe I was hoping this would happen since that first time."

West's soft eyes crinkled half-shut with laughter. "As if I'd let you leave. And no need to figure it all out tonight. Right now we should go to sleep because I'm tired, and you must be as well."

Of course as soon as he said it, I yawned. "Kind of, but I need to wash up." I wiggled my fingers. "I'm a little sticky."

With a rueful smile, Weston flung off the covers and circled the bed to my side. "I'll help you. Plus, I have to clean up in the living room." He offered me a hand, and I gingerly swung my legs to the floor and stood. I made to reach for my crutches, but Weston held me. "You don't need them. Not while you're here. Lean on me." At my hesitation, he squeezed my shoulder. "I'm not asking you to marry me, Brenner. Don't make a big deal out of it."

"I'm not." I glared at Weston, and he snickered.

"Has anyone told you you're cute when you're annoyed?"

"That means I must be fucking adorable whenever I'm with you," I shot back, but of course Weston ignored me. He left me in the bathroom to wash up, and after I finished, I thought I heard the television on low. Holding on to the wall, I crept to the hallway and peeked into the living room, where Weston sat on the couch, watching his father's victory speech for the second time. Try as he might to deny it, the hurt ran deep from his father's words.

There were different types of abandonment. Some of us were rejected by our parents, or put in impossible situations that risked our lives. Others, like Weston, had to learn to deal with a parent who gave everything except what a child most desired and needed—unconditional love; a parent whose main concern was himself, his wants and needs, not those of his child.

I returned to the bedroom as quietly as I could, and with my ribs and heart aching for both of us and what we'd lost, got into bed. I closed my eyes, waiting for Weston to return. I must've fallen asleep because I awoke to complete darkness and Weston lying curled up in a tight ball, miles of empty space between us.

******

It had been odd between us since that night together. There'd been no repeat, no kisses or touching. In fact, it almost seemed as though Weston had been going out of his way to avoid me, and now, at the end of the second week, I made the decision to return to my apartment. There was no need to stay with Weston any longer, and I needed my life to return to normal, whatever that meant.

My doctor appointment went smoothly. The bruising around my ribs looked worse than it felt, and he put me in a small, soft brace for my ankle and said I should be able to put weight on it again. Before returning to the office, I stopped at a sandwich place and picked up something for lunch. At first it was weird not using the crutches, and I moved slowly, but when I didn't fall, I gained more confidence and waited for a car. This proved to me I'd made the right decision to go home. I couldn't depend on Weston anymore.

But Weston didn't see it that way. "Why did you go without me? I said I'd take you. My meeting got held up but only by a few minutes." His eyes shot fire at me from across the desk.

"It wasn't a big deal. The bruising is healing nicely, and my ankle is much better." I made an attempt at a joke. "Look, Dad, no crutches."

"You're not funny."

"I think I'm hilarious." Struggling to understand why I was so afraid to tell him I was leaving, I decided to blurt it out and get it over with. "I'm going home tonight. I appreciate everything you did, but I think it's time."

Expecting an argument, I received a shock when all Weston did was shrug. "Suit yourself. If you need help bringing anything, let me know."

"It's not much. I can handle it."

Weston opened his mouth as if to say something, then changed his mind and gave a sharp nod. "All right." He turned to leave.

"West, please wait." Using the desk to brace myself, I got to my feet and walked to where he remained standing, stiff and still as a soldier. "Is everything okay?"

"Yeah, sure, why wouldn't it be?"

"That's why I'm asking. Ever since...that night, you've changed. I thought...I don't know. I thought things were going to be different between us. Better."

"Nothing's changed. It's been a busy week, and I'm tired."

My door was closed, so I took the chance and touched him. A simple hand on his arm, but I heard his breath hitch. "Talk to me. Tell me what's wrong."

"I said *nothing*." He wrenched away and opened the door. "Have a nice weekend."

I watched him leave without trying to stop him. If he'd wanted to talk to me about it, he would have. I had no desire to chase after him. One thing I'd learned in our brief time together was that despite our differences, we were very similar. If we didn't want to talk about something, we wouldn't, and no amount of pressure would change our minds.

Of course I'd forgotten about my friend Christine, who called to find out how I was feeling. At least that was her claim, but I knew otherwise.

"Darling, that's wonderful. I'm glad you're healing. And how is that gorgeous roomie of yours?"

"He's not my roomie, as you so quaintly put it. In fact, I'm moving home tonight. I just have to pack up some things."

"That's not a good idea. What if you fall? Who'll be there to pick you up?"

I laughed. "I'm not a frail ninety-year-old. I'm fine."

"And how does your friend feel about it?"

"Weston? He doesn't care. I'm sure he's glad to have the place to himself."

"I wouldn't be too sure. Anyway, let me send you Omar to help with your things."

I was about to protest but decided not to. It would be bulky to have to wheel my suitcase and carry my laptop as well. "Okay, thanks."

"I'm shocked. You finally agreed to something without me having to twist your arm."

A swift check of my watch showed it was close to three p.m. "I'll be ready around six. Can you send him to Weston's building then?"

"That's perfect. *Ciao.*"

I hung up, no longer in a bad mood. I finished up my work for the day and left for the weekend. Weston's office door was closed, and I didn't bother to knock to tell him I was leaving. We'd said everything necessary. By six I was ready and waiting in the lobby, and I watched as a black car pulled up. Omar the mountain man came and took my belongings to the trunk, then opened the car door for me.

I slid inside, and why was I not surprised to see Christine in the back seat with me? "Funny, I had this feeling..." I shook my head.

"Does that mean I'm becoming predictable? I need to step up my game." We took off, and we were soon bumping downtown on the FDR drive. "You had to know I'd have questions."

"And you think I'm going to give you answers?" I joked.

"It didn't take a mind reader to see that something was going on between you and Weston."

While weighing how to answer, I cast a glance toward the front seat, and again Christine read my mind. "There's a divider. He can't hear anything unless I push the button."

I heaved a long sigh. "I'm not sure what's going on. We're friends but not really."

"I'm not talking about friendship. Are you lovers?"

Recalling Weston's mouth on my dick and his unbridled, passionate response, I wanted to say yes, but it wasn't my place to talk about his sex life. Besides, *lovers* wasn't the right word, though I didn't know what was.

"No. We aren't lovers."

"But—"

"No. Please, Christine. It's not only my life here, but Weston's too, and I don't feel right talking about it. I answered your question, and I think that should be enough."

She took my hand and squeezed it. "We met because we both suffered losing our mothers to a horrible disease. But you know that you're my friend. And if something bothers you, I want you to feel like you can talk to me."

I smiled at her. "I appreciate that, and I consider you a good friend as well. But some things are better left alone."

She frowned. "You sound like Archer. He kept his whole life a secret, thinking he wasn't good enough, when he was better than anyone I knew. You are the same. A wonderful man who deserves to be happy, if you'd allow yourself to accept it."

I stayed silent for the remainder of the ride. We reached my apartment in DUMBO and Omar helped me upstairs. Of course Christine came prepared with food to fill my refrigerator.

"Thank you again for everything." I kissed her cheek. "I'll call you. I know the fund raiser is coming up, so I'll see you then."

"Yes, you will and maybe before. Try and get some of your new partners to come. I'm sure they'd be happy to donate to a worthy cause. In any case, I'll talk to you in a few days."

After she left, I FaceTimed Bill.

"Hey, kiddo. How're you feeling? The ankle better?"

"Yeah, definitely. No more crutches. Just checking in to make sure you're doing okay."

"I'm good. Meant to ask you how that date went the last time we talked. You still seeing her?"

"No, it didn't work out."

"Ahh. Too bad. On to the next one."

I chuckled. "Probably gonna wait until I'm fully healed."

"They get those SOBs yet?"

"Yep, they're going to do some quality time." The police had swiftly made arrests, and with the entire attack on camera, they'd pled guilty to assault and a whole host of crimes.

"Why dontcha come down here and recuperate? They musta given you time off."

"They did, but I don't want to take it. Better to keep busy."

Always sharp, Bill zeroed in on my words. "Why? What's wrong?"

"Nothing, nothing. I just started, and I don't want to get off on the wrong foot."

"You're a great lawyer. They're lucky to have you." Bill had always been my staunchest supporter.

"Thanks." A text popped up from Weston, and my heart slammed. "I, uh, better get going. Lots of stuff to go through, like the mail and my fridge. I'll talk to you soon."

My palms were sweaty when I picked up the phone to read.

> *Couldn't wait for me to come home to say good-bye at least? There are still some left-overs in the freezer.*

I gnawed on my lip.

> *I had Christine and Omar help me. The food is for you. She gave me more.*

The texting stopped after that, and I decided to do what I'd told Bill—go through two weeks' worth of mail, which turned out to be mostly advertisements, catalogs, and some other junk. My fridge had plenty of lunch and dinner food but nothing for breakfast and no milk for coffee, so I placed a delivery order. I changed out of my suit and into shorts and a T-shirt, figuring I'd have a drink, sit out on the terrace, and watch the lights of the city come up. My apartment was small, but the view was killer—floor-to-ceiling windows brought the bridges and Statue of Liberty right to my face wherever I turned. It didn't get any better than that.

The buzzer rang. "Brenner?"

My delivery must have come faster than usual. "Yeah, John. Let them up."

"Oh, okay."

I waited by the door and opened it at the soft *rap*.

Weston stood in front of me.

"What the hell are you doing here?"

That cocky grin surfaced. "I ran out of parmesan."

CHAPTER SIXTEEN
WESTON

Had I made a mistake? Coming home to find the apartment empty and Brenner moved out, I'd blown up, cursing him for leaving. Eventually I'd stopped ranting, pulled my head out of my ass, and thought about it like a rational person. I'd acted like the spoiled, petulant brat he'd always accused me of being.

Brenner wasn't some hookup I'd never see again or a mistake I'd made while drunk. I'd known exactly what I was doing when I'd sucked his dick. This was more than lust or desire. It was a feeling of rightness. I wanted him. Maybe the reason I'd pushed him away all those years ago was because I'd known this was who I was and hadn't been ready or able to accept it.

Now I had to own up to this—to me. Brenner was a success-ful attorney, not a scrappy foster kid with something to prove. Nor was he someone I had to protect. The man was smart and quick and could handle himself. The truth hit me like a punch to the jaw: I wanted him with me. I liked having someone to sit and talk with after the workday was done. I missed our banter over dinner and his smartass comebacks. Once we'd stopped acting like dicks to each other, we'd discovered that a lot more brought us together than separated us. I walked through my apartment, and it felt empty...hollow.

And so did I.

"Aren't you going to let me in?"

But Brenner didn't move, and my hope faded that we could recapture what had happened between us. I didn't know how or why being with him turned me on, and it didn't matter. I'd had a fucking week, and all I wanted was to be with the one person I could be real with.

"I don't know. Why are you here?"

Bullshit didn't work with Brenner, so I needed to lay it on the line. "I'm sorry I was a colossal jerk. Stuff happened that I don't know how to handle, and instead of dealing with it, I took it out on you and pushed you away."

God, being honest hurt like hell. Maybe that was why people hid the truth. Unless you had someone to put your trust in, how did you know you wouldn't get hurt? I'd taken that first step when I'd told Brenner about my father.

He remained silent, staring at me with confusion and hurt in those big blue eyes.

"I need to talk to someone I can trust, and you're the only one."

Being with Brenner opened me up to such scrutiny, and though it made me squirm, I was willing to let him take the lead. All I wanted was to babble my way out of the situation, but I shut my damn mouth and waited. And thank fuck he didn't slam the door in my face but instead opened it wider. I didn't stride right in, staying by the tiny entrance, which still allowed me a glimpse of the spectacular views of the skyline and the river through floor-to-ceiling windows. It hit me—the scenery might be incredible, but my concentration remained solely on Brenner.

"Do you still want to tell me about it?" Brenner asked, his lips tugging up in a smile I could see he was trying but failing to suppress. "Or did you really come all the way to Brooklyn for cheese?"

I grinned, and the tightness in my chest unraveled. Suddenly I could breathe. "Maybe I want a taste of both? Cheese and..." I left the second part unspoken, but the flush painting Brenner's cheeks left little doubt he knew where the second part of the sentence led.

Why and how had it come to this point where I needed to share the most personal part of my life with Brenner Fleming? Grady had been after me all week to talk about my shitty mood, but as close as we'd become, and despite knowing he cared, the words stuck and I couldn't speak. But here, with Brenner, the pain easily flowed from heart to mouth.

"Come." He led me through the tiny space of his one room to the couch, where he sat by my side and didn't let go of me. "You can have it all—the cheese and me. But you need to get something off your chest first, so let it go."

His hand burned in mine, and like the other night, his mouth called to me. I didn't understand it, didn't try to explain or justify it, but instead cupped his cheek and guided our lips together. The moment his touched mine, that switch flipped on, flooding my darkness with light, and all I could think about was tasting Brenner's tongue in my mouth.

"Bren, I need you. Please." Words I never thought would pass my lips escaped, and I pulled him close, sucking his tongue, swallowing his gasps. Brenner's hands rested heavy on my shoulders and pushed me off. Panting, I gazed into his stern face.

"Talk to me."

Pleasure drained from me. "It's my father."

Concern replaced annoyance in his eyes. "I kind of guessed that. What happened?"

I didn't know what to do with my hands, my heart pounded, and a knot formed in my stomach. Not since my mother went into the hospital had I felt so lost and sick to my stomach.

"After the primary results and my no-show, I received a formal letter that he's removed me from his will. He's cut me out."

"West, I'm so sorry." Brenner pulled me close, lips resting in my hair.

"I should've expected something like this. He's always been a vindictive bastard."

Brenner massaged my shoulders. "You have every right to be upset."

"I shouldn't be, right?" Unwanted tears burned my eyes, and I grew angry with myself.

"Who says so?"

"I mean...we haven't spoken in years. I defied him, and he's made these threats countless times. I don't need his money. I guess I just never thought he'd follow through, but he's got his new family now. By getting rid of me, he can completely erase the past. Meaning me."

Brenner tipped my chin and met my eyes. "I can't imagine anyone who knows you ever forgetting you."

I didn't answer...couldn't. I trembled and couldn't trust my voice not to crack. When I leaned in close, I still wasn't sure he'd meet me, but the touch of his lips on mine stole my soul. Soft kisses grew lingering, our tongues tasting, then chasing, until we couldn't hold back.

"Bren," I gasped and held his face between my palms, anchoring him to me. "I need you. So damn much."

"God, West," he moaned, and I'd never wanted anything more than to hear him say my name.

Brenner pulled my shirt up and over my head, our lips disconnecting for only a second before he took my mouth again, and damned if I didn't like his bossy, demanding side. My dick stiffened and ached to the point of pain.

"Please, Bren. Please."

"Yes." The husky rasp traveled straight to my balls. "Everything. God, do it." Our clothes went flying, and he grabbed my hand. "This way."

In my fevered mind I remembered his injuries and held him, letting his body weight lean on me. Around a half ledge, his bed sat tucked into a nook, and we tumbled down together, legs and arms tangled. Our full, leaking cocks rubbed together, and though it felt fucking amazing, it wasn't enough.

Not anymore.

As if reading my mind, Brenner propped himself on an elbow, and I brushed the burnished dark hair tumbling over his brow.

"I want you. All of you." I leaned in to press a kiss to his red, swollen lips, their softness fast becoming an addiction.

"Me too." Red-faced, he ducked his head, then peered up at me through those thick lashes. When the hell had he gone from annoying to adorable? "I'm still so confused how all this happened and why."

"I'm not sure we'll ever know definitively why we're attracted to whom we are. And does it matter? I never imagined wanting to be with a guy, but all I know is that if I see you, I have to touch you. Kiss you." I mapped the hard dips of his muscles with my fingertips, feeling the rough, wiry hair of his chest and thighs. All new and so damn tempting. "So how could that be bad?"

"It isn't. And I don't want you to stop." The honesty of his words stunned me. "I-I want you inside me. I fucking ache for you, and I don't know what the hell it means because you're a man, but I can't find one damn reason it should matter." His fingers skimmed my face. "You being here with me makes everything right."

The buzzer rang and Brenner's eyes grew wide, then crinkled shut with laughter. "My food delivery. That's who I thought you were and why I allowed you up." He hesitated, then leaned in for a kiss. "Be right back."

Was I going to lose my nerve? I could make a joke about it and leave, but when he returned from putting the milk in the refrigerator, all I wanted was to kiss him again.

So I did.

We broke apart—I was breathless and shaking yet never more certain that this was so damn right. I hadn't a clue how to get started, but we could figure out the mechanics together. "Do you have lube? I guess I need to prep you...you know." My gaze flicked to his ass.

Those big blue eyes fired with unmistakable lust. "Yeah. Do that. It's in the drawer next to the bed."

I crawled to where he pointed and took it out, plus a couple of condoms. I figured it would be no different than rubbing one out, so I coated my fingers and pointed to the bed.

"Lie down and open wide."

"The last person who said that to me was my dentist, and he gave me a root canal."

"I'm gonna drill you a different way." I ran one finger along the shadowy cleft, and Brenner's eyes clashed with mine. I went to two, liking the sound of his sharp, indrawn hiss and how he instinctively opened up to me.

"I hope your technique is better than your jokes...ahhh," he cried out as I slipped one finger past the rim of his tight hole. "Warn a guy first."

"Going in," I murmured and pushed in farther, fascinated and turned-on by the hot clasp of his muscle squeezing me. "Whoa, you should feel this." I moved it in and out, watching Brenner twist under my busy fingers.

"I do," Brenner panted. "Please. Another finger."

I couldn't imagine how it would fit, but I managed, and Brenner moaned and worked himself on my hand. "Damn," I whispered to myself, watching his face, and without even realizing it, I was stroking my dick as I finger-fucked Brenner. It was the hottest thing I'd ever done or seen. Brenner wrapped his hand around his shaft, and his mouth fell open.

"West, please. Fuck me. Oh, God."

I pulled out my fingers, my dick leaking everywhere, and with shaky hands, opened the packet and rolled the condom on. I poured on some lube, then added even more. My control teetered on the edge of something irrevocable, and instinct took control. I pushed his legs up to his shoulders, gritted my teeth, and nudged the head of my cock in past the rim.

"Oh shit, that hurts."

Despite the urge to go deep, I stopped. "I'll slow down." Little by little I slid in, stopping every few seconds. "Are you okay?" I placed a kiss on his lips.

"Yeah. It hurts but feels good at the same time. God," he groaned as I slipped another inch farther. "So fucking good. All the way."

I sank in fully, and a deep flush covered Brenner's face. "So good. You're pulling me apart...how can I still be together...? I fucking need it, West." His eyes widened as I pushed and met resistance. "Oh, fuck. Fuck me. Do that again. Please."

Damn, hearing him tell me how I made him feel was the biggest turn-on. I normally didn't like sex talk, but listening to Brenner got my blood going. I thrust, gently at first, but when he began to claw my back and his head thrashed side to side, I moved faster.

"I don't want to hurt your ribs." I braced on my hands and held off from grinding into him like I wanted to. My dick was wrapped in a silken fist of fire, and seeing Brenner lose control under me brought out a wild, primitive side I'd never known existed. I wanted to take him and fuck him until he passed out.

"Screw my ribs. Move, dammit. More."

That bossy growl sent me into a frenzy, and I pumped into him, lost in a possessive, driving haze of lust. I barely heard him cry out as he climaxed, splattering come over the two of us. Sweat poured off me, and our bodies slapped together. I heard his moans and felt the squeeze of his ass on my dick.

Fucking hell, this is the sexiest thing that's ever happened to me.

The roar of my orgasm tore through me, and I came so hard, I thought my heart stopped. Blinded for a moment, I managed the little self-control I had left to not collapse on top of Brenner, waiting on trembling arms for my brain to unscramble.

My wits finally in order, I pulled out as slowly and gently as I'd pushed in, took off the condom, and tossed it into the trash. Brenner's eyes remained closed, his chest heaving, rivulets of sweat running down his bright-red face. I crawled next to him and kissed his cheek.

"How do you feel?"

He turned his head and opened his eyes. They glowed like twin sapphires. "Like a fucking king."

I rested my head in the crook of his neck. "You are. And you're sure I didn't hurt *you*? What did it feel like?" I ran my foot up his leg.

"Full—like being split in half yet more whole...more *me* than I'd ever been before with anyone else. Then I was flying, and I didn't ever want to come off from that high. It hurt, but I forgot the pain when you hit my prostate. I remember Bailey trying to get me to understand what happens, but I couldn't imagine what he was talking about.

Damn, he was right. Oh, my fucking God." Laughter bubbled up from Brenner, and I cocked my head.

"What?"

"This." He waved a hand in the air. "Us. Imagine what Bailey would say if he ever found out."

"Knowing him, he'd want to join in," I joked. "Or watch." I played with the swirls of Brenner's dark chest hair. "Are we telling anyone about…us?"

Brenner winced as he shifted to his side and faced me. The question in his eyes matched the tumult running through my head. "What are you thinking?"

"I don't have anything to hide, and I don't give a fuck what anyone thinks, but I'd rather not, at least right now. Not because I'm ashamed of what we've done or afraid of what people might say, but because I kind of like it being just the two of us." I kissed him. "Against the world."

Apparently, that was the correct answer, because a smile claimed Brenner's face. "I agree," he murmured. "I have another question."

I yawned. "*Mmm*, what?" My eyelids weighed a thousand pounds.

"Stay here tonight?"

I took his arm and draped it over my shoulder, then snuggled in close. "Try and get rid of me. Besides, you owe me cheese."

CHAPTER SEVENTEEN
BRENNER

I opened my eyes to gentle snoring. The sun hadn't yet risen, but predawn light laid a filter over the sky, softening the harsh, hard edges of the skyscrapers shooting upward outside my windows.

I inched away from Weston and gazed at him sprawled across my bed, and it gave me a chance to stare at—okay, ogle—him. He was naked, his cock half-full and resting on his thigh. His body was beautiful—flat, muscled abs, golden hair lightly covering his chest. A shocking bolt of lust streaked through me, and I cursed the fact that I still hurt and felt open and sore from having him inside me. A hungry ache throbbed low in my belly. I wanted him to wake up, but the snoring continued, and despite my rising lust, I grinned. I couldn't wait to tell Mr. Perfect what a noisy sleeper he was.

"*Mmm*, Bren? Where are you?" he mumbled, sweeping a hand across the empty space I'd vacated. He cracked open one eye. "What time is it? Why're you awake?"

Much less tender, my ribs gave only a slight protest when I bent to place a kiss at the base of his strong neck. His pulse jumped, and I didn't miss the catch in his breath. For someone so purposeful and driven in his everyday life, Weston's emotions lay surprisingly close to the surface, and I liked being the one who left him trembling with desire.

"I thought a rhinoceros had entered my apartment." I smirked. "You snore."

At that, his eyes popped open. "I do not."

My smirk broadened. "You do. Like a freight train. Or an elephant." I fell on the bed, making snorting noises, and he growled and straddled me, his now fully erect cock hitting my stomach, which fluttered. It was my turn to lose my breath.

"Take it back." His nose brushed mine, full lips close enough to feel the vibration of his voice.

"No."

A dangerous glint lit his eyes. "I don't snore. You're lying."

"I don't lie." I cackled. "You snore. Loudly." I made some more garbled noises.

The delicious friction of his dick against my raging hard-on proved too much to ignore, and I gripped us both. Weston grunted, and his chest rose and fell rapidly as I began to pump us.

"You're trying to distract me from your insult," he panted.

"*Mmm*, how's that working for you?"

"What? It's—*ohhhh*," he groaned as I squeezed our red, sticky heads in my fist, remembering he'd liked that.

His mouth took mine in a hard, almost savage kiss, and I fucking lost it. Our teeth clashed, and our tongues, slick and hot, slid and tangled. Weston rode my hand, a low growl escaping him. He trailed wet kisses along my jaw, buried his face in my neck, and sucked and nipped the skin before biting my earlobe.

"Fuck," I gasped, and he did it again and again until I lay beneath him, pleading. "West...God...oh, fuck."

On fire, my body seized and I exploded, coming undone. My cock jerked and spilled out streams of come, and Weston followed a moment later, shaking and moaning. The sun rose, glittering fire on the water and a ship's horn sounded in the distance.

I forgot about my ribs and wrapped my arms around him, hugging him tight.

"I don't want to hurt you," he murmured, kissing my cheek.

The rapid pump of his heart matched mine. "You couldn't."

Sticky with come and sweat, we stayed locked together. I had no idea what was running through Weston's mind, but mine was galloping. This insatiable hunger for each other had proven not to be a one-time thing, nor something that happened only when we'd had too much to drink. I wanted Weston, but that damn devil of insecurity over our differences made it hard for me to believe he could want me too. I thought about that even as he kissed my shoulder and I sighed with contentment.

The man came from a billionaire dynasty—oil, cattle, politics—while I'd been found in a drug raid, abandoned by my mother, no father. Only through sheer luck had I found Pearl and Bill.

"I can almost hear your mind spinning." Weston rolled off me but lay on his side. Sharp eyes I was used to seeing across a conference table held my gaze. "What's wrong?"

A shadow crossed his face. "Are you having second thoughts about this? Us?"

"No." My swift response drove away his frown.

He skimmed his fingers from my abs to my chest, tweaking my nipples lightly. "Then what? And don't say nothing, because I know you."

I shook my head. "No, you don't. That's the thing. I don't even know who I am. And I know you say it's all bullshit, but I'm not sure it is."

"Have you ever tried looking for your mother? Do you know anything about her?"

I broke away from that intense scrutiny and stared out the windows to the river. Good thing I was twenty-six stories up with no direct view into my apartment. Only the birds got an eyeful of Weston and me.

"No and no. My foster parents didn't even want to tell me the truth until I forced them to. They always said she must've had a rough life and didn't know any better, but she kept me, which meant she wanted to be a mother. She just didn't know how. Drug addiction is a terrible sickness. I just wish she could've gotten the help she needed."

He brushed the hair off my face. "That's true. The easy thing for her would've been not to have you. I'm sure she loved you."

"It took me years to come to that realization. When I was young, I never wanted to meet her because I wouldn't know what to say. I resented her for choosing drugs over her own child. I know now that she was so young and had no support. I don't blame her anymore. Maybe she left me behind, hoping I'd end up with a better life than the one she could give me." Weston tried to hold me, but I pushed him away. "I don't want your pity," I grumbled, embarrassed at letting down my guard.

"Shut up." He put his arms around me, and this time I allowed it, but I still couldn't relax. "You made it out when so many don't, and you are a success. I don't pity you. At all. I admire you. There's a difference." His eyes narrowed. "Is that what's bothering you? That I come from money and you don't?"

I rolled my eyes at his words. "Jesus, West, could you be any more simplistic? That's like saying a diamond and a piece of glass are the same, just a little different. You come from a family dynasty. I'm from a foster family."

"Who loves you unconditionally," West stated quietly, and it broke my heart.

I couldn't argue with that, but I still had reservations. "Your father is a United States senator running for the presidency. What if someone found out about us? It could make trouble for him. I know you say you don't care, but–"

"Fuck that," he snapped. "I don't live my life according to how it might affect my father. I do what I want. Let's shower. I need coffee."

About to protest that we weren't finished, my skin started to itch. He was right. We were both a mess. "This conversation isn't over."

He rolled out of bed. "It is for now." And walked away toward my bathroom, leaving me fuming.

I muttered to myself, "One day I'll come out on top with this bastard."

But I followed him, and soon we were wet and soapy and I forgot about my complaints.

**

We lazed around all day on my terrace, and as someone who spent most of his weekends either at the office, working, or alone, it was nice to have someone to share my time with. We took a walk to pick up lobster rolls and fries and decided to eat them by the river. Weston finished his first, and watching him looking at the boats sailing past, I licked the butter off my fingers.

"What would you be doing if you weren't here with me?" I asked him just as he picked one of my fries. I glared. "I hate when people eat off my plate."

"And I love doing it. Besides, you're too slow. It becomes fair game after twenty minutes. That's the rule." He snickered. "And what would I be doing? Probably sleeping away the morning, then seeing if anyone wanted to have lunch or go out tonight."

"You go clubbing every weekend?" The distaste in my voice couldn't have been more obvious. Or was it condemnation? I wasn't a prude, but I imagined Weston with a different woman every weekend, and my stomach turned.

"No, but I hate being alone on the weekends." He nudged my foot with his. "Hey. Listen, I know what you're thinking, and it's not true."

Doubtful, but I was curious to hear what he had to say. "Now you're a mind reader? What am I thinking?"

"That every weekend I pick up random women and hook up with them."

Hmm. Maybe he was more insightful than I thought. "Well, I mean, that's what it sounds like."

"I'm no Boy Scout, Bren, and I never claimed to be, but that doesn't mean I bang every woman I see." Pink dusted his cheeks. "Besides, after that time...with the two of us...you know, last year? I was only with a few other people, but it never came anywhere close to what it was like between us. What about you? How do you spend your weekends?"

He reached for another fry, and I pulled away the basket and took some, not because I was hungry, but to give myself a chance to think. "Work. Working out. Sometimes a movie or a date." I mustered a smile. "King of the dating apps here."

Weston didn't seem fazed. "It's the way of the world now."

"I guess." Finished with my food, I tossed the bag into the trash bin. "Want to take a walk? It's not too hot yet."

We strolled along the river, then through the Time Out Market, where we had a few beers before deciding to splurge on ice cream. Cones in hand, we made our way down Front Street, where visitors and influencers jockeyed for space to pose and take that iconic shot with the Manhattan Bridge behind them. Weston leaned in close and licked my cone, and my eyes widened with shock.

"What the hell was that? Did you just lick my cone?"

He snickered. "You're so upset. I wanted to taste your flavor to see if I like it." He did it again. "Besides, I've sucked your dick. Licking your ice cream cone should be nothing."

A man with a huge camera, who was taking a picture of two men, obvious influencers, whooped with laughter. "That's the best thing I've heard all day."

I punched West in the shoulder. "Ignore him, he's an idiot."

Weston winked, and we strolled away.

Back inside, I turned on the ball game, and we settled on the couch to watch. The afternoon melted into the night, and West frowned.

"I don't want to go home, but I don't have any clothes."

"You could wear mine." The words fell from my lips without me even thinking, and a wicked grin tipped up Weston's lips.

"You don't want me eating your fries or licking your ice cream cone, but you don't mind me wearing your clothes? Or sucking your dick?" He ran his foot up my leg, his tongue sweeping along his lips, and my cock hardened. "Make it make sense."

"I don't have to. Take it or leave it." I had to admit I kind of liked the thought of him wearing my clothes. I'd never let West know that, and I immediately shut that thought down as way too fast, too soon.

We're just having fun here.

"Oh, I'll take it."

We ordered in Mexican and ate tacos on the terrace. Weston finished his beer and sighed.

"This is damn nice. I've never seen the city from this side."

"Yeah, it's pretty spectacular. You should see it when they have fireworks for the Fourth."

"Maybe you'll invite me for a special viewing." His eyes sparked hot.

"Maybe I will."

My phone buzzed with a text, and I grimaced. Weston arched a brow. "Problem?"

"Christine."

"Ignore it." He set his bottle on the table and rose to his feet. "You're busy." A devilish light sparked in his eyes. "I talked a lot about sucking your dick. Time to put up. Or out."

"Sounds like a good idea." I joined him, and he slipped his arms around my waist. The bulge of his erection pushed against my own. I'd never been a person who thought about sex all the time, but Weston changed that. Fact was, he'd changed everything I'd ever known about myself.

The buzzing stopped, and Weston nuzzled my neck. "See? I'm always right." His hands tugged at my shorts.

"Wh-what're you doing?"

"Up, up, and away." He hummed in my ear, then took my shorts and briefs with him as he sank to his knees. My cock swung free, and I was on the verge of protest but he took me into his mouth, and my objection turned into a long, drawn-out moan.

"West...ah..." I clutched at his hair as he sucked hard, his tongue lapping every inch of my throbbing dick.

My phone rang, and Christine's name popped up. "Shit...she, uh...she's calling now." It continued to ring and ring, but I was too lost in sensation, drowning in a wave of desire I willingly let pull me under.

He growled and sucked, adding his hand in a rapid motion. I trembled from head to toe. The sound of people laughing from the terrace below, the knowledge we were out in the open, even as hidden as we were by the wall, was so dangerously exciting, I flung my head back and cried out as I came. West coughed and sputtered, come dripping from his lips.

"Guess it'll take me a while to master the technique."

Unable to catch my breath, I collapsed in the chair while West took a bunch of leftover napkins and wiped his face.

"You hear me complaining?" I reached for him, ready and eager to return the favor, but another text came through, and this time I read it.

> *I know you're upstairs. Your doorman told me. And that you have a visitor. Tony and I are waiting downstairs to take you out for drinks. Both of you. *devil-horns emoji**

I groaned out loud. "Fuck my life."

"What is it?" Weston asked. "What does she want?"

"To take us out for a drink—I mean, to take me out for a drink, but she's outside with Tony and said she knows I'm upstairs with someone..." My face grew hot. "And she added a devil-horns emoji."

Weston snickered. "She's a trip." He helped me pull up my shorts. "So let's go." He kissed me. "You can pick up where you were about to start later."

I gaped at him. "Uh, hello? It's Christine. I thought we were keeping this to ourselves for now."

"And? Why can't two guys just hang out to watch the game? Maybe we were gonna go out after. Don't make it a big deal, and she won't either." His nonchalance was something I wished I could learn.

I chewed my lip. "I guess so."

"Answer her."

Sorry. Was on the terrace. Be there in a few.

"We better change."

In record time, we put on jeans. I lent Weston a button-down, and I couldn't help staring—he'd rolled up the sleeves and the sight of his forearms with the dusting of golden hair over his tanned skin was the sexiest thing on the planet.

Did being attracted to men make me an arm man? I gazed at his ass in my pants, and it was pretty nice, but it didn't give me the same vibe as his powerful arms.

"What're you staring at?" Weston asked as we waited for the elevator.

I jerked my gaze up to his smirk, and I thought, *What the hell am I so worried about?*

"Nothing."

A black car sat idling in front, and the window slid open. Christine stuck her head out the window. "I knew it."

I opened the car door. "Knew what? Hey, Tony," I greeted Christine's husband.

"Bren, how're you feeling?"

"Much better. No more headaches, the bruising is almost gone, and my ankle is holding up. I have this brace from the doctor. It gives me more stability. This is my friend, Weston Lively."

"How's it going?" Tony greeted him, and I would bet my ass Christine had already given him West's pedigree and shoe size.

"Good. Nice to meet you, and good to see you again, Christine."

"It's great to see you. What have you two boys been up to?"

I watched as Weston practiced his bullshit, and he was a master. "We watched the game and had some Mexican. I've never been to this part of Brooklyn, so Brenner showed me the view from his terrace. Pretty amazing."

Her eyes narrowed as she studied the two of us. My intuition told me she didn't buy it but couldn't say anything outright. "It is."

"What brings you here?" I asked." You're city people."

Tony chuckled. "Madden's company put up a new mixed-use building in Greenpoint, and we're opening a Gigante's in it, so we're celebrating. We figured as long as we're on this side of the bridge, you should join us. Archer and Madden are meeting us at the restaurant."

"I didn't mean to barge in on your celebration." For the first time, Weston looked uncomfortable. "I can go home."

"Don't be silly." Christine reached out and squeezed his arm. "I have a feeling we're all going to end up great friends." Her smile was pure mischief, but I refused to engage. It didn't matter because she wasn't interested in me anyway. It was Weston she was after. "Weston, I want to make sure you know about my fund raiser, and that you plan to come."

Looking a bit lost, Weston glanced at me. "Fund raiser?"

She explained, and Weston's whole demeanor changed. The light in his eyes dimmed, and his mouth drooped. "My mother passed away from blood cancer. I'd like to help any way possible."

She took out her phone. "Give me your contact info. I'll make sure you're on the list. Brenner always comes, so you'll have a friend to spend the night with."

The car arrived at the restaurant, but before we entered, I took Christine by the arm. "I know what you're doing."

"Do you?" She patted my cheek. "I thought you would. I always say listen to your heart, darling. It won't steer you wrong." She sashayed off and slipped her arm into Tony's.

With laughter and hugs, Madden Steele and Archer Strong greeted Christine and Tony at the door. Madden was worth billions, and Archer was an attorney, formerly an escort. They'd been together for years, and when their affair had first hit the gossip pages, it was a shocking scandal, but now they were a power couple in the city. Maybe I was overthinking and worrying more than necessary. If Madden Steele could be out and proud, Weston wouldn't have a problem.

If things worked out between us.

If he wanted to go that route.

If I did.

If. If. If.

Did I want that?

Why wouldn't I?

Shit. This was a lot to handle.

Weston waited by the door. "Everything all right?"

"Yep. Everything's great."

He gave me a slow, sexy smile. "It sure as hell is."

CHAPTER EIGHTEEN
WESTON

It had been hard as hell leaving Brenner Sunday afternoon, but I'd had to go home and get ready for Monday morning. I had a deposition, two client meetings, and agreements to review, and I always used the night before to prep.

I sat staring at my computer, the files up on the screen, but my mind was miles away—specifically those miles that separated Brenner from me.

"Jesus, get a grip. You're not a teenager." I buckled down and took the notes I needed, read through the questions I anticipated, then took a break, checking my phone. A text from Grady popped up.

Wanna watch the game?

*Have another hour of work, but come on by.
Bring beer. I've got an empty fridge.*

I received a thumbs-up emoji and checked the time. Six o'clock, and that late bagel brunch we'd devoured seemed a long way away. As did Brenner. After two days and two nights with him, my apartment was way too quiet, and despite telling him I had tons of work, I sent him a text.

What're you doing?

To my surprise, he answered almost immediately.

Texting you. I thought you had to work.

I grinned and decided to push his buttons because it was so easy to get a reaction.

Miss me already?

You're the one texting me. So I think it's you who misses me.

Well, well. Brenner was learning.

I am working. Took a break. Grady is coming over later to watch the game. You could stop by if you want.

I hadn't intended to ask him, but what the hell. He was there alone, and I was here alone, and that was stupid.

Can't. I've got lots of things to do here. Still learning my way around the firm.

It was true, but I didn't have to like it.

Fine. See you tomorrow.

Don't pout. Maybe dinner during the week?

No maybe about it.

I tucked the phone away and tackled the rest of my files. When the doorman buzzed to announce Grady, I saved everything, closed my computer, and stretched. On my feet, I groaned at my aching muscles, but it was with a smile on my face. It had been a long time since I'd stayed up all night with a lover, and Brenner had matched me with a strength I hadn't anticipated I'd find so damn sexy. I didn't know what to expect with a man, but I wanted more of Brenner. What would he feel like inside me? A deep pull low in my belly was the answer.

"Damn. For someone who never thought of sex with a man, you can't stop thinking about it."

I answered the door, and Grady breezed in, carrying two six-packs. "This should hold us, especially if the Mets blow their lead like they always do." He peered at me. "What's going on?"

Jesus, maybe it had been a mistake inviting him tonight. The man was way too perceptive.

I laughed, uneasy, and quickly shut the door. "Nothing. I've been working for the past several hours, and I have to switch gears, is all. Want to order pizza? And let's put the beer in the fridge."

"Sounds good."

He followed me to the kitchen, and I took the six-packs from him.

"So what'd you do this weekend? Beautiful weather," Grady said.

"Not much. Hung out mostly. How about you?" I put all the beers save two to keep cool and handed one to Grady.

"Saw my brother, and he took me to a club. I met a friend of yours."

My brows pinched together. "You did? Who?"

"Bailey Marks."

I smiled as I scrolled through my delivery apps to order us food. "Bailey's a fun guy. Smart lawyer. He's got a solo practice in the city. We saw each other about a year ago."

"Yeah. He mentioned that." He took a pull from his beer. "Said the last time you were trashed."

Heat flashed through me. "Uh, yeah. Just a bit. I lost track after four Tito's." I grinned. "Or was it five?"

"Damn, man. That could be dangerous."

You have no idea.

"Well, you know how it is at conferences. Pizza should be here in about twenty minutes. Want some chips?" I busied myself, pulling out a bowl and a bag—anything rather than focus on where the conversation seemed to be headed. Bailey had seen Brenner and me dirty-dancing.

Grady blinked. "Bailey mentioned you and Brenner were going at it."

My face burned. "Going at it? What the hell does that mean?" I drank half my beer in one long pull.

"West. Take it easy. I'm not here to give you the third degree."

"Sounds like you are. There's nothing to talk about. Yeah, Brenner and I were going at it like we usually did. Sniping and one-upmanship. But I told you, we've decided that's childish and stupid and made a pact to be civil."

With a face full of skepticism, Grady met my eyes. "Okay. That's good. I guess the days he spent here after the attack were productive."

"Yeah, you could say so. Let's go in the living room. Game should start soon."

I grabbed the bowl of chips, and Grady had his beer. My phone buzzed with an unfamiliar number.

"Problem?" Grady asked around a handful of chips in his mouth.

"Must be the pizza delivery guy. Maybe he can't find the place. Hello?" I knew I sounded like a dick, but I was hungry and impatient.

"Is this Weston Lively?"

"Yes. Who's this? Are you the delivery guy?"

"No." The yet unidentified person laughed. "I'm Noel Lane from *Politiclout.*"

"Okay. That doesn't help me much. I still have no idea who you are. What can I help you with?"

"We're a political news source, and—"

"Let me stop you right there. If this is about my father, my only response is no comment."

"But don't you want—"

Cutting him off again, I tried as best I could to keep a tight rein on my anger. "No. I don't. I have no input or any insight into my father's campaign. I'm completely removed from politics." The buzzer rang. "If you'll excuse me, I have someone at my door. Good-bye."

I ended the call and answered the buzzer from the lobby announcing the pizza had arrived. After I carried it to the coffee table, I gazed down at Grady. "Another beer?"

"Yeah, sure."

I brought them along with some paper plates, and we each took a slice. "God, I'm starving." I eyed the set. "Damn, the Mets scored in the first inning? When the hell was the last time that happened?"

"Who was that?"

I chewed and swallowed. "Some journalist—*Politiclout,* I think they said they were from—asking about my father. I never speak to the press about him. Ever." I took another slice, eating at a more human speed.

"*Politiclout* is a queer news source. Why would they be calling you?"

Inviting Grady was a mistake. I possessed a damn good poker face at the office, but that obviously wasn't carrying into my personal life. Grady knew something was going on, but without me as a willing participant, he wouldn't push me beyond what was comfortable.

"I don't know. Can we watch the game now?"

Grady dipped his head. "Yeah, sure."

Of course the Mets gave away the lead they'd held throughout the game, and it was extra innings before they finally put it in the win column. It was a little past ten when the game finished, and by then, Grady and I had finished a six-pack between us. I was a little buzzed and ready for a shower and my bed.

"Thanks for coming by. I needed this break after staring at settlements all evening."

He flashed a smile. "Always willing to help. I'd better go. I have a foster family coming in at nine a.m. who are considering adopting siblings. I'm hoping they go through with it."

Curious to know more, I leaned against the kitchen island. "Why wouldn't they want to?"

A cloud settled over Grady's face. "Because once you adopt, you can't give them back. And that's always a foster child's greatest fear. It's why we're so often people-pleasers or nonconfrontational." His dark eyes glittered. "We never feel safe."

Those words had me recalling my client Steven Culver and how desperately he wanted to hold on to the child he and his soon-to-be ex had fostered then adopted. Again, I admired his tenacity to fight for his child.

"Were you or your brother adopted?"

"Nah. Keston was an even wilder child than me." His eyes dimmed. "Still is. Owns a tattoo parlor."

"You, your brother, Brenner...amazing that you all managed to beat the odds."

Grady's good humor faded. "That's an anomaly, as I'm sure you know. Most don't."

"I'm sure."

I couldn't imagine the terror of living with that uncertainty every day, not knowing if the bed you woke up in in the morning would be the one you'd fall asleep in that night. For all that my family was dysfunctional, I'd never had to worry about survival.

"I'd better get going. See you in the morning."

"Take it easy."

I cleaned up, took a shower, and went to bed, wondering what Brenner was doing.

**

At eight thirty the next morning, I sat sipping coffee and reviewing the file for my first meeting.

"Wow. Weston Lively in the office so early." With a smile in his eyes and on his lips, Brenner strolled into my office and kicked the door shut behind him. My brows rose.

"You know what they say. The early bird gets the *cock-a-doodle-doo*." I met him halfway for a kiss.

"That's not how I learned it. Must've been those fancy prep schools you went to." He cupped my ass, and I rubbed up on him.

"*Mmm.*" I kissed the spot under his ear I'd learned made him quiver. "Why're you here before nine?"

"Couldn't sleep," he panted and pulled away. "We can't go further."

"You started it. And why couldn't you sleep?" I snickered. "Miss me?"

Laughing, he moved to a safe spot in the corner of the room. "You're right. I shouldn't have."

My personal phone rang, and when I saw it was my father, my head began to pound. Monday morning and my father. Two things that sucked. The ringing stopped, then began again, and I grabbed it. "What?"

"Don't you talk to me like that, you stupid fool," he hissed. "Since when are you a fairy?"

Stunned, my gaze found Brenner who, sensing something was going on, moved closer. "What're you talking about?"

"I got a call from a reporter who had a picture of you walking with a man. Said his photographer spoke to you this weekend, and you said"–he paused, and his voice dropped to a whisper but his drawl became more pronounced–"he said you sucked another guy's cock. Is that what you are? A cocksucker? Queer? What the fuck is wrong with you? You're doing this to sabotage me, aren't you?"

Unbelievable. Everything revolved around him and his campaign. "Is that how you think I live my life? Dreaming up ways to screw you over? News flash, *Dad*, I don't. I don't think of you at all. I stopped caring about your opinions when I discovered you screwing other women while my mother was sick. You pig. What makes you so sanctimonious? It's none of your business who I sleep with, but I'll tell you this. He's ten times the man you've ever been."

"So it's true. My only son, one of them. Thank God I've kept you away from Emily."

My heart squeezed tight at his admission. "I knew it. You deliberately prevented me from meeting my little sister. What kind of monster are you? What father would keep his child from knowing her brother?"

"She's innocent and too young to understand. I'm the best father because I'm protecting her from people like you. Paige wasn't sure if I did the right thing by cutting you out, but she will. Your mother coddled you, and this is the result. A weakling."

My stomach bottomed out.

"Don't worry," I snarled. "I don't consider you a father, so you can forget about me. You and your young wife can have more babies. Maybe you'll have a son you actually love."

I ended the call and threw my phone onto the desk, where it landed with a crash. Wary, Brenner put a hand on me, but I shook him off.

"West, I—"

"Don't. Leave me alone. I have work to do." I couldn't fall apart. Not in the office with everyone watching.

The fierceness in Brenner's glare was a palpable force, reaching through my hurt and anger. I wanted him to hold me but knew he couldn't.

"So that's how you deal with things? By shoving aside the people who care about you?"

"Bren. I—he blindsided me."

"What exactly happened?" Brow puckered, Brenner's gaze remained laser focused, but his voice gentled as he took my arm again. This time I let him. "Did he find out...about us?"

I sank into my chair, and Brenner parked himself on the desk. "Remember when we passed by those two guys posing for pictures and I made a joke about you not wanting me to lick your cone?"

His cheeks fired red. "Yeah."

"Seems the photographer—who also works for a news outlet—took our picture. Of course they connected me to my father, and with the joke I made..." I blew out a breath. "So much for keeping it to ourselves."

"Does that bother you? That people will find out?"

Before I could answer, there was a knock on my door.

"I have a nine a.m. It's probably about them."

Except it wasn't.

"West?" Grady stuck his head in. "Sorry to interrupt, but you might want to hear what I've got to say."

"Already know." I waved at him to come in. "This must've been what that call last night was about." I explained it to Brenner, who shook his head in disgust.

Grady remained by the door. "There's a blind item online about a presidential hopeful's straight son having an affair with a man." His eyes flickered between Brenner and me. "I'm assuming you two?"

"Surprise," I said weakly with a rueful smile. "Or not." Brenner raised his brows, and I shrugged. "We thought we were being smart, but Grady is smarter. He figured it out a while ago."

Grady's brow puckered. "Whoa, wait. How long have you two—never mind. That's not the issue."

"So what is? Who cares? I sure as hell don't." The initial panic had worn off, and I was in my I-don't-give-a-fuck mode. I looked to Brenner, whose face reflected some concern. "But you do?"

He chewed on his bottom lip. "Not sure. I haven't thought about it. Are you ready for what might come your way?"

"Because of my father?" At his nod, anger swelled inside me. "The last time I cared about what my father thought I was fifteen, in a hotel hallway, watching him stick his tongue in another woman's mouth."

"Are you sure? You were pretty angry during that phone call. Maybe there's more there than you think."

I picked up my iPad and slid my phone into my pocket. "I have work to do, and I presume you both do as well. My father can go to hell."

I left them in my office and headed to the conference room, but I was waylaid by Daniel. His concerned gaze met mine. "Weston. We'll talk later. Stop by after your meeting, please."

"Sure. No problem."

Did the firm have a no-fraternization policy? I hadn't a clue, and to me, it didn't matter. Neither my father's threats nor Daniel's rules would keep me from being with whom I wanted to be with. But was Brenner having second thoughts?

CHAPTER NINETEEN
BRENNER

The weight of Grady's gaze rested solely on me.

"I should get back to work," I told him. My damn ankle still made movement slow-going, which gave Grady the chance to put in his two cents.

"I'm not judging you. I hope you know that. But it could get complicated."

"I'm aware. Because of his father."

"Indirectly. But being with a high-profile person such as Weston, even though it's not his choice, means more eyes on you as well."

"I have nothing to hide." The conversation was getting a little too personal for my liking. "I appreciate your concern, Grady, but I don't think it's going to be a big deal. West is a politician's son, but he didn't do anything wrong.

I'd better go. I have a client meeting at ten." Before Grady could respond, I escaped to my office, making sure I shut the door behind me. For only a moment, I hesitated, then placed a call.

"I need your advice."

"What for?" Christine purred. "Your man looked totally smitten—he couldn't take his eyes off you."

Even with the situation brewing, I couldn't help the happy bounce of my heart. "Uh, well, it's not about that. Well, maybe it is..." I floundered, and she jumped in.

"What's the issue?"

When I explained, she sucked in a sharp breath. "Poor Weston. I think you should meet with Madden. He's lived through a scandal, and he knows how to handle the press."

I hadn't thought about that. "Good idea, but I'm not friends like that with him. We're more business acquaintances. Wouldn't it look odd to just call him up to discuss his personal life?"

"Well, of course, sweetheart. That's where I come in." Her laughter lightened the lead weight in my gut. "We'll have lunch. I'll arrange it and let you know when and where."

"I appreciate it, but I'm sure a man like Madden Steele has his time booked up. This is a time bomb." I leaned my forehead on my hand. "I can only imagine if they find out who I am, a foster kid whose mother was a drug addict..."

"Stop that," she snapped. "I won't let you go down that black hole. We'll fix this. Let me go and make my calls."

I sat at my desk, grateful for my friend but uncertain she could pull off a miracle. I should break my rule of ignoring my past and find out who I was before someone else did it for me, so I called ACS, and after a few minutes of being transferred between departments, I finally found a person to help me. He put me on hold, and I waited, listening to the canned music.

"Mr. Fleming? Thank you for waiting."

"No problem. Did you find anything out?"

"Being that your case is over thirty years old, none of the files are computerized. They'd be in a warehouse, and we'd have to put in a ticket number to retrieve them. Those files would contain notes from the social worker who worked on the case."

I winced. "I see. So there's nothing you can tell me?"

"Just the basics that you likely already know. You suffered from secondhand exposure to various drugs and spent some time in the hospital. You were made a ward of the state when she was sentenced." I could hear the clicking of the mouse. "That's all we have in summary."

"Thank you." Frustrated, I rubbed my face. I had to get my mind into my work. People depended on me. My phone buzzed.

> *Madden will meet you at the Mark at 2.*

My lips twitched. If I could pick anyone to have on my team, it would be Christine.

**

At exactly two p.m., I spotted Madden Steele striding through the restaurant, and I rose from my seat.

"Good to see you again." I shook his hand. "Although I hadn't anticipated it to be so soon."

His eyes twinkled. "I thrive on spontaneity, and Christine told me it was a matter of some urgency, so why don't we order and get to the point?"

"Shouldn't we wait for Christine? She said she'd be here."

His gaze was steady. "She assumed you'd be more comfortable with me alone."

The waiter appeared, and we ordered—Madden the chicken club, and me only a soup because my stomach couldn't handle much else.

I explained my relationship with West, from law school to the hotel hookup and our reconnection. Madden listened intently until I was finished. "So now that Weston's been outed, you think they'll come after you?"

"Listen. Weston knows I was a foster kid. But I'm worried they'll come after him by using my birth mother's past—and by *they*, I mean his father or the press. Or both."

Madden's lips thinned. "Trust me, I know all about family deceit and sabotage. And I've heard of his father." Distaste dripped from his voice. "Enough said. Archer and I faced similar issues—his escorting background was fodder for the tabloids for weeks, and my aunt fed them every juicy bite they wanted. You need to get ahead of the information so they can't hit you with a surprise."

"I agree. I called ACS, and they could only tell me my mother was incarcerated after the drug raid on her house."

Madden pulled out his phone. "Give me names, dates, and any other information you've got. I'll have it checked out and call you when I have something. I'll put a rush on it, and it'll be confidential."

The knot of anxiety that had gripped me since the morning loosened.

We finished our lunch, and Madden paid the bill.

"Thank you, Madden. I appreciate your help."

"Neither you nor Weston should have to live under the threat of whatever it is that's coming." We walked out to the street. "Who contacted Weston? Was it a news organization?"

"It's called *Politiclout*. Weston was so upset about the phone call from his father, he didn't want to talk about anything else. He has no idea I'm talking to you."

"I've heard of them." I could almost see the wheels turning in Madden's head and remained quiet. As head of a multibillion-dollar real-estate enterprise, Madden Steele was as savvy a businessperson as they came, and I'd welcome any and all suggestions.

"I'll have my publicity people nose around and let you know." His smile was grim. "I'll be in touch. And for what it's worth, don't let small, petty-minded individuals determine how you live your life or whom you want to love. Surround yourself with people you can trust to always be in your corner and have your best interests at heart."

"I think I have." I extended a hand, and we shook. "Thank you."

He walked away, leaving me wrestling with my thoughts. My calendar was light that afternoon, and Weston was running on back-to-back meetings, so there was little chance for us to connect. In my office, I called Bill.

"Hey, kiddo. What's goin' on?"

"I have some questions. I'm asking them for a reason that I'll tell you about, but not right now."

"Uh, okay. Shoot."

"What do you know about my birth mother? Did you ever get any information on her? I-I need to know where she lives, or just anything."

"Listen, kiddo. Your mother and I didn't ever wanna say anything because we didn't wanna upset you."

"Upset me about what?" I grimaced. "What could be worse than what I already know?"

He sighed. "She—Alicia—she died."

Even though I had no recollection of her, hearing the words hurt. "Do—do you know how?"

"She spent nine years in prison, and when she got out, a coupla years after her release, they found her stabbed to death under the Gowanus, near Thirty-ninth Street."

"Jesus." I sucked in my breath. "She never really had a chance, did she?"

"Maybe not, given what she'd been through—she was only sixteen when she had you, an addict...but you did. You were the most important thing to us, and we didn't want you to be upset, so we decided not to tell you. I'm sorry, Brenner."

"Don't be. I'm not angry with you." It was true. "Funny enough, I'm not angry with her either. Not anymore." Grief sheared through me. "Her life was over before it had a chance to begin."

"Why the questions about her all of a sudden?"

I hung my head. I wasn't ready for this conversation. Especially not without talking to Weston first.

"I can't get into it now. But soon."

"Okay, I guess. You ain't in trouble, are ya?"

"No. I'm good. Talk to you soon. Love you."

"Bye. Call me."

I sat, my head in the clouds. My phone buzzed. "Yes?"

"It's Daniel. Can you come to my office, please?"

My heart sank. "Be right there."

Feet dragging, I walked the halls until I reached Daniel's office.

Joanne, his secretary, held up a finger. "I'll let him know you're here." She spoke into the phone, then looked up at me. "Go right in."

I mustered a faint smile and tried to ignore the pounding of my heart as I entered.

"Sit, please." Daniel pointed to the chair at the conference table and joined me. "I've already talked to Weston, but I'd like to hear what you have to say."

"About what?"

Daniel's lips twitched. "Well played. I knew you were a good attorney." He took off his glasses and rubbed his eyes. "I'll tell you what I told Weston. I don't care what people do in their spare time unless it's illegal or negatively impacts the firm. I wasn't aware that you and he were more than friends, and I suppose there's no reason I should've been. We don't have a no-fraternization policy, and there's no intention to start one."

Even the tips of my ears burned. God, to have Daniel talking about my sex life made my skin crawl. I was certain my face was bright red.

"That being said, Weston has told me there have been some...inquiries about your relationship. I expect you'll keep the firm out of the press."

"Of course. And please, I don't want you to think Weston and I—"

Daniel held up a hand. "Brenner. You don't owe me or anyone else an explanation. You have a right to be happy."

Inexplicable tears burned my eyes. "Thank you."

I left the office and headed to Weston's to see if he was finally free, but his paralegal stopped me.

"He left about an hour ago."

"How did he...was he okay?"

Delia raked me with a frank gaze. "What do you think?" She tucked a long strand of hair behind her ear. "I'm sorry. I just feel so bad for Weston. He's so upset about everything." As she was about a foot shorter than me, I leaned over to hear her lowered voice. "I've been with him since he joined the firm and relocated with him from Boston. West likes to pretend nothing affects him and he's above it all, but the truth is, he's very sensitive. That's what makes him so good at his job. He's very attuned to people and their problems."

"Thanks, Delia."

Back at my office, several texts from Madden popped up. *Damn, that was fast.*

> *I have some information.*

> *Your mother was incarcerated for nine years on drug and prostitution charges. She lived in Brooklyn after release.*

The news, while not unexpected, hit me like a punch to my chest. I knew about the drugs but not the prostitution.

> *I'm working on some other angles to get more detailed information and find out what she did after she was released.*

Great. More terrible news to come. With nothing on my schedule for the rest of the afternoon, there was only one place I needed to be.

******

The doorman waved me up without calling, perhaps thinking I was still staying with Weston. I rang the bell and heard footsteps approach. An unfamiliar pain wrapped around my heart at the sight of Weston standing there, shadows holding his bright eyes captive. Normally so filled with light and life, Weston's expressive face was all too somber for me.

"West, I–"

"Shh. I had a feeling you'd come." He moved in close to murmur in my ear. "Be prepared." And pressed a quick kiss to my lips without giving me a chance to react.

"Prepared for what?"

"Not what. Whom." And before he could say more, Bailey appeared behind him.

"Brenner. You dog. Come in here and plant me a wet one."

West shrugged. "He called me, and I couldn't say no."

I allowed myself to be hugged, and then Bailey pushed me away. "I can't believe this. The two of you? When? How? Are there pictures, videos?" He waggled his brows, and despite the ugliness of the day, both Weston and I burst out laughing.

"Bailey, don't be gross."

"Are you kidding? Two insanely gorgeous straight guys I've known for years, guys who swore they hated each other, are now hooking up, and you don't expect me to have questions? Not to mention, just thinking about the hate sex gives me a stiff one. Jesus, it's like a fantasy come to life." He eyed us. "So...which one made the first move? Come on. You can confess to me."

West nudged me. "Maybe if he keeps talking, he'll wind down and eventually shut up."

"I heard that. So?" Bailey's eyes gleamed. "Is it serious?"

I wanted to die of embarrassment, but West took my hand and shocked me for the umpteenth time that day.

"Can Bren sit? You ambushed him without giving him a chance to breathe." Still holding my hand, which Bailey had zeroed in on with a grin, West took us into the living room, where we sat—Bailey in the club chair, West and me on the couch. "Bailey read the blind item in *Politiclout* and called me." To Bailey, he said, "*Politiclout* called me last night, trying to ask me questions, and I cut them off. I thought it was about my father's campaign, and I wasn't going to talk to them."

"In a roundabout way it is." Bailey informed me. "Your father runs on a very conservative platform. But he also stresses love for his family. By having a son involved in a sexual relationship with another man, it throws a bomb-shell into that scenario. What is he going to do?"

"I already know," West responded with bitterness. "He cut me off. He'll find some way to make it my fault and claim he's simply protecting his family."

Bailey turned to me. "You're awfully quiet. What are you thinking? This affects you as well." The jokester had vanished, and Bailey presented as the sharp-eyed lawyer we'd heard he was.

I hadn't planned on revealing in front of Bailey what I'd learned about my birth mother, but Weston, again proving his innate sensitivity, squeezed my hand. "Brenner doesn't have to say a thing. This is my fight."

"Bullshit," I snapped. "We're together, right? How long do you think it'll take them to figure out who you're with and start digging into my background? I refuse to be a liability to you."

Weston's eyes smoldered with a dangerous light. "Liability? Is that what you think you are to me?"

My voice hitched. "I-I don't know."

"I think you do." The intensity of his gaze left me reeling.

"Oookay. I'll talk to you guys later. I'm definitely not needed here." Bailey slipped out, and I heard the door lock click.

"I thought he'd never leave," Weston murmured against my mouth, and I grinned.

"He'll be back."

Weston pressed a kiss to my lips, and I couldn't stop trembling. "I'm sure. If only to get more of the story of us."

"The story of us? What's that?"

He cupped my face between the palms of his hands. "Stick with me, and we'll find out together."

CHAPTER TWENTY
WESTON

Brenner gazed at me with trepidation. "I discovered some things today that might change your mind. About me, I mean."

This wasn't Brenner stepping aside to be altruistic. He was truly concerned, and I needed to put him at ease once and for all.

"Have I given you any indication that I want to walk away for you...from us?"

"N-no, but—"

"No buts. We are in this together. You. Me." I didn't know where all this possessiveness sprang from. When Isobel and I had been lovers, I'd known she was with other people, as was I, and it had never bothered me. But the thought of someone else touching Brenner sent my blood to the boiling point. "I'm not looking for anyone else. Are you?"

I held my breath, waiting for Brenner's response.

"No. I just don't understand how it happened. And why you?"

"*Hmm.* Maybe I'm irresistible?" I cast my eyes upward, unable to keep the smirk from my lips. "If memory serves, you always wanted the best."

Surprising me, Brenner took my mouth in a bruising kiss. "That was my line. And I think I got it."

"Think? You think you got it?" I sucked his tongue hungrily while pushing his suit jacket off. I ran my hands over his firm biceps. "I know I have. You are whom I want. Whom I need. No one else."

Bright-blue eyes latched on to mine, and his fingers never fumbled when he undid the buttons of his shirt. I removed my T-shirt, desire escalating at the roughness of Brenner's chest hair and his scruff rasping against my hot skin.

"I need you too, West. How it happened or why doesn't matter. I don't want to let you go."

I held him close, the thump of his heart echoing in my chest. "Not happening."

Brenner held me at arm's length, sorrow chasing away the lust. "It might, once I tell you what I learned today."

My breathing returning to normal, I tangled my fingers with his, the heft and strength of a man's hand in mine no longer an oddity. It was right. Real.

"Go ahead, but it takes a lot to shock me."

Hearing Brenner hesitantly relay his mother's heart-breaking story made me want to put him in bubble wrap so nothing could ever hurt him again. When he finished, he kept his head bowed, refusing to meet my eyes. "So you can see, it's not simply me being a foster kid."

I tugged him near. "There's nothing simple about you. You're a fighter, and you have more integrity than anyone I know. Let them try and come after you. They'll have to get through me first." My phone buzzed, but I ignored it, my focus on Brenner. Unfortunately, whoever was trying to contact me was persistent, and when I picked it up, shock sent my heart racing. Missed calls and a text from my father.

"What is it?" Brenner inched closer. "Did something happen?"

Numb, I showed him my phone screen.

> *I'll be in New York City on Saturday. If you'd like to meet your sister, come to the Waldorf.*

"I'm not sure what to think. With my father, it could be a trap."

"Or it could be an olive branch. He did mention your sister."

If he was playing on my heartstrings, it was working, the bastard. He knew my one weakness was Emily. They might not have wanted me in her life, but that didn't stop me from sending her a gift for her birthday and at every Christmas.

"You think I should go?"

Brenner cupped my cheek. "Don't you?"

Sweat dampened my shirt. "I want to, but I don't want to fuck up."

"How could you?"

Brenner pulled me close, and I rested my head against his shoulder. "I've been angry with him for so long, and Emily's just a little girl who loves him. I can't be certain I'll be able to keep my emotions in check." We sat for a moment, Brenner stroking my cheek, and I thought how nice this could be. Permanently. "Come with me?" I blurted out, and Brenner's arm tightened around me.

"What?" His laugh was uneasy. "No way."

"Why? You'd keep me from saying something stupid."

His chuckle rumbled deep in his chest. "Since when do you say stupid things? Come on, West. What's this really about?"

I sat up, facing him. "I-I'm afraid." At my confession, Brenner's eyes widened. "Yeah. Imagine that."

"There's nothing wrong with being afraid. Trust me, I know."

I took him by the shoulders. "Exactly. You understand me. I don't want to fuck it up with her." Something bright yet terrifying twisted in my chest. "Please, Bren? I-I need you."

I'd never said that to anyone before, but the truth was, since I'd begun this relationship with Bren, I'd discovered a new side of myself. One that when I was younger I might've rejected but now couldn't deny.

"I'm not sure I can do this on my own."

"You make it impossible to say no."

"Don't." I kissed him. "Say yes. You want to be with me, right?"

His lips moved against mine. "Yes. I—yes."

I pressed kisses to his mouth and cheeks, nipping at his throat. He swelled hard and thick underneath me, and I fell into his blue, blue eyes. "I want you inside me. I need to know."

"You want me to fuck you?" His expression turned fierce, his gaze heated. Bren licked his lips, and a bolt of lust shot through me, leaving no doubt.

"Yeah," I confessed. "I've been thinking about it all day."

He followed me to my bedroom, where we undressed, and in between kisses and touching, Brenner laid me on the bed. "You're sure?"

I fixated on how thick and heavy his cock was. My ass clenched, not from fear but desire. I needed to belong to

Brenner completely. "Do it," I rasped, my dick throbbing and leaking on my stomach. "Please."

But Brenner never rushed anything—not his work, nor his lovemaking. First he slid that fabulous mouth over my dick, sucking me hard, then licking me gently. He fisted the length of my aching shaft, lapping at the head.

"Tastes like heaven."

"Bren, do it," I urged. "Everything."

With avid, hungry eyes I watched him lube his fingers and slip one, then two in me, stretching and twisting. So good, so goddamn right and perfect.

"Fuck, that's it. There," I moaned, wishing he would stuff me full, but he moved slowly, deliberately, eyes never leaving mine.

"It's hot like fire. Soft and hard at the same time." He played with me, and I lost all semblance of dignity.

"Fuck me already. Goddammit." I ripped at the sheets. "Please, please." My pleading echoed in the room, but I didn't care. All I wanted was Brenner.

I watched his every move as he rolled the condom on his heavy shaft and positioned himself between my legs. I never thought I'd beg for another man's dick, but here I was, dying for it. The full head breached me, and I cried out from the pain. He hesitated.

"Don't you fucking stop."

Solemn and intense, he inched in, splitting me in half, until his balls rested against my thighs and I realized he was fully seated. He kissed my trembling lips.

"Okay?"

I grabbed his shoulders, digging into the muscles, slick with sweat. "Yeah. Hurts like fucking hell, but I feel like I need more."

"Like this?"

He moved, and my eyes rolled to the back of my head. "Fuck yeah, do that again."

He grinned and bucked his hips in short, shallow thrusts. I rode his dick, and a feral smile curled his lips.

"Fuck me, you should see your face…" He gained more confidence and began to pump into me fast and hard, and I loved every fucking second of it. I grabbed my dick and thumbed the crown, picking up slick to make it easier for me to rub.

"Harder. Yeah. There. Right fucking *there*." There was no beginning and end to Brenner and me, we were one as we moved together, and I passed the point of no return, my orgasm hitting, breaking me into one single element. Desire. For Brenner. My dick pumped out thick streams of come between us.

Brenner grunted and hammered into me. I reveled in his strength and held on, still breathless and woozy from my climax. His jaw ground tight, and he groaned loud as he came, filling me with heat. With a sigh, he lay on top of me, and I held him close, my face buried in the curve of his neck, tasting his sweat.

"You can't leave me now," I whispered.

"I can stay the night, if that's what you want." Brenner eased out of me, and I shivered at the emptiness he left behind. He got rid of the condom, and I held out my hand.

"Please." He slid under the covers, and I curled around him. "Please come with me on Saturday?"

"Are you sure?"

"Yes."

"Then I'll go."

Relief swept through me. "Thank you. It means everything to me that you'll be there."

"You shouldn't have to face it alone."

Weariness overtook me, and I closed my eyes. I thought I felt his lips on mine.

**

"Weston. Weston Lively, is this your boyfriend?"

"How long have the two of you been together?"

"Where did you meet?"

"Your father voted down every LGBTQ bill in his state. How does he feel about you and your boyfriend?"

Brenner's hand in mine, we raced to the car waiting for us by the curb. With the news outlets reporting on our relationship, it was now no longer a guessing game. Brenner and I had been outed in the press, and they were hungry for any sound bites they could get. Sex always sells, and the story of a presidential candidate's supposedly straight son in a relationship with another man was as juicy as they came. All week we'd managed to duck the media circus by coming and going to the office at different times and staying in my apartment after work. Today, with me meeting Emily, we'd had to emerge, and the vultures had been waiting.

Before we closed the door to the sedan, a microphone was shoved in our faces. "Do you think it'll hurt your father's campaign to have a gay son dating a man whose mother was a prostitute and a drug addict?"

"No comment," I snarled and shut the door in their faces. "Let's go," I shouted to the driver, and we took off.

Huddled in the corner, Brenner said nothing for the first few minutes, while I attempted to figure out what I was going to say. But Brenner beat me to it.

"I told you this would happen. I knew they'd use my past against you."

"Against me? How so?"

Mouth set in a firm line, Brenner laughed with little humor behind it. "Are you serious? Didn't you hear what that reporter asked?"

"Yes. And?" If I was to convince Brenner that their questions meant nothing, I'd have to be the best I could be. I might've teased and taunted him in law school, but no one had ever pushed me to be a better lawyer than Brenner Fleming.

"A*nd*? Come on. They've obviously been doing some digging into my past, and they plan to use it against your father."

"Bren, have you told me everything you know?"

"Yeah, of course."

"And I don't care. Their questions are directed toward my father's campaign, not our relationship. He has nothing to do with us."

"No, that's not true." Exasperated, he made a fist and banged his knee. "You're trying to reconcile with your father. I can't stand in the way of you having a relationship with him and your sister and ruin his campaign. It's not fair to you."

"Whoa, whoa, hold up." I unbuckled my seat belt. We were fast approaching the Waldorf, and I had only minutes to speak. "First of all, I'm not trying to reconcile with him. I'm going to meet my sister. Second, I don't give a damn about his campaign or what he thinks about my life. There's only one person who matters when it comes to that."

Brenner shook his head. "But if you have the chance...if he asks you to make that choice—"

"You. I choose you. Now, today, next week, next month, next year. I'll always choose you. I took my first step in this new life with you. Now I'm ready to walk the path together."

The car stopped, and I held out my hand. "Are we good?"

He sighed. "I guess so."

I tugged at his hand. "The Brenner Fleming I knew in law school wouldn't take shit lying down. He'd fight for what he wanted."

We entered the hotel and received side-eyes and outright stares, but I ignored everyone. My mission was to meet Emily, and if my father chose to be a civil human being that was a bonus, but nothing more. His earlier ugly words still burned sour in my gut, and I had to wonder if the turnaround was real or merely for show.

Several security people lounged outside his suite, and when I showed them my identification, their brows rose high, but they stepped aside. My heart banged as I knocked on the door. It opened, and Paige stood before me.

"Hello, Weston. Please come in." Her eyes widened. "Oh, you brought—"

"Brenner. Yes. May we come in?"

"Of course."

We entered the suite, but my father wasn't there. She motioned for us to sit.

"Please. I have water, coffee, juice." A charcuterie platter was on the table as well as one of fruit.

"Nothing for me, thanks." Brenner shook his head as well. "Is Emily here?" I glanced around. There were no toys or dolls or anything that might've indicated a child was staying there.

"Yes. My nanny is just getting her ready." On cue, the bedroom door opened, and an older woman appeared, holding a little girl's hand. She ran into Paige's arms but kept shooting me looks from under her lashes. Joy leaped through me, and I wiggled my fingers at her. Paige smoothed her curls.

"Emmy. This is Weston."

I licked my dry lips. "Hi, Emmy."

She snuggled into Paige. "Hi," she said after a few seconds.

"That's a pretty dress."

Her face brightened. "Daddy gave it to me." She fingered the lace at the bottom, then pointed to Brenner. "Who's that?"

Tension radiated from Brenner, but I kept my cool. "This is my friend Brenner."

"Is he your best friend? My best friend is Mandy. She's going to be five."

I looked to Brenner. "Yes. He's my best friend."

"I got a new dolly yesterday. Wanna see?" Without waiting, she dashed into the other room and returned with a large doll with long, sun-streaked blond hair and big green-gold eyes. Like Emmy's.

Like mine.

"She looks like you. She's very pretty."

Emmy stroked the doll's hair. "Daddy had them make it up special."

I really had no clue what to say to a four-year-old. "You must have lots of dolls at home."

She nodded vigorously. "Uh-huh. And some here." Again she sprinted off and came back with an armful of dolls and stuffed animals. "Wanna play with me?"

I glanced at Paige, who gave me a tentative smile. I had none for her, but I sat on the floor with Emily and listened to her explain the toy family. Brenner watched us without participating, but every once in a while, when I caught his eye, he grinned.

The door clicked, and my father walked in. Emmy tossed aside the orange elephant she was playing with and ran to him. "Daddy, Daddy."

He picked her up and kissed her, laughing until he spotted me on the floor. The color and good humor drained from his face, and Emily slipped from his hands. "What're you doing here?"

"Daddy. Weston's my new friend."

I rose to my feet. "What do you mean, what am I doing here? You invited me to meet Emily."

An ugly flush rose over his face. "I did not. You're lying. Get out of here." Brenner got to his feet to stand by me, and my father's eyes bugged out. "You had the nerve to bring him here? How dare you?"

"Daddy, don't yell. Mommy, Mommy." Visibly upset, she ran to Paige, who held her tight.

"I invited him. It's wrong to keep Weston from seeing his sister."

"How...when..." he sputtered. "I never would've permitted this."

Paige remained calm. "You're always on your business phone, so I texted him from your personal cell."

His eyes spit fire. "We will talk about this, and I'll deal with you later. You had no right. Look at what he's exposing our child to."

"Rosa?" Paige called out, and the nanny reappeared. "Please take Emily to her room."

"But, Mommy—"

"Don't worry, honey. It'll be okay." She kissed her, but Emily persisted. She was my sister after all.

"I wanna play with Weston."

I crouched in front of her and Paige. "Do what your mommy says. We'll see each other again." I kissed her forehead. "Bye, Emmy."

Big eyes filled with tears, but she allowed Rosa to lead her away, and I remained silent, waiting for the door to her bedroom shut.

"I should've known something wasn't right." I turned to Paige. "Thank you for making the attempt. I appreciate it."

Paige addressed my father. "Weston is your child as well. Whether or not you agree with his life, he and Emily should know each other."

"Like you said, he's *my* child. Not yours." He pointed at me. "Leave."

"Gladly. But don't think you'll stop me from seeing my sister again."

He advanced on me with his finger in my face. "You keep away from my daughter. You and your sicko friends."

I tipped my head to Brenner, and we left. I didn't start shaking until we walked out onto the street. Brenner put his arm around me and pushed me into the waiting car. Christine, Tony, Madden, and Archer were all inside. I gazed at Brenner, who squeezed my hand.

"I figured you could use the support right now."

I blinked at the sudden rush of tears. "Thank you."

Christine patted my knee. "It's what we do for family."

I leaned on Brenner's shoulder as the blocks faded away, leaving a piece of my heart behind.

CHAPTER TWENTY-ONE
BRENNER

Once his father began raving at Weston, I'd texted Christine, who'd started messaging me that morning as soon as she'd heard where we were going. I'd ducked her calls all week, unwilling to get into a discussion on the phone of my rela-tionship with Weston. Even so, she was right there when I needed her, and I was never more grateful to have people like her in my corner. I knew the worst thing would be for Weston to be alone afterward, where he'd work himself up to a fever pitch of anger. Several reporters waited outside Weston's building, shouting questions as we passed, but Weston ignored them. We walked into Weston's apartment, and Madden took my arm.

"Hold up a second. I need to talk to you."

"About?"

We paused in the entranceway while the rest of the group headed toward the living room. "It'll only be a minute. For now."

"What is it?" I asked once we were alone.

"I did some more digging into your mother." I winced, and he shook his head. "Don't make any judgments until I finish. My people made inquiries into her death, and it seems the investigation was swept under the rug. The detectives took at face value what the arresting officer said—a drug deal gone wrong—and closed the case. They knew she had no family, no one who cared, so they didn't even bother to do much of an investigation. Sloppy, shitty work."

"And? Why do you sound like you think it's something else?"

"The tox screens were clean. Your mother wasn't doing drugs. And she wasn't a prostitute. She worked at a big-box store in Brooklyn, right off the BQE, near where her body was found."

Stunned didn't begin to describe my state of mind. "Wh-what? What're you saying?"

"The cop who found her body was later convicted—he took drug money and let the gangs rule the streets. There's a possibility, because of her background, the cops used her as a confidential informant. Maybe she was going to report on someone." He paused. "I think your mother was murdered by that dirty cop. The gangs are brutal, and that cop was afraid of being exposed."

My head spun. "I-I don't know what to say."

"Nothing yet." Madden was grim-faced. "I'll have my people dig further. Listen. I know what it's like to grow up without a mother. But yours was young and didn't have people she could count on. Yes, she screwed up big-time, but afterward she tried her best to turn her life around. There's nothing you can do to help her now, except think more kindly of her."

Weston appeared in the hallway entrance. "Hey. Everything all right?"

"We're coming," Madden said, and as he passed by me, he squeezed my arm. "I'll be in touch."

I joined Weston, who put a hand on my shoulder. "Something's going on. What is it?"

"Nope. This time is for you. We'll talk later."

Archer and Madden sat on one end of the couch, in conversation with Christine. They all quieted down when Weston and I approached.

"Thank you, everyone, for being here." Weston might not be a politician himself, but he'd grown up in that world. "Obviously, you've heard the news, so there's no need to get into it."

"On the contrary, Weston," Christine called out. "I thought you two were only friends. That's what you told us."

Weston grinned. "I lied. Sue me."

Archer snickered. "He's got you there. And for the record, we knew."

My brow furrowed. "How? You don't believe two men can be friends without anything sexual going on between them?"

"Of course they can. But friends don't kiss each other like you did that night we met for dinner. You thought we couldn't see you after our car picked us up, but they don't call me Eagle-Eyes Archer for nothing."

"Who calls you that?" Madden joked and whispered loudly, "I have other names for you."

"Darling, not in mixed company," Christine teased, then grew serious. "I'm thrilled for Brenner to have met someone, but all this politics and ugliness makes me angry and upset. Family should never come in second."

More somber than I'd ever seen him, Weston met my eyes for a moment, and my heart lurched at the devastation he tried so hard to hide from everyone. But I saw it. We hadn't been lovers that long, but he'd weaved his way into my life so seamlessly, now I couldn't imagine being without him. I wished I could take away all the pain of his father's cruel words. I wanted to protect him. If we were alone, I'd hold him and tell him I'd never hurt him. That I loved him.

"I agree, but my father—" His voice caught, and he took a sip of water. "My father does not." A slight smile softened the taut lines of his face. "Do you know Emily is four years old, and today was the first time I've seen her in person? We were having fun, playing with her dolls when he came in, and as soon as he saw me, he flipped out." He huffed a sigh. "The biggest shock is that Paige went behind his back to arrange it. I wonder why."

"Maybe she's finally seen how wrong your father's been," I murmured. "I wonder if their marriage is as perfect as they'd like everyone to believe."

"Why would you say that?" Weston asked.

"Because of how he spoke to her. Telling her he'd deal with her later when she told him she was the one who invited you, sounded ominous."

"If I ever said that to Christine, she'd have my balls," Tony remarked.

She pressed a kiss to his lips. "So right, my love. But let's discuss what's happened today." She directed her question to me. "How are you feeling, now that everyone knows about your relationship?"

West sat, eyes fixed on mine, waiting for my answer.

"I'm fine with it. It was never a matter of hiding what we were doing because we thought it was wrong. It just sort of happened between us, and we wanted the alone time to be able to figure things out."

West laced his fingers with mine. "If anyone thinks I'm going to pull away now, you're wrong. What happened between Brenner and me has been brewing for over a year.

Maybe even longer. There's a lot we need to talk about, but we have time."

We shared a knowing look. Weston's phone buzzed, and I swore everyone in the room tensed, but he shrugged. "It's Grady. Excuse me a minute. I should take this." He left the room.

"You're in love with him, aren't you?" Christine posed the question to me.

"What?" I laughed her off. "Don't be ridiculous. We've barely been together."

"You know that's bullshit. I fell for Tony the first night I met him, and I knew he was going to be mine forever." She pointed to Madden and Archer. "These two were instantaneous as well."

Madden's cheeks grew red. "Our situation was a little different."

She gave an unladylike snort. "Do tell, darling. That's why you couldn't keep away from him at your niece's sweet sixteen and my fund raiser."

Archer patted Madden's cheek. "She's got eyes everywhere. Don't you know by now? But Christine is right. We had a spark I'd never felt with anyone else, and it made just one night with him impossible."

Since there wasn't a chance in hell I'd discuss my feelings with them before Weston, I kept my mouth shut and changed the subject.

"I wonder how this will all play out in the senator's presidential campaign. He is the leading candidate so far in the primaries."

"I don't see why it should make any difference what a president's child's sexuality is."

Weston returned and sat next to me with a sigh. "It does if your party's platform is against it and you've spent your career talking shit about it. I'd rather not dwell on this anymore. My main and only concern was Emily, and that hasn't changed. I need to find a way to connect with Paige to see if she'll allow me to continue to have contact with my sister."

"I'm sure we can find her cell phone number. Nothing is truly private on the Internet." I squeezed his hand. "Meanwhile, I think we should have some lunch and ignore the hate."

"I agree," Christine declared. "But this is where we leave you. Weston deserves peace and quiet with you. The fund raiser is only a few weeks away, and I have tons to do."

She kissed Weston and then me. "Talk to you later."

Madden gripped my hand. "We'll be in touch. I hope to have more information for you soon."

"Thank you. It's a lot to take in."

Weston waited until I closed the door. "Are you going to tell me now what the hell you two were talking about?"

"My mother." It still seemed surreal to be discussing her and what Madden had told me. "When it was obvious the press was going to dig and find out about us, and use my past against you, I asked Madden to help find out information. I figured he's got the resources."

"Come into the kitchen. I need a drink. And it looks like you might too." Weston handed me a beer, and we sat at the island.

With his usual intensity, Weston listened to my story. My throat was dry and scratchy by the time I finished, and I took a long drink. "So now I'll wait to see what else Madden's people can dig up."

"It's terrible what happened to her, and to you as a result of her actions, but can you forgive her now?"

"It took me a while, if I'm being totally honest. When I was a kid, no. I was very unforgiving, very hurt, and I blamed her for all my problems. Now I can see how addiction is an illness and without a support system—pregnant and all alone at sixteen—what chance did she have? If I hadn't lucked out in the foster-parent lottery and ended up with Bill and Pearl, who knows where I might be now? Being a mother is a hard enough job when you've got it all. When you've got nothing?" I shrugged. "So yeah, I forgive her. But not the system that turned its back on her."

West's chair scraped the floor, and a moment later he was holding me. "Yes. And fathers need to take responsibility too. Sometimes they fuck up because they don't know any better. And sometimes they just don't care."

I rested my head on his shoulder. "Both of us got the short end of the stick in the parental department." My phone rang, and seeing Bill's name pop up, my heart sank. "Shit. It's my father. I-I never told him about us."

"Do you want me to leave?" West asked.

"It's your apartment." I hit the screen. "Hey, Bill. Sorry I didn't call you."

"Yeah? I gotta say I'm a little PO'd with ya."

I hunched my shoulders." I know. And you have a right to be. There's just been a lot going on."

"So. Talk to me now. Tell me about this guy." I heard the swishing of the ice in his cup and the television on in the background. "Is this something new? I've only heard about you dating women."

Weston had left me alone, and I heard him in the bedroom, opening and closing drawers. He reappeared in the living room in a T-shirt and sweats and lay on the couch to watch television.

"Yeah. It's...uh...new. I've never dated a man before or even thought about it. But Weston and I have known each other a long time. Superficially. It's only recently we've gotten...close." God, this was embarrassing. Talking about my personal life wasn't high on my list of things I liked to do with anyone, and with my father? Yeah...not a fan.

"And his father is running for president?" Bill whistled. "That's a whole other kinda stress. You ready for this?"

In the living room, Weston pumped his fist. "Yeah. Go Mets!" Maybe he felt my stare, because he looked my way, and brightness beamed from his face. Foolish me, thinking I had a choice in the matter. My heart turned over.

"Yeah, I am. I'm in it for the long haul."

"If you're happy, kiddo, that's all I care about."

"I think I finally am."

We ended the call, and I left my phone on the island and joined Weston on the couch. He put his legs in my lap, and amused, I pretend-glared. "Am I an ottoman now?"

He rolled up to sitting and grasped me at the nape. "You are so much more. My safety net. The one I know will be there for me, like I'm there for you. I don't care anymore either how or why this happened. It did, and I hope you know I'm all in with you."

I ran my nose down his cheek. "I liked being all in you."

"Oh God, that was so bad." Groaning, he fell back, taking me with him so I lay prone. Weston took my face between his hands. "You are everything. I don't think I could've made it through today without you there. I wouldn't have been able to face him."

Knowing Weston, that admission and his vulnerability only made me love him more.

"You're strong. You can do whatever you want." I kissed him.

"I want to do you. How about that?"

I laced our fingers together. "Stop talking and start doing."

******

We spent the rest of the weekend lazing in Weston's apartment, making love and watching television. We shut out the rest of the world, ordering in breakfast, lunch, and dinner, and turned off our phones, concentrating only on our desire for each other. Sunday night came way too soon, but we remained in our cocoon, greedy bastards for each other. When Weston reached for me again, sometime in the predawn hours of Monday, I mumbled, "I surrender. I'm done. Just a couple more hours of sleep."

"Bren?"

"*Hmm?*" I murmured, my eyes closed, ready to drift off.

"Is it too early to say I love you?"

My lids flew open, and all thoughts of sleep fled. "What?" I whispered as he lay on his side, facing me with eyes soft as twilight. Silence weighed heavily between us.

"You know I always have to be first." He kissed me. "So? Is it?"

I nudged his cheek. "Not for me it isn't. And since you didn't exactly say it to me but asked the question, I love you." I kissed the tip of his nose. "Now I said it first."

"I've got you, so this time I don't care if I come in second." Weston claimed my mouth in a breath-stealing kiss. "I'm not that kind of guy to argue a point, especially when I'm on the winning side."

"I think for the first time, we both came out on top."

CHAPTER TWENTY-TWO
WESTON

Even having to sidestep the photographers camped outside my apartment building, shouting questions about my sex life, I was in a damn good mood. The ugly confrontation with my father had faded away, replaced by the absolute perfection of having Brenner there with me all weekend. I strolled into my office alone, Brenner and I continuing to arrive separately so as not to raise suspicion. After our talk, neither of us had been able to sleep, so Brenner had gone home to change, and I'd decided to come to the office early. I'd assured Daniel that our relationship would have no impact on the firm, and I intended to keep that promise.

Yawning, I pushed open the door to my office, only to be greeted by Grady sitting at my conference table, a cup in his hand and a grin on his face.

"Well, well. Good morning, sunshine. How the hell are you, or do I even need to ask?"

I plucked the coffee out of his hand. "Thanks. And things have only gotten better since we last spoke." I set my bag on the desk and sank into the chair. I took a sip of the coffee and almost died. "What the hell is this shit?"

"Turkish coffee. Drink up. It'll put hair on your chest and keep you up all night." His eyes twinkled. "Although maybe Brenner takes care of that?"

I handed him his cup. "My chest is hairy enough, and I'm not hearing any complaints from Brenner, thank you very much." I smirked and got busy with my coffee machine.

"You two had a good weekend, I presume? No other repercussions from the meeting with your father?"

My good mood faded. "I wouldn't exactly call it a meeting. More like a clash. He thinks I'm with Brenner to sabotage his run for the presidency." I snorted. "I haven't let my father influence my decisions in any part of my life since I was fifteen and caught him cheating on my mother when she had just been diagnosed with cancer."

"Good," Grady said, serious. "Brenner is a really good guy, and I'd hate to see him hurt."

That stung. "Hey, what the hell does that mean? I'm a nice fucking guy too, you know. Why would I want to hurt him?"

"I'm not saying you do. But you like to party, always up for fun and games. Brenner's quiet. He's the guy who never fit in."

"He fits with me. I know you don't get it, and frankly, neither do we, but the two of us...we work. I couldn't have faced my father if Brenner wasn't there with me. But I hate having to duck and run from photographers all the time.

And it's not fair to Brenner. He didn't sign up for this." I pressed my lips together until they hurt. "But I'd run through fire to make sure he doesn't ever feel less than wanted again."

"You're crazy about him." There was no question. Grady knew.

"I fucking love him. I'm not afraid to say it."

"You've told him?"

I took a sip of coffee. "Yeah. This morning. We said it to each other. But I gotta tell you...it's almost like something I was waiting for. It happened so easily between us, maybe it was always there and we weren't in the position or mindset to recognize it."

Grady shrugged and finished his vile cup of death. "Sexuality is fluid, always changing. I'm proud of you two for accepting what I could see from the beginning."

Someone knocked on my door.

"Come in."

Brenner walked in but stopped when he saw Grady. "Oh, sorry. I didn't mean to interrupt."

"Don't be ridiculous. Grady was giving me the third degree about us."

"Hey," Grady protested. "No way. I think it's great. And I called it right away."

Brenner's face was red, which was cute. That shy uptick of his lips and the way he ducked his head? Adorable. And mine. Damn, I had it bad. No one but Brenner had ever brought out that possessive side of me.

And I liked it. I caught Grady's eyes on me, and scowled at the shit-eating grin on his face. *Dammit.* I'd better brush up on my poker face.

"I just wanted to say hello. I have a mediation to prep for, so I'll see you later."

"Lunch?" I called out.

"Can't," he answered with regret. "I have depositions downtown. Dinner?"

"Of course."

Brenner left, and Grady clapped. "I'm impressed. That was a master class in how to have a mature relationship with someone you work with."

"Oh, be quiet. Don't you have work to do?"

"Yeah, but this is more fun." He snickered, and I flipped him off. "Since your man is busy for lunch, how about me? I don't mind being second string."

"Deal."

Grady left, and I sipped my coffee, grateful for a light Monday. My personal cell rang, and it was Isobel. I rolled my eyes in anticipation of a third, fourth, and fifth degree.

"Hello, Izzy."

"Hello to you too." She sounded amused. "When were you going to tell me?"

I scrolled through my emails. "Tell you what, and isn't it early for you? Shouldn't you be asleep?"

"I'm in DC for a conference, and the tongues are all abuzz about your father's campaign. And you."

I frowned. "You know I have nothing to do with him."

"That may be true, but everything you do affects him. Never mind that. A man? Since when?"

"I don't know, Izzy. It just happened." Frustrated, I tossed the pen I was holding across the desk. "I'm kind of getting sick and tired of having to explain it. Even to you. It's really no one's business whom I date or why."

"Don't bite my head off. I'm on your side. Have you been getting pushback from the firm? Only because you work together. I can't imagine Daniel Roth would care. He's a reasonable man."

"It's only been out a week. He and I had a decent talk, and it should be okay. As for how my father will handle it, I neither know nor care."

Not exactly true. A small, vindictive part of me wanted it to hurt him, but I kept that to myself. It had nothing to do with my relationship with Brenner.

"I didn't call you just to gossip. I'm your friend, and I wanted to let you know I'm here to support you."

"Thank you. I didn't realize it would be such a big deal news-wise, but I suppose I was being naïve."

"Um, come on, West. The leading candidate for president's son starts dating a man during his campaign, and you don't think it's news? Especially since his party's platform isn't exactly welcoming."

"I guess, but it shouldn't be that way. And even if my father and I were on good terms, my life shouldn't have any bearing on his candidacy."

"Everything everyone in his life does reflects on him. Even if you're estranged. Now tell me about Brenner. From what the papers have dug up, he works with you and was a foster child growing up?"

I tensed, hating how Brenner's life became gossip fodder simply by association with me. "I'd rather not get into it. He's a very private person, and his life shouldn't be put under a microscope."

She laughed. "You really are a Boy Scout. Listen, honey. I know the way this town works. Things can get very ugly. You should be prepared."

"I'll keep that in mind. I'd better get to work."

"Talk to you soon."

That conversation stuck with me throughout the morning as I handled a couple of client calls. In the halls, some people gave me the odd stare, and I caught a few smiles and whispers, but I ignored them. These people weren't my friends.

I had a particularly long and arduous call with a client who'd discovered his wife had been cheating on him for years. Fearful that their children weren't his, he wanted to know if he could force a paternity test and the legality of taking his name off their birth certificates. Add divorce proceedings to the mix, which would entail forensic accounting of their assets, and my brain was a bit fried. As I'd listened to the client, I was sad for the children. Did they know what happened? How would they feel knowing the man they'd always thought of as their father could so nonchalantly walk away from them? That was something I easily related to.

I'd been hoping to escape for a cup of coffee and was at the elevator when Manny stopped me.

"Weston, I was looking for you."

"To what do I owe the pleasure?" His behavior at the retreat still rankled, and I was polite but wary. "I was about to step out for a moment."

"Can we talk?"

The doors to the elevator opened. "We can." Yes, I was a wise-ass, but he'd pissed me off, and I was a bit of a grudge holder. I walked inside, and he followed me.

We arrived at the lobby, and realizing it would be a dick move to walk away from him, I figured to make peace. He was a friend to Brenner and had offered him his support after the story came out. "I'm getting coffee. Want to join me?"

He nodded, and we went to a little diner I liked to slip into when I needed to escape the hustle and crowds. We ordered, and he fidgeted across from me.

"I think I need to apologize."

"You think?"

He flushed. "Okay. I'm sorry for the way I acted toward you at the retreat. I didn't know you and Brenner were together but not out."

"Not that it's your business, but we weren't together then."

Skeptical brown eyes met mine. "You sure acted like you were."

It was my turn to get red in the face. "Yeah, well...I was concerned about him."

Manny's lips curved, and his eyes warmed. "Or more likely, you liked him even then but didn't want to. Or didn't know what was happening and how to handle it. I get it."

I shrugged. "Nothing to get. We've worked out our differences."

Our coffees came, and I took a sip.

"Brenner's a great guy," Manny said after a few minutes.

"The best."

"You know, sometimes parents can change. I know your father's probably not supportive now, but maybe–"

"But maybe what? That was rhetorical because frankly, I don't give a damn what he or anyone else thinks of our relationship." My patience had worn thin, and I was damn sick and tired of talking about my father and his election. "Being Brenner's friend, I'm sure you mean well, but I learned a long time ago that my happiness depends on me. I'm tired of people thinking my father and I can somehow magically work things out. We had no relationship before Brenner and I got together, and that's not going to change. Got it?"

"I think he's got it." At the amused voice behind me, I turned in my seat. Brenner stood behind me with a smile and eyes dancing.

"Hey. What're you doing here?"

"I finished with my depositions, and your paralegal told me you went out for coffee. Figured I'd join you."

Manny gulped his down. "Here. Take my spot. I gotta get back." He slid out of his seat and held out a hand to me. "I'm sorry if you thought I was out of line. I'm just very protective of my friends."

"Eh, don't worry about it." I shook his hand. "We all need someone looking out for us."

Manny and Brenner exchanged a fist bump, and then he sat across from me. "You and Manny?"

"He wanted to apologize for acting stupid when you were hurt." I gazed into his face. "You look tired. And not from me keeping you up half the night."

"That kind of missed sleep I don't mind." He shifted and murmured, "Although I'm gonna have to get used to...you know..." His cheeks turned pink. "Finding a comfortable way to sit afterward."

"I know. But the discomfort is worth it, don't you think?" God, I wanted to reach across the table and hold his hand. Was I being a total sap? Yeah. Did I care? Not one damn bit. So I did it. Only briefly, but it was enough.

Brenner's eyes grew soft. "Yeah. That kind I don't mind."

I hated that he'd had a life filled with so much turmoil. "I don't ever want to hurt you. I hope you know that."

Brenner's brows drew together. "Why do you think you would?"

"I'm just not sure how to do this." I lowered my voice. "I've never been in a relationship. You mean too much to me to fuck up what we have."

"It's not going to happen."

I wished I could be as sure as Brenner. "My father might say some things....I'm not sure what, but I wouldn't put it past him to have been in strategy sessions figuring out how to handle the situation." Brenner's blue eyes flicked to mine. "Yeah. You and me."

"I don't want—"

"If you're going to say you don't want our relationship to prevent me from getting closer to my sister, I'm hoping that won't happen. But don't for a second think about stepping aside for 'the greater good.' " I took his hand again. "Because I'm no good without you anymore."

A camera was thrust in our faces, and before either of us could react, the shutter reeled off snaps. A smarmy face peered over the lens.

"Thanks, guys! You just got me an exclusive and made the front page of the *New York Express*." With a wink, he scurried away.

"Fucker," Brenner spat out and half rose, but I tugged his hand, and he sat.

"Don't."

"Why'd you stop me? He shouldn't be spying on us."

"No, he shouldn't." I clasped my hands. "But this is how it's going to be until the primaries are finished, and if my father is the nominee, it will only get more intense. Worse." I hated to say the words, but as much as I didn't give a flying fuck what the press or anyone else had to say about Brenner and myself, it wasn't only up to me. The one thing I'd learned being in a relationship was that I didn't come first. Being a couple meant making decisions together. "I don't care what people say about me, but I need to know how you feel. You're a private person. How do you feel about our relationship being splashed in the news media and gossip columns?"

Brenner shook his head and gazed at the sticky Formica table. My heart in my throat, I waited for him to respond.

CHAPTER TWENTY-THREE
BRENNER

"I'm not going anywhere," I stated firmly, and the relief in Weston's face broke my heart. He'd lost the person who'd loved him without question, and the other person who should've been there for him had failed him. "If you think I care about the opinions of people I've never met, you're wrong."

The bill was slapped down on the table, and Weston grabbed it. "I'd better get back to the office. Do you want your coffee to go?"

Now it was my turn to play with his fingers. "I didn't come for the coffee."

Sparks fired the gold in his green eyes until they blazed. "You are so gonna get lucky tonight."

I squeezed his fingers before letting him go. "I already am."

At the office we separated, and I spent the next hour at my computer, filling out my case notes. It had been a rough deposition for the client, and I could only hope that the children wouldn't suffer. My cell phone rang, and seeing it was Bill, I gladly took the break.

"Hey, how're you doing?"

"Shouldn't I be asking you that?" Bill said, unusually subdued, which startled me.

"What're you talking about?"

"I been thinkin' about your boyfriend. He's the son of the potential president. Are you sure you're ready for your life to be exposed in the newspaper and television?"

Thinking of the scene in the coffee shop, I gripped my phone tighter. "I don't pay attention to gossip. And neither should you."

"It's got nothin' to do with gossip. It's a lot to handle for someone you don't know."

"What makes you think I don't know him? We went to school together, and we've reconnected."

"*Mmmhmm.*" Bill didn't sound convinced.

"Listen." An idea popped into my head. "Why don't you come up for a visit this weekend? Meet Weston, and you can see for yourself."

"Ahh, I don't know. I haven't been in the city in years, and—"

"And it's about time you did. I can't take time off to come visit this year with the new partnership." I used my most persuasive voice. "C'mon, Dad. I haven't seen you since Christmas, and that was over six months ago. I'd really like you to meet Weston."

"I'm no fancy guy. You know that."

"He's just a regular guy, like us."

Bill snorted. "Yeah, with a coupla hundred million in the bank and a father who might be president."

"Trust me," I assured him grimly. "Weston is nothing like his father."

**

"Are you sure he's okay with us?" Weston and I waited at the arrivals gate at JFK. Friday evenings were crowded as usual, and of course the plane was delayed, which only made Weston more nervous.

"Yes. I told you. His concern isn't that I'm with a man. It's more how the relationship will affect me because of your father...and all your money."

Brow puckered, West frowned. "I can't do anything about that." He grew agitated, but then his shoulders slumped. "I don't throw away my money or live some crazy, lavish life-style." At my steady stare, he crossed his arms. "What should I do, Bren? Give up my mother's apartment and go live in a one-bedroom? Not accept the trust fund my family set up for me? That's ridiculous, and you know it."

"I'm not saying that. But he does remember seeing you and your Mercedes and hearing you talk about your fabu-lous vacations." Bill had always insisted on driving me up to school after summer break or winter vacation, so inevitably, he'd run into Weston. And my digs about him didn't help, so his opinion wasn't crafted from thin air.

"Again, nothing I can do about it now." Worried eyes met mine. "Is he going to hold that against me?"

"There he is." I waved to Bill, who pulled a small carry-on behind him. "We'll find out soon enough. Bill," I called out, and he broke out into a big smile. "Don't worry about it. He'll love you."

But I could see Weston's concern in how he didn't respond with his usual snarky reply. I grabbed Bill in a bear hug, grateful to feel his strong arms around me. The smell of his Old Spice aftershave mixed with Irish Spring soap was like coming home.

"How you doin', kiddo? You're lookin' good."

"I'm great. You remember Weston? West, this is my dad, Bill."

"How are you, sir?" Weston shook his hand. "Good to see you after all these years."

"A surprise for sure. Nice to see you too."

"I have a car waiting for us in the garage. Why don't I take your suitcase, and you and Brenner can catch up."

Knowing the loss of his relationship with his father was never far from his mind, I could see how West wanted Bill to like him, and it only made me love him harder.

When we'd settled into the car, Bill clasped his hands and gazed from me to West, who shifted, uncharacteristically nervous. "So tell me about yourself. When did you realize you were interested in Brenner?"

I coughed. "Damn, nothing like getting right to the point. You couldn't have waited until we got home?"

"It's okay, I don't mind answering." Weston huffed out a sigh. "I'm not sure. Maybe the reason I came at him so hard when we were in school together was because I was fighting an attraction I wasn't even aware of."

That explanation startled me. "You...were?"

Weston's eyes crinkled with his smile. "I've been thinking that might be the case. But you wanted nothing to do with me, so I guess it worked a little too well. To answer your question, last year, we were at the same conference, and things just...happened. When Brenner joined the firm, neither of us intended for a recurrence, but he got hurt and..." He shrugged and met my eyes tenderly. "I realized what I was feeling wasn't merely concern for his health." Facing Bill with an earnest, determined expression, Weston leaned forward. "I know you have concerns because we're different. I come from money and a family with political power. But because of that I'm very aware of how the game is played, and I promise I will do anything and everything I can to protect Brenner."

The conversation about me was annoying. "Excuse me, but I'm a grown man who can take care of himself. I don't need you to speak for me or protect me."

"Hold up, kiddo. I get what he means." Bill regarded Weston thoughtfully. "How do you plan to do that? Your father is a senator. He might be president. I'm sure he's not happy about your relationship with Brenner."

"My father only cares about his image. He's been hiding his affairs with women for years." Weston's lip curled. "If he so much as tries anything to hurt Brenner, I'll go to the press and tell them everything I know."

I took his hand. "Don't. If you do that, there's no coming back. You and your father will never reconcile."

Weston said nothing for the rest of the ride to his apartment.

A long, low whistle escaped Bill when we walked inside. "Park Avenue. Fancy stuff."

Now that he was home, Weston was more relaxed and kicked off his sneakers. "It's the same four walls to make a room as anywhere else. The people are what makes it special."

Bill's eyes dimmed. "My wife useta say something like that."

I squeezed his shoulder. "Are you hungry? I can order whatever you'd like. Tomorrow we'll go out for a real diner breakfast like we used to."

"Nothin' like it. And you don't gotta entertain me." He walked through the rooms, admiring the apartment. "You got a nice place here, but shouldn't I check into my hotel before they give my room away?"

"No way," Weston called out from the kitchen, returning with three bottles of beer. "I have a second bedroom. You'll stay here." He handed them out.

"I-I couldn't. That wouldn't be right."

"Says who?" With a wink, Weston tipped his bottle to us.

"Besides," I added in. "I didn't reserve a room. I wanted you to stay here with us."

Weston nodded vigorously. "We can order a pizza, and I'm sure Bill will want an early night, but tomorrow I've got tickets to the Mets game. Right behind home plate."

"Wow, uh, that's nice of you. I never been in one of them."

I handed Bill the remote. "Make yourself comfortable." And left him happily reuniting with all his old stations. "West, can you help me in the kitchen for a sec?" West trailed after me, and I faced him once we were alone and out of earshot. "What're you doing?"

His eyes narrowed. "I'm being nice. Why is that a problem?"

I put a hand on his arm. "No, of course not. But you don't have to throw all these expensive things at him. Just be you."

He slipped his arms around my waist. "That thing you said in the car? About never being able to reconcile with my father? That ship has sailed."

I kissed his cheek. "Are you sure?"

"I tried so hard to be the son he wanted when I was young. I wanted to be just like him. Until I saw who he really was, and then I wished I'd never met him." His cheek rested against mine. "I don't have a father anymore."

"What about your sister?" The little girl was the real reason Weston had tried at all.

"Paige texted me that she'll let me talk to Emily and see her." He smirked. "Seems Emily hasn't stopped talking about our visit."

"So maybe it's me, not you."

"Well, you are pretty cute," Weston teased. "And sweet." He kissed me. "And don't forget sexy." He kissed me again. "So, so sexy."

I let him nuzzle my neck and rubbed my cheek to his, reveling in the raspy skin. "Just be yourself with Bill. I fell for the Weston you are right now, not that guy who once thought he needed to show off who he is. Your star already shines bright."

"But I told him about the game."

"I know, and he'll love it. Are you sure you want to go out in such a public arena? The press might be up in our faces."

His smile was grim. "I refuse to live life hiding in shadows. I'm not ashamed of being with you."

Damn, I was a lucky guy.

"But let's have hot dogs and junk food at Citifield, not some fancy dinner in a stuffy restaurant."

He kissed me hard, leaving me breathless. "Anything you want."

**

"This is great," Bill said happily, chewing his hot dog. "Thanks, Weston. I ain't been to a ball game in years. I miss it." It was the top of the eighth inning, and the Mets were leading.

"Anytime you want, come up. I've got season tickets."

"No shit, whoa. Great."

I relaxed in my seat with my hot dog and beer, soaking up the late-afternoon sun. It truly had been a perfect day.

"Weston Lively? What do you think of your father's repudiation of your relationship?" A burly, middle-aged man with a press pass around his neck leaned in to talk to him. "He's ahead in the polls for Tuesday's primaries. Are you choosing your boyfriend over your family?"

I rose to my feet as Weston's lips drew up in a snarl. "I'm a private citizen, and you're harassing me."

"Come on, Weston. Is this the boyfriend? Does it bother you that his mother was a drug addict and a prostitute?"

My stomach went into free fall, and Weston jumped to his feet, his fist cocked. "Get the hell out of here," he snarled. "Now."

I sank to my seat. Silent. Frozen.

"He said get outta his face," Bill shouted.

With a smirk on his lips, the reporter strolled away, and Weston put a hand on my shoulder. "Don't listen to what that idiot said. I don't give a damn, and neither should you. We know your mother had left all that behind."

"What's he talking about?" Confused, Bill looked to me for an explanation.

I hadn't told him what Madden had revealed, and I wasn't about to do it at Citifield, with fifty thousand people surrounding us. "Let's go home. I'll explain there."

We left our seats, and Weston called for a car while I steered Bill with my hand on his shoulder. The traffic was predictably awful, and the drive to the city took more than an hour. Weston tried to keep us amused with stories of his failed attempts at little league and water polo, but I was too tense to enjoy it.

At the apartment, I sat beside Weston and retold the story Madden had relayed to me. To my surprise, tears ran down Bill's face, and he covered his eyes with his hands.

"What's wrong?"

"A couple of years after you came to us, a woman called. She said she was your mother and wanted to see you. We were so hesitant because we didn't know if she was telling the truth—how did she get our phone number? Plus, even if it was true, we didn't know if she was still on drugs, and you were having all that trouble in school. We called the social worker, but they were so jammed up, it took several weeks before we tried the number she left, but it was disconnected." Anguish tore at his voice. "Maybe...maybe if we'd known she wasn't on drugs and said yes, things would've been different."

Grief, shock, and sadness swept through me, and it took a few seconds to process Bill's words. I left Weston to crouch by Bill's chair, gazing up into the face of the only father I'd ever known.

"I-I don't blame you. You couldn't have known, and you were only trying to protect me. I understand." Bill rested a hand on my head. "Most likely I wouldn't have wanted to see her anyway. I was so angry with her when I was young for taking drugs and abandoning me. But eventually I forgave her. It's taken this long for the truth to come out, and I don't have it in me to hold it against her. Who knows what she went through?" I wiped at my eyes. "She could've gotten rid of me, and I'd never have been born. So no matter how hard I had it, I'll always be grateful to her."

The intercom buzzer rang, and frowning, Weston went to answer it. I heard his harsh voice, but he was too far away to make out what he was saying. I stood, and Bill heaved himself out of the chair.

"If you don't mind, I think I'm gonna take a nap."

Concerned, I held him by the shoulder. "Are you all right?"

"Yeah, sure, kiddo. I'm good. Just a lotta runnin' around. I'm used to snoozing by the pool." He patted my arm and trudged to the bedroom.

The bell rang, and I walked toward the foyer and stopped in my tracks. Preston Lively stood at the door.

"I'd like to come in and talk, Weston."

Jaw clenched, Weston stepped aside to let him in. "What do you want? We have nothing to say to each other."

"That may be true, but I have a proposition for you." Preston strode inside, and spotting me, veered away. "This is your friend."

"He's my boyfriend. My lover." Weston took my hand. "What proposition?"

I whispered in Weston's ear, "Maybe you and your father should talk privately."

"I have no secrets from you," Weston murmured to me. He addressed his father. "You can't be here to pay me off because I have enough money that nothing you could offer would matter. So what is it? And please be brief, because we have company."

Preston cleared his throat. "It's very bad for my campaign that I'm at odds with my child."

"Oh, Daddy, dearest. I didn't know you cared," Weston sneered. "And?" He folded his arms.

"But I can't condone this...this situation you've decided to embroil the family in. So I've come to put this forward as a way to make it work: you and your...friend stay out of the public eye, don't make any statements to the press—or better yet, you can state you're single again. In exchange for that, I will let you see Emily as often as you want."

Evil comes in all forms, but to use the love of a brother for his sister was so diabolical, so disgusting, I shook my head. "Jesus, that's cold."

"No one is asking you," Preston snapped.

Weston had remained silent, and I waited, wondering what he'd say. Much as I knew he'd stand up for us, giving him the space to build a relationship with his little sister was paramount.

"It's amazing that you've managed to prove you're a worse person than I'd even imagined. You'll do anything to win this election, even use your children. What an awful, terrible man you are."

Preston cleared his throat. "We both get what we want. I don't see the problem."

Face filled with thunder and eyes blazing, Weston advanced on his father. "You don't, but I do. Your threats won't work on me, old man. God forbid someone like you becomes president. You have no feelings for anyone else, and you've just proved you'll do and say anything to get what you want. And what's worse, you'll use coercion and lies." His lips thinned. "Not a good look for you."

"So you've made the decision that your sex life is worth more than Emily. I should've known."

A flush rose over Weston's face, and his hands balled into fists. "Don't you ever say that. I love Emily. But I won't be bullied or blackmailed into pretending I don't love Brenner. I'll never deny him."

"You stupid fool. You'd have the world at your door. You could be president one day if you'd only see it my way."

"What way is that?" Bill called out from the opposite side of the room.

"Who the hell are you?" Preston demanded.

"I'm Brenner's father. And you better not threaten either one of them."

Preston snorted with laughter. "Now who's threatening whom? What do you think you can do about anything?" With an arrogant smirk, he gave his back to Bill who, to my surprise, grinned.

"I might not've gone to fancy schools, but I watched enough television to know what to do." He held up his phone and hit the screen. A video appeared, and Preston's voice came out of the speaker.

"But I can't condone this...this situation you've decided to embroil the family in. So I've come to put this forward as a way to make it work: you and your...friend stay out of the

public eye, don't make any statements to the press—or better yet, you can state you're single again. In exchange for that, I will let you see Emily as often as you want."

Bill silenced the video and walked to Weston and me as he talked. "So here's how I see it goin' down. You're gonna let Weston here see his little sister, and you ain't gonna make him and Brenner hide that they're together."

Preston grew red. "Are you blackmailing me? Me?"

Holding tight to his phone, Bill crossed his arms. "What's good for the goose, ya know? Now whaddya say?"

"How do I know you won't use this against me for anything else?"

"Well, now, I guess you don't. But see, here's the difference. Unlike you, I love my son and I'd never do anything to hurt him, or Weston." Bill glared at Preston.

The senator adjusted his shirt cuffs and huffed. "You can arrange all correspondence regarding Emily with Paige." Without another word, he walked out of the apartment.

Weston's shoulders slumped. "Thank you. That was...wow. I've got nothing."

I hugged Bill. "Thank you. Where did you learn about doing that?"

"I told ya. I watch a lotta television. *FBI* and *Law and Order* are my favorites." He snickered.

Weston hugged him. "Thank you, Bill."

"That's what you do for family."

CHAPTER TWENTY-FOUR
WESTON

"Aren't you a handsome devil." I ogled Brenner's ass while he buttoned up his shirt. Our tuxedos were hanging in the closet, and I'd just come out of the shower. "You should wear a tux more often." I smirked. "Or nothing at all."

It was the night of Christine's annual benefit, and Brenner and I were getting there early for a pre-party drink with her and her family.

"Yeah, sure. I'll casually stroll into the office in formal attire." He slung the bow tie around his neck.

"I wouldn't mind." I grabbed the tail of his dress shirt and tugged him close. "Although I do like you better naked." I cupped his rapidly stiffening cock and smiled at his sharp inhale. My lips found the rapidly beating pulse at the base of his neck, and I sucked and bit the skin, loving the sound of his harsh breath and the jerk of his thickening dick against my thigh.

"Two can play this game, you know." Brenner grasped my dick, but I pushed him away.

"This is no game. This is everything." I sank to my knees and took him between my lips, the salty taste of his precome filling my mouth. His moans rose in the quiet, and those long fingers tangled in my hair as he fucked my mouth.

"West, God."

I peered up to see his head flung back, mouth open and panting, that beautiful face flushed with passion. Jesus, he was gorgeous when he was lost in himself. Knowing it was me doing that to him, giving him pleasure, turned me on. I slid my fingers along the smooth skin under his balls to tease the crease of his ass.

"*Mmhmm.*" I sucked and licked up and down his shaft, using my hand to follow my mouth. "Those two words go perfectly together." A gentle tug of his balls while tonguing his slit brought a cry of pleasure and another burst of precome in my mouth. I lapped at the wide crown and gave it one final kiss before getting to my feet.

"What the...? West," Brenner whined. "Are you kidding? I was so damn close."

"I want you in me. Now."

A feral, hungry spark lit those bright-blue eyes. "Yeah." He licked his lips and stroked himself. "Let's do that."

We moved to the bed, and I handed him the condom and lube. I ached for him. "Hurry. Fuck me."

Brenner's chuckle sent a shiver through me. "Not so fast. I'm going to make sure you feel me all night."

"Promises, promises, uhhh," I groaned as his lubed fingers breached me, thrusting in and out of my ass, teasing and taunting, and I rutted on the bed, craving friction on my erection. "Please, please," I gasped. "Now." I couldn't remember ever being so desperate, so needy for someone. There'd never been anyone who'd changed me from the inside out.

The packet ripped, and a moment later the head of his dick nudged past my rim. Pleasure tore through me, and I backed into Brenner, my head spinning as his cock filled me, inch by glorious inch. He rested the heel of his hand against my spine as he glided, pushing into my willing passage.

"Oh yeah, you're so perfect." Brenner grunted as he thrust, and I held on to the headboard as he pumped hard and fast. "Fuck, West."

"Oh God, yeah." My nails dug into the headboard, and my ass throbbed, muscles clenching around the thick length plowing me. Brenner's fingers grasped my hips, holding me steady. When he covered me, his heavy body pressing me down, he bit my shoulder and whispered, "You're mine. All mine. Forever."

Those words thrilled me, giving me life. My head spun, I couldn't catch my breath, and my heart pounded. "Bren, Bren," I called out, dimly hearing the splintering of wood.

"Mine," he growled and gave one last, deep thrust, sending me tumbling into an orgasm so explosive, I screamed as my legs gave way and I collapsed. Brenner came, hot and hard, and fell on top of me, his heart beating fast and furious.

"*Mmhmm.* Yours." I closed my eyes and sighed.

We lay like that for a few minutes, sharing gentle kisses. Brenner slipped out of me. "That was incredible. It's always wild when I'm inside you." He nudged my cheek with his nose. "But tonight I want you in me."

"I'm not gonna say no—oh, shit." I sat up in bed, narrowly missing smacking Brenner's nose with my head. "Tonight. We're supposed to be leaving for the benefit now."

With an arched brow, Brenner stretched and swung his legs over the bed. "We need to shower again."

"No time. The car will be here in five minutes. We'll use a little extra cologne. No one will know." I scrambled to the closet to get dressed.

Slipping my feet into my loafers, I checked my watch. "Only half an hour late." I fixed Brenner's collar to hide the red mark where I'd bitten him, and I reached for his hand. "Not too bad."

"Oh, trust me. We're going to hear about it."

**

Upon entering the restaurant, Christine called out, "There they are. Hello there, lovebirds." She sauntered over to us, slim hips swinging, a glass of wine in her hand. "Whatever were you doing that made you so late?" She kissed Brenner first, then me.

Pretending innocence, I shrugged. "You know Saturday night traffic. Such a mess."

She narrowed her eyes and whispered in my ear, "Really, darling? You'll have to do better than that." Her hand waved in front of her face. "You smell like each other. All those hot alpha hormones. Whew." Her grin was wicked, and I laughed.

"You are a bad girl."

Brenner rolled his eyes. "Why are you playing along with her? She's the worst influence."

"I'm the best. Now come say hi to Archer and Madden."

The dynamic duo waved to us from the bar, and hand in hand, we greeted them. Recalling our drinks from the times we'd met, Archer ordered me a vodka and Brenner a beer.

"How goes it?" They lifted their glasses. "Cheers."

We clinked our glasses.

"It's going." I took a sip, still buzzing from Brenner's possession of my body.

"Have you heard anything more about my mother?" Brenner asked, and my heart broke for him.

"The detectives said the files are hard to locate–they're old and all paper, and there was a warehouse fire about ten years ago that destroyed boxes and boxes of old cases." He shook his head. "We may never know."

My phone buzzed with a text. It was from Grady.

> *I know you're at a benefit, but your father is making a speech you might want to hear.*

"What's wrong?" Brenner put a hand on my shoulder, and I swallowed the bile that rose in my throat.

"My father's on television. Grady said I should watch."

Archer waved at me. "Come into Tony's office. He has a TV."

We hurried with him to the rear of the restaurant, and all of us crowded together. Archer turned on the set, and my father's face filled the screen at a rally. Cheers rang out, and he soaked in the adulation of the masses.

"Why is Grady telling me to watch?" I muttered. "I don't need this shit."

My father raised his hands to quiet the crowd.

"My fellow Americans. I'm happy to say that I've received the endorsement of Reverend Austen Carlyle of the Conservative Coalition. If I'm elected president, I promise to restore faith in our schools and keep our children safe from outside influences that threaten our traditional way of life."

I went cold, and Brenner's hand crept into mine, his fingers squeezing tight. "You shouldn't have to listen to this shit."

"I want to. I need to."

After the clapping subsided, he continued. "You might've heard rumors that my son is engaged in a relationship with a man, and I want to assure you all that his choice of that lifestyle will never influence me. I am against it, I repudiate it. And I promise that if you elect me, I will always keep this country on the path to righteousness. God bless you, and God bless this country."

"Turn it off," I snapped, and downed my drink in one gulp. Without another word, I wrenched my hand out of Brenner's and slammed out of the office, heading straight to the bar. "Vodka. Double. Fuck it. Make it a triple."

The bartender filled the tumbler with ice, then poured the liquid to the top. I gulped it, hissing at the burn. I sensed Brenner behind me.

"Let's go home. You shouldn't be out tonight."

I scrubbed my face and drew in a deep breath, trying to clear the rage and pain from my head. "No. I'm not going to hide. I have no reason to."

"Of course you don't, but you might not want to be in the spotlight." Brenner held my waist. "Let me take you home."

"I said no." Lashing out at the person I cared about most in the word wasn't helpful, and I faced him. "I'm sorry. I shouldn't have yelled at you. But the worst thing I can do, and what he wants, is for me to live in the shadows." I lifted my chin. "And I refuse."

Admiration shone from Madden's and Archer's eyes. "Good for you. Get in front of this and take control."

With a wink at Brenner, I tipped my head to them. "I'm all about taking control." Brenner shook with laughter.

"I can't believe you're handling this so well."

The reality was, inside I was falling apart, but not in public. I'd never allow that. The time might come where

I'd shatter completely, but Brenner would be there to pick up my pieces and help put me back together. The same yet different. Forever changed.

My mind ran in a hundred directions as to the best way to handle the situation. One thing I'd learned growing up in a political family was to make sure you always had an answer prepared.

"I'm not, trust me. But I'm staying."

The room filled up, and I recognized New York's social elite, board members of museums, the opera and ballet, plus a mix of television and Broadway stars. Of course the press was close by, always sniffing for a juicy tidbit or scandal. Brenner remained steadfast by my side, hand in mine. I nudged his cheek with my nose.

"You look like my bodyguard instead of my boyfriend. That glower is killer." I lowered my voice. "And fucking hot."

"Weston Lively?" A husky voice interrupted my flirting, and I tensed, ready for battle. A tall man, midforties, tanned and trim, with flinty gray eyes, stood poised with his phone at the ready.

"Yes, that's me. And you are?" I raised a brow, using my don't-fuck-with-me voice.

"Chuck Peterson, Channel Eight news. What did you think of your father's speech in North Carolina today?"

"What do you mean?" I sure as hell wasn't about to volunteer anything. Let him ask the question.

He blinked. "Your father accepted the endorsement of the very right-wing, evangelical, influential pastor, Austen Carlyle."

"Quite a lot of adjectives for one man." I chuckled, but Peterson didn't join in.

"Mr. Lively, how do you feel about your father rejecting you because you're gay?"

A small crowd had gathered around us—Madden and Archer a step behind us while Christine hovered with Tony.

A woman close to my age with similar facial features as Madden stood by Christine.

"First of all, I'm not gay. I'm bisexual. I've dated women my whole life, but I happened to fall in love with a man. And you know what?" I tapped my jaw, pretending to be deep in thought. "I find it funny that you're asking me that question. Maybe I rejected *him* and his refusal to accept my relationship. You see, I don't grovel for anyone's attention."

Eager to get what he perceived as a scoop, Peterson continued on. "Is that what happened, Mr. Lively? Did you tell the senator that unless he approves of you and your boyfriend, you're not going to participate in his campaign?"

Like sharks smelling blood, several more reporters circled us, one with a camera filming, and I had the audience I needed to make my statement. I didn't ask for this fight, but my father had provoked and pushed me to my limit. He'd poked the bear, and I was ready to growl in return.

My grin was broad and bright. "Oh, no. I never had any intention of voting for him. He stands for everything I'm against. In fact..." I paused for effect, squeezing Brenner's hand. I always did enjoy a bit of drama, and from Brenner's dancing eyes and how hard he pressed his lips together, he knew. "If he does win the primary and becomes his party's nominee, I plan on actively supporting his opponent in the general election."

The uproar I'd counted on occurred, with the reporters shouting question after question at me. I held up my hands to quiet them.

"I have to insist you stop making this night about me. This is an incredible charity event for a very worthwhile cause. My mother, Melinda Weston, whom I'm named after, passed away from an aggressive form of blood cancer, as did Brenner's foster mother. I'm very grateful to Christine and Tony Gigante for inviting me tonight, and I plan to set up a trust in my mother's name, which will donate to this yearly fund raiser. If you truly want an important story, speak with Christine, as she can tell you about all the research funded by the money raised each year from this event. Now, if you'll excuse me, we'd like to move on and enjoy the rest of our evening. Good night."

The questions didn't stop, but I walked away, and with Brenner at my side, escaped to the opposite side of the room, where another bar awaited. I let out a long sigh, tension uncoiling from my stomach, and took the drink Brenner handed me. The glass trembled in my hand.

Brenner said, "I guess there's no coming back from a speech like that."

Surprised by his remark, I set the glass on the bar. "Why would I want to? I refuse to be a pawn in his political game. What he asked—for us to hide our relationship—is abhorrent. He doesn't care for me or anyone else. Power is his one true love."

Still, Brenner continued asking questions. "But Emily? Don't you think this might hurt your chances to see her, even after what he said?"

I loved how despite all the terrible things that had happened between my father and me, Brenner's wish was to keep my family intact because he understood how much my little sister meant to me.

"Are you forgetting Bill's recording?"

"No, I'm not forgetting anything. But I wonder if your father will find a way to wiggle out of that promise he made you."

"Paige is her mother, and she has a say as well. I'm not saying we're going to be best friends or anything, but she's the one who initiated the first meeting. I think we can work it out."

Brenner smiled. "If anyone can, it's you."

I fluttered my lashes at him. "Was that a compliment? That deserves a kiss."

I touched my lips to his, intending for it to be brief, but Brenner held me, and as always, the wildness took over and I lost all sense of time and propriety. The sound of cameras clicking and excited voices filled the air, but I didn't pay attention. All that mattered was his sinful tongue sweeping through my mouth, teasing and playing with mine.

Brenner whispered in my ear, "You realize the press is taking this all in? I thought you wanted to keep this discreet?"

"Discreet?" I grinned and winked. "You should know me better than that by now. You've got the wrong man, 'cause I am not that guy."

EPILOGUE

One year later

BRENNER

I stood on the shoreline with Bill, watching Weston and Emily frolic in the waves. Her shrieks of delight rose in the air when he scooped her up and spun her.

"Mommy. Look at me."

Shading her eyes, Paige sat under an umbrella and waved to them. With Weston's father back in the Senate after losing the election, Paige had created a firestorm of her own by filing for divorce and moving out. She and Emily were spending time with her family in Florida, which happened to be only twenty miles away from Bill's retirement community.

"Things working out with Weston seein' his sister?" Bill adjusted the ball cap to keep the sun off his nose. "They look like they're gettin' along good."

"They are. Weston calls them once a week, and when Paige's family had a birthday party for her, he flew in for the day to be there."

Bill frowned. "And nothing from his father?"

"No. Paige has custody, and the senator sees her on the agreed-on holidays and part of the summer." Election night, Weston and I had been at home with a bunch of friends, watching the results, and though we were all thrilled his father lost, it had taken a toll on Weston. There had been no contact since that night he'd come to the apartment. "He says it doesn't bother him, but I try not to bring it up."

"That's good."

A wet and giggling Emily darted past us, and Weston strolled up, grinning behind his sunglasses and baseball cap. I couldn't help but admire him at his approach. Water dripped down his broad chest, setting off his tanned, glowing skin. Sun-kissed ringlets of hair lay plastered to his face, and a lazy smile curved his lips. Thick, powerful thighs filled out his colorful board shorts.

"My two favorite guys." He slipped an arm around my waist. The past year had given us time to grow more comfortable with public displays of affection. "Paige and Emily are meeting her family a little later on for a barbecue, but what do you say the three of us go to lunch now?"

A certain sparkle in his eyes told me something was up, but I didn't have a clue. I peered over my sunglasses. "You don't want to eat on the beach?"

"Nah. I know a better place." He took my hand. "Come on. Bill, you ready?"

"Yep. I'm starvin' like Marvin." He walked ahead and began to pack up.

I held West's elbow. "What's going on? Why do I feel like you're keeping something from me?" One annoying thing about my boyfriend was if he didn't want to talk, he wouldn't. Maybe if I got him naked, but that wasn't about to happen on a public beach.

"Who me?" That guileless grin of his didn't fool me, and though I narrowed my eyes at him, he merely patted my cheek and kissed me. "Don't be so suspicious."

We put our things in the trunk, and West drove north on A1A. We passed by countless restaurants, but he didn't stop. After twenty minutes, he pulled into the circular driveway of a luxurious high-rise on the water. Palm trees soared to the sky, and I spied the glitter of a huge pool on the side of the expansive grounds, while the ocean beckoned from behind the tall tower.

Bill's bushy brows drew together. "I don't think there's a restaurant here."

"Nope." Weston left the car with the valet. "Come and see anyway."

He greeted the concierge as if they were old friends, and we zoomed to the top. Weston knocked on the only door on the floor, and it opened to a smiling woman in a sleek tan dress.

"Good afternoon. Welcome to Versailles on the Water."

My eyes bugged out at the sight before me. Floor-to-ceiling windows faced only turquoise ocean and an endless cerulean sky. The floors were pale-blond wood, and the furniture was done in neutral tones of beige, blue, and sea green. The room had to be at least forty feet long, with twelve-foot ceilings. A chef's kitchen was dominated by an immense nine-foot island of gleaming white.

Bill whistled. "Man...this is...I ain't never seen anything like this except in the movies. Who lives here?" He ran a hand over the spotless quartz.

"Nobody now. Five bedrooms and four bathrooms. But…" Weston's eyes glittered as bright as a rising sun. "I'd like to buy it. For us." His gaze met mine. "We shouldn't have to stay in a hotel when we visit Bill. Plus, when we come for vacations, it'll be nice to have a home base to bring everyone together—us, Bill, Emily, and Paige. Once the divorce is finalized, she told me she's planning on living here and coming to New York for the summers. She's already looking into schools for Emily. And for holidays, we can invite Manny and his husband, Grady, Mads and Archer, Christine and Tony if they're around."

"Don't forget Bailey. He and Grady's brother, Keston, have been seeing each other."

Weston chuckled. "There's a pair I never saw coming. Bailey Marks, lawyer and nice Jewish boy, with the wild-child, motorcycle-riding, tattoo-artist Keston." His hand crept into mine. "What do you really think?"

I leaned against the counter. "I think it's beautiful, but what're the carrying costs? I'm still paying into the practice, as you know."

"And as you know, I have more money than I know what to do with. I'll buy it, and you pay the carrying costs. You have the proceeds from the sale of your apartment."

After several months of back and forth between my tiny one-bedroom and West's spacious co-op, I'd succumbed and moved in with West. I sold my condo and while it had been at a premium, it still didn't go far living in the city.

His nonchalance about money was the one thing that always stood between us. "Yeah, but between paying the costs for your apartment and also into the practice, I'm tapped out as to how much I can contribute toward every-thing else."

"Can I stick my nose in, if you don't mind?" Having wandered through the spacious living area, Bill took a seat by the island.

"Opinions are always welcome, and yours more than anyone's." West hopped up onto the island and sat. "Lay it on us."

Despite the seriousness of the conversation, I had to smile. Weston and Bill had a great relationship.

"I didn't know what to think when Brenner told me he was involved with a guy. And then finding out who you were and how much money you got? Made me wonder if you was just playing at it as something to do to piss off your old man."

Grim-faced, Weston gazed at the floor. "Anything I can do to shit on my father makes me happy, but I would never, ever have used Brenner for that purpose. I fell for him. Hard. Like face-smashed-into-the-ground-at-a-hundred-miles-an-hour hard. I didn't plan for it or even think about it."

"I know that now, son. I can tell the real deal. That's why I'm trying to plead your case."

"You are?" West and I echoed each other.

"Listen." Bill turned his attention to me. "In relationships, there's always gonna be someone who's got more of something—money, patience, smarts..." His eyes twinkled. "Although God knows both of you are too smart for your own good sometimes." His tone gentled. "West isn't doing this for any other reason than he cares about you. Like what he did for your mother."

My throat closed, and West slipped off the counter and put his arms around me. "I did it because I love you. And because what I do for you is also for me. Us. She deserved peace, and so did you."

"I know." Weston had put some pressure on the police department and found out where my mother had been buried. He'd bought a plot for her near Pearl's, and we'd had her exhumed and had held a proper funeral. West didn't ever use the power of his father's name. Weston Oil had enough influence to move mountains and get results. "I'll never forget it. Giving her a proper final resting place means a lot."

"And you mean everything to me. So let's do this together. Your first big bonus, you can give me a chunk of change—whatever you want, I don't care." Weston squeezed me. "All I want is us together."

I took in the sun-drenched space, thinking of long-ago days when I was a kid, first bounced from family to family, then as a teenager, sitting alone in my room while everyone else was at the cool kids' parties. Never belonging. Always yearning.

"It's more than I ever dreamed possible."

"Anything is possible. If we want it bad enough, we can make it happen. This will be something that's ours—something we do together. It would be putting down roots. Creating a future." Weston squeezed my hand. "Our future together."

Bill gave a slight nod. "C'mon, kiddo. Lookit this—it's gorgeous. We could do all the holidays here, insteada my dinky one-bedroom."

"Exactly. Imagine Thanksgiving and Christmas, with a tree in the corner," Weston said, and his excitement was contagious.

"Emily would love it."

"Yeah. She would. And maybe one day..." He raised a brow, and that lazy, wicked smile sent a rush of heat and anticipation through me. His lips hit my ear. "Say yes. Let's do it."

I pretended an exasperated sigh. "Who could say no to you?"

Weston kissed my cheek. "It only took you a year to figure that out?" The devilish grin that never failed to make my heart pound tugged at his lips.

"Ironic, isn't it, that the boy I couldn't stand to be in the same room with now becomes the man I can't live without."

Our fingers laced together, Weston held up our entwined hands. "And that's the only guy I want to be. Yours."

******

Thank you for reading *Not That Guy*. I hope you enjoyed Weston and Brenner's story and enjoyed the cameo of Archer and Madden (and of course, Christine) from my Lambda Literary Award nominated book, *Just One Night.*

If you have the chance, I'd love for you to leave a review. Reviews are like M&Ms (chocolate only, no peanut, please.) There can never be enough.

And it's not the last you'll see of this dynamic duo, as they appear in the second book of this duet series, *The Lucky Ones.*

The Lucky Ones is the story of Weston and Brenner's friend, Bailey Marks and Grady's brother, Keston. It's a story of hope, acceptance, family, but most of all, the power of love.

FELICE STEVENS writes romance because what is better than people falling in love? Her favorite part of a romance novel is that first kiss...sigh. She loves creating stories of hopes and dreams and happily ever afters. Her stories are character-driven, rich with the sights, sounds, and flavors of New York City, and filled with men who are often deeply flawed but always real.

Felice writes gay romance because she believes that everyone deserves a happily ever after. Having traveled all over the world, she can safely say that the universal language that unites people is love.

Felice has written in a variety of sub-genres, including contemporary and paranormal, and she has a mystery series as well. You can find all her books listed on her website.

Felice is a two-time Lambda Literary Award nominee and a Lambda Award winner in Gay Romance for her book *The Ghost and Charlie Muir*.

BOOKBUB

https://www.bookbub.com/profile/felice-stevens

NEWSLETTER

https://tinyurl.com/y85e69ab

READER GROUP

https://www.facebook.com/groups/FelicesBreakfastClub/

FACEBOOK AUTHOR PAGE

https://www.facebook.com/felicestevensauthor/

INSTAGRAM

https://www.instagram.com/felicestevens

GOODREADS

https://www.goodreads.com/author/show/8432880.Felice_Stevens

WEBSITE

felicestevens.com

PAYHIP STORE

https://payhip.com/FeliceStevensAuthor

TIKTOK

https://www.tiktok.com/@felicestevens